LOSING BECK

ALSO BY SUSAN HAHN

NOVEL

The Six Granddaughters of Cecil Slaughter

POETRY

The Note She Left
The Scarlet Ibis
Self/Pity
Mother In Summer
Holiday
Confession
Melancholia, et cetera
Incontinence
Harriet Rubin's Mother's Wooden Hand

PLAYS

The Scarlet Ibis
Golf

LOSING BECK

a triptych

Susan Hahn

🐦 Red Hen Press | *Pasadena, CA*

Book design by Ann Basu

Library of Congress Cataloging-in-Publication Data
Names: Hahn, Susan, author.
Title: Losing beck : a triptych / Susan Hahn.
Description: First edition. | Pasadena, CA : Red Hen Press, [2018]
Identifiers: LCCN 2018031076| ISBN 9781597096317 (tradepaper) | ISBN
  9781597096324 (ebook)
Classification: LCC PS3558.A3238 L67 2018 | DDC 813/.54—dc23
LC record available at https://lccn.loc.gov/2018031076

The National Endowment for the Arts, the Los Angeles County Arts Commission, the Ahmanson Foundation, the Dwight Stuart Youth Fund, the Max Factor Family Foundation, the Pasadena Tournament of Roses Foundation, the Pasadena Arts & Culture Commission and the City of Pasadena Cultural Affairs Division, the City of Los Angeles Department of Cultural Affairs, the Audrey & Sydney Irmas Charitable Foundation, the Kinder Morgan Foundation, the Allergan Foundation, the Riordan Foundation, and the Amazon Literary Partnership partially support Red Hen Press.

First Edition
Published by Red Hen Press
www.redhen.org

ACKNOWLEDGMENTS

(in order of appearance)

Grateful acknowledgment is made to the generous editors of the publications in which the following poems, or versions of them, appeared:

Unlatched

"Her Purse At The Winter Solstice" is reprinted from *Holiday* by Susan Hahn. Reprinted with permission of the author. Published by The University of Chicago Press, 2001. This poem was first published in *Poetry*.

"Mother In Summer I" is reprinted from *Mother In Summer* by Susan Hahn. Reprinted with permission of the author. Published by Northwestern University Press, 2002.

Nijinsky's Dog

"Petit Point III" is reprinted from *Mother In Summer* by Susan Hahn. Reprinted with permission of the author. Published by Northwestern University Press, 2002. This poem was first published in *88: A Journal of Contemporary American Poetry*.

"Nijinsky's Dog" is reprinted from *Confession* by Susan Hahn. Reprinted with permission of the author. Published by The University of Chicago Press, 1997. This poem was first published in *The American Poetry Review*.

Specula Karma

"The Woman Who Loved Halloween" is reprinted from *Holiday* by Susan Hahn. Reprinted with permission of the author. Published by The Univesity of Chicago Press, 2001. This poem was first published in *New England Review*.

"The Pornography of Pity VII" is reprinted from *Self/Pity* by Susan Hahn. Reprinted with permission of the author. Published by Northwestern University Press, 2005.

"Pity Jerusalem" is reprinted from *Self/Pity* by Susan Hahn. Reprinted with permission of the author. Published by Northwestern University Press, 2005. This poem was first published in *New England Review*.

"Directions To Where I Live" is reprinted from *Incontinence* by Susan Hahn. Reprinted with permission of the author. Published by The University of Chicago Press, 1993. This poem was first published in *Poetry East*.

"Goose Pity" is reprinted from *Self/Pity* by Susan Hahn. Reprinted with permission of the author. Published by Northwestern University Press, 2005. This poem was first published in *The North American Review*.

"Lady Trick IV" is reprinted from *The Scarlet Ibis* by Susan Hahn. Reprinted with permission of the author. Published by Northwestern University Press, 2007. This poem was first published in *Michigan Quarterly Review*.

I am most grateful to the Ernest Hemingway Foundation of Oak Park, Illinois, where I was their first Writer-in-Residence at the Hemingway Birthplace Home for the year 2013–2014. Much of this manuscript is the result of my residency there.

≈ ≈ ≈ ≈ ≈

For a true writer each book
should be a new beginning where
he tries again for something
that is beyond attainment.
He should always try for something
that has never been done before
or that others have tried and failed.
Then sometimes, with great luck,
he will succeed.
> —Ernest Hemingway

For All Their Support

For Them With Love

Fred and Rick

Jeanne

Jean and Jacob and Charlie

CONTENTS

In the fullness of time all will be revealed.

—Lettie Shershevsky Silver
    as told to her by Sister Teresa Marie

How many genres will it take?

—Jennie Silver

INTRODUCTION

In "Unlatched," a year-long diary and the first section of Susan Hahn's innovative and hypnotic new novel, *Losing Beck*, the author introduces us to Jennie Silver, a well-regarded young poet trying without success to recover from a disastrous and intense sexual affair with Benedict "Beck" Eck. Along with being a chronic womanizer, Beck is a respected literature professor at a prestigious Midwestern university with a long career of preying on graduate students and discarding them as soon as their novelty wears off. Jennie isn't so easily discarded, however, and part of the novel's suspense hinges on whether or not she'll report him to university administrators for assaulting her in his office early in their affair.

Another significant component of the novel's tension arises from the question of whether Jennie will follow the same doomed trajectory as the troubled poet Sylvia Plath. Jennie is fortunate to have Neil, however, a husband who has gracefully weathered the vicissitudes of their marriage and stayed by her side, though his ability to save her from her darkest impulses is of course in question from the very beginning of "Unlatched."

Throughout "Unlatched," Jennie is also grieving for her mother, who died almost exactly a year before Jennie's diary begins, and coupled with this loss is the more dramatic, much earlier loss of Jennie's beloved older brother John, who killed himself when Jennie was still a girl, this tragedy forever tainting the lives and psyches of the surviving Silvers.

In the novel's other two sections, the experimental two-act play "Nijinsky's Dog" and the novella "Specula Karma," Hahn recasts her heroine Jennie Silver as Lissa and Idy Cometh, respectively, and approaches the story of Jennie's abusive affair with Beck from different angles, while also dramatizing the days preceding Jennie/Lissa's mother's death from cancer. As *Losing Beck*'s other two sections also do, the play interrogates the effects of inherited trauma—from the millions murdered in pogroms and death camps before and during the Holocaust to the often painful adjustments and fractured relationships many immigrants (untold numbers likely suffering from survivor's guilt, Hahn posits), were forced to confront after emigrating to the U.S. and taking on new identities in a foreign country.

Along with the titanic and violent forces of history and their effects on individual lives, *Losing Beck*'s three sections are each perhaps most invested in exploring the effects of obsessional desire and how Jennie/Lissa/Idy's creativity and relationships with men have been influenced by her grief over her lost brother and mother, her anger at her estranged father, Joe Silver, and her experiences as a poet and public figure.

The final section, "Specula Karma" circles back to characters who are introduced in "Unlatched," most notably Dr. Sam Guttmacher, a retired therapist Jennie greatly admires, and Avigdor Element, a legendary novelist, and like Beck, a serial womanizer and academic. *Losing Beck* ultimately is a mystery, one that, in addition to the other narrative paths it takes us on, immerses us in the literal trenches of World War I where we learn Dr. Guttmacher, who has strong ties to Element, was saved by the poet Wilfred Owen, and the metaphorical trenches of Jennie Silver's grieving mind, which for so long has been seeking beauty and release from the burdens of her family's tragedies.

In *Losing Beck*, Susan Hahn has offered readers an extraordinary work of prose and poetry, one that ranges widely across a unique and memorable literary landscape.

—*Christine Sneed, 19 September 2017*

LOSING BECK

The Diary

Unlatched

by
Jennie Silver

This is the loss that conjures up all the rest.
—Jennie Silver

Day 1

Astrid Olson's secretary at the university just returned my call, saying, "Astrid Olson will see you immediately." I am grateful, although I couldn't bring myself to tell her why I called—why I called Friday, called back and canceled, and then called again today, Monday. My voice probably sounded even more desperate than it did seventy-two hours ago. I used the last name "Tin," rather than my maiden name and the name I publish under, which is "Silver." I do feel as cheap and empty as a beggar's cup. I told the secretary I couldn't make it today after all, but asked her to please keep a record of the call—of all the calls. I called three years ago, too. I told her that today—it's the best I can do. She calmly replied, "We've started a record as of last Friday." I also asked, "If I do come in to speak with Astrid Olson, will I have to name someone?" In other words, I'm not able to name Beck—or rather, Benedict Eck. She gently said, "No." But I know eventually they'll want a name.

(Only I called him Beck, after the postmodern musician known for his alternative rock and psychedelia. How his thick skin flushed when I gave him that nickname at the beginning of our relationship. How well it played into his ego.)

≈ ≈ ≈ ≈ ≈

The bald spot atop the center of my head is rubbed clean of the pathetic hairs that had broken through and begun to grow. The past few days I've mostly just sat in my chair, touching the bristles roughly, so it's no surprise that by today none have survived. Last night before I went to bed I banged the top of my skull six or seven times against the bathroom tiles. It actually felt good—at least the pain felt localized. I could point to it. *Here. Here, Mommy, is where it hurts so much.*

In little more than a week it will be the one-year anniversary of her death, and next month my sisters and I are finally dividing up her clothes. It's taken me almost a year to agree to this and still, I know I'm not ready. John won't be there. No, our brother just won't be—he's been gone over twenty years. Right now, it is easier to force my focus away from him and pour all my devastation into losing Beck and trying not to call him.

I know that he cares little for me, although Jason insists it's quite the opposite—that Beck cares too much, is too attracted to me, and one way for him to cope with this is to try to control me. I'm seeing Jason tonight. At some point during the session he will insist that Beck *will* call. He will promise me this, saying, "He always does; just be patient." But I know this time is different, even though I don't have the full story—the full story of the rumor that has made him so angry. I don't know who started it and what twist of it has gotten back to him—what he heard that has made him furious enough to bash the phone in my ear. When he did this, it felt like how a gunshot must be—the noise, the shock of being hit, then the aftermath—the awareness of a sudden mess and the excruciating injury.

≈ ≈ ≈ ≈ ≈

His cardinal rule was secrecy, so he would not like me starting this record—*or* the play *or* the novella, the latter of which I've been writing for a while, for I have in fact been losing Beck for some time. No, he would not like me writing *any* of this, given they all are the basis of what went not-so-suddenly wrong. Although I suppose almost everything went wrong from the very beginning.

≈ ≈ ≈ ≈ ≈

I waited in the vestibule of his apartment building for almost an hour the first time he invited me for dinner. When he finally did show up, there was a woman with him and as we were climbing up the three flights of stairs, I thought she was a neighbor who lived on the same floor. But no, she, too, was his guest for dinner. He had just begun an affair with her. That was five years ago—history. She's long gone—Sophia. He had gotten her a quarter-long lectureship at the university. Days later he told me over the phone, "Her vagina's too baggy—no friction. It lessens the excitement." Then he laughed. Just that should have put a very early end to the relationship. But it didn't.

≈ ≈ ≈ ≈ ≈

Now, instead of focusing on his research or on academic matters, he spends most of his free time at a boxing gym. That's when it's not his turn to take care of his daughter, Maxi. And when he's not at the gym, or with Maxi, or teaching his class, he sleeps with, or "fucks"—as he puts it—his current female graduate assistant.

Yes, losing Beck should be easy—and I haven't even written of the worst of it—but it's just not. I wish he'd call. But he won't. Jason's wrong. I've transgressed. Maybe I did tell someone *some* of the truth, or maybe *too much* of the truth. I can't remember right now. I'm too upset. Soon it will be the first full day of chronicling the losing of Beck. The phone is right next to me. I've been calling just about everyone I know—Mandy, Sallie, and the rest—even Hedy. I tell them I've lost Beck. The chorus of voices is in unison, all hymn or hum—an a cappella choir singing "Hallelujah."

Day 2

Ignoring Jason's and everyone else's advice, I went to Beck's apartment. I called first and left a message that I wanted to talk with him. Of course, he didn't call back. As I waited and waited for the call I knew would never come, I started getting dressed—just blue jeans and a white T-shirt. Actually, the same outfit I wore to the cemetery on my mother's birthday—her first birthday beneath the ground, sealed in a vault, locked in a coffin with the Star of David carved onto the top of it. No shopping for a gift this year, no shawl or scarf or bracelet to buy, just a handful of flowers placed next to her temporary marker—too soon for the heavy plaque to be anchored into the ground with her name deeply embossed into it. I haven't been able to put on those particular clothes since—odd, that's what I chose to wear today. *Grief Clothes*. In addition, I grabbed a red sweater—the color my mother chose. A red wool suit in the coffin, in the vault, in the ground on that hot July day of her birth. Why *that* color?

She never spoke to me directly about death. Those last days I was reading Seamus Heaney's poems to her until, quite high spiritedly (her spirit was just about all that was left of her, but how fully fleshed it was), she said she was sick of listening to his "digging around in the dirt." I told her his father was a potato farmer and she smiled. We ignored what she really meant—and I quickly switched to another book, Helen Hayes's autobiography. We ended our last afternoon together with me reciting Emily Dickinson, "I'll tell you how the sun rose— / A Ribbon at a time . . ." The rabbi read those lines at her funeral a few days later. I had added, "Her smile was that to us," and he fit it in well enough. He told me, "You shouldn't speak—you should mourn silently." I'm sorry now I didn't insist—that I'd allowed him to silence me. He also read a section of Wallace Stevens's poem "Sunday Morning" at my request:

> Divinity must live within herself:
> Passions of rain, or moods in falling snow;
> Grievings in loneliness, or unsubdued
> Elations when the forest blooms; gusty
> Emotions on wet roads on autumn nights;
> All pleasures and all pains, remembering
> The bough of summer and the winter branch.
> These are the measures destined for her soul.

I had read those lines to her before her failed surgery. She listened quietly as she looked out the window of her hospital room that mid-April afternoon and then said, "Lovely, just beautiful." But I'm sure the rabbi was not at all pleased by their postmodern no-one-God focus, their complete emphasis on the natural world.

She was being choked by the cancer and couldn't eat. The doctors said that with the operation she'd have several years, without it, six months.

She had the surgery—recovered from most of the horribleness of it in two months—and died four months later. Six months.

≈ ≈ ≈ ≈ ≈

The final days of her life, my mother's head looked so large and leonine—in part because of her disappearing body. The cancer was busy eating her body, but it never reached her brain. She was smarter than she'd ever been. Heaney, Hayes, Stevens, Dickinson all spoke on her tongue. We even talked about Nijinsky, Pavlova, Isadora Duncan—how my grandmother had wanted her to become a dancer, because that's what her own mother had wanted for her and her brother and twin sisters before the train carried them all to their deaths, my grandmother being the only one sent away and saved. But when my mother's four-year-old self didn't take to dance, my grandmother thought an actress "good enough."

She told me about the American theater in the 1940s and 50s—the plays she'd seen, the recitations she'd given. How at ten she was introduced to Helen Hayes at the Ambassador Hotel, wearing summer—"Jennie, bouquets of flowers encircled my delicate, pastel, polished-cotton dress!"

≈ ≈ ≈ ≈ ≈

That last day Joe Silver called the hospice people. My mother didn't want them in her house, but she had grown too weak to beat back her husband's insistence. Reality had grown too heavy against her almost nonexistent body. I left her with the hospice nurse. I didn't know I shouldn't have left. Or did I? I went down the stairs and then ran back up and said, "Mother, I'll see you tomorrow." All she did was turn toward me and wave—her arm and hand so fragile, her wave so graceful. The next day when I awoke, in between my messages from Mandy and the dentist, there was one from Joe Silver. All he said was, "It's your father, Jennie. It's all over." I turned off the recorder, sat in my chair for almost an hour, and let the phone ring and ring. Finally, when I answered, it was my sister Hedy, asking frantically, "Do you want to see her?" "See Who?" I said, bewildered. She answered,

"Mother." Apparently, the hospice people were waiting for me—for me to have the chance to come over and see my now-dead mother.

I dressed in jeans and a T-shirt, not dissimilar from what I wore today to see Beck, except in almost a year I've never worn *those* particular clothes, even the shoes. Probably never will. Today, I just wore my cemetery clothes.

My mother had told Hedy what she wanted to wear: red suit, white silk blouse, black patent leather pumps. Where did she think she was going? And now, for the first time in eleven and three-quarter months, I grabbed the color red. I grabbed *my* red sweater. I don't know why and at some level *that* frightens me, but these last few days, especially, most of what I think and do has a frightening aspect.

≈ ≈ ≈ ≈ ≈

He hung up on me when I dialed his code in the hallway of his apartment building. I thought that would happen. I then called his telephone, but he'd turned his answering machine on. I left a pathetic message. "Please, Beck. Please. See Me," and waited. I knew he had to pick up Maxi from school. After a few minutes, I panicked, thinking he might have left the building through a back door. I ran outside and, sure enough, there he was getting into his car. I approached it as he kept waving at me. Different from my mother's wave. These were jerky and angry. I ran to his car. He had locked himself in and I couldn't hear what he was saying. He also kept putting his hands over his mouth. Finally, I realized he was saying that he didn't want to talk to me. I should move away. I wouldn't. His face was flushed and ballooned up—like a stop sign with its edges rounded off. I kept begging, "Please. Please. Talk To Me." He then said something I couldn't quite hear. I shouted, "I can't hear you." It was only then that he rolled down his window. I breathed. I thought this was a step, but he just yelled, "Go Away." I pleaded, "Please, Beck. Please. I can't handle this. I don't know what to do." It was then he screamed, "Write me a letter saying I never attacked you, hadn't pursued you afterward, that my calls to you were *not* unwanted, that I hadn't tried to suppress your work, and that the

poems you've written about some monster of a man *aren't about me*." HE
WANTED A DISCLAIMER.

I took a too-shallow gulp of air, coughed, and then said in a thin voice,
"I'll give you some names of who might have started the *rumor* that you
had tried to suppress my writing." But from what he had just said, I knew
more of what he'd done than just trying to censor my writing had gotten
back to him. "Please," I repeated. "Please Talk To Me." He reiterated in
a more controlled—pedantic, professorial, arched—way, "I have to pick
up Maxi, you do *know* this, do you not?" But I couldn't move. Maybe I
wanted to be run over—that's what he'd been trying to do to me for years
anyway, both physically and psychologically.

Finally, he seemed to soften and said, "Call Me." I stepped aside and
he drove away.

≈ ≈ ≈ ≈ ≈

I then waited two hours and went to the playwriting class I was starting
at the university. I was wearing my red sweater, when we were asked to in-
troduce ourselves. I began by talking about my mother. How she had been
a child actor, had done solo performances at downtown theaters. It was
the first time in days that what I said felt right—with *that* color wrapped
around me, talking about her, and Beck's words, "Call Me," I felt calmer.
However, at the same time I had to keep pushing those two historically
grisly words—"Call Me"—from John's life out of my mind.

When I see Jason, I'll have something positive to tell him.

Day 3

Jason said, "If you really *need* to call Beck, you shouldn't wait too long,
that when Beck said 'Call Me,' the implication was to call him soon." I
thought I should wait a week. I was just happy—or rather, more stable
than I'd been in days—with his "Call Me." As if there could be a new beginning in those two monosyllabic words—a seed where I thought there
had been a bullet. I felt more rested—dormant and perennial with hope.
Yet, in the deepest pit of my gut I also knew that any "new beginning"

could have little longevity—most especially because of the play and the novella I'd been working on. On "smart" days, I know they're more important than losing Beck. Through their invention they are the most precise emotional records of the acts against me by Beck. "Tell all the truth but tell it slant," as Emily Dickinson had written.

The second reason I know we really have little future are the things he said to me the last time I saw him—before yesterday. Ten days ago, when we had walked along the lake, he stated, "I'm having these fantasies—fantasies of you getting your breasts tattooed with my initials on them. I want to watch." Being a writer, I listened and thought, what material. He then asked, "What do you think of that?" I just answered, "Interesting." His voice was quiet and gentle.

The next day I woke up repulsed. The day after, I was once again intrigued. I couldn't keep up with my emotions and I was lonesome. He knew that my relationship with Neil was pocked with emptiness, making his parting, tender words with their well-cushioned iron hook—"Jennie, I think about you all the time"—once again, pull me back to him.

≈ ≈ ≈ ≈ ≈

I called him at 12:30 p.m. He answered the phone quickly—one ring—as if he had been waiting. I was excited that he picked up the phone. I could tell it wasn't going to be his answering machine. We were about to start over. I said, "Hello, Beck," and as soon as he heard me—with my voice all hopeful and girlish—he bashed the phone into my ear. I sat immobile in my chair for over an hour. Stunned, like when Joe Silver called with that message, saying, "It's your father, Jennie. It's all over." In between all the mundane messages of that morning from the dentist and Mandy (once again doubting if Sy would ever leave his wife), somewhere between them in time and space, my mother left.

Tomorrow I have an appointment with a new therapist, whom Mandy got for me from a friend of hers.

Day 4

Tonight I feel a little better, but I can't say it has anything to do with the new therapist—in fact, it's quite the opposite. I called the novelist A. (The initial of his last name begins with A.) It was, I think, a way of saving myself after the two phone calls I made just after I awoke. These last days, as soon as I open my eyes, my whole body starts to tremble—feels like it's about to quake. Although, it didn't happen yesterday when I thought Beck was going to talk with me. I truly didn't believe I was being set up for another slam—slam of the phone, slam of me. I'm still stunned. Today's morning rage was not confineable. I called Beck and left a message: "I know you are going around saying I betrayed you, when in fact I'm the one who's been betrayed and I am going to tell everyone." As I write this, the words sound so dumb—as if they're from a hormonally unbalanced preteen. I then called Astrid Olson's secretary to make an appointment to finally file a complaint against him—a multifaceted one. As I was making up my list, I realized the one that would jeopardize him the most: three years ago, he invited me to his office after a class of his that I was sitting in on, and he locked the door and lunged at me. Or rather, at my breasts. I was sitting down at the time and I kicked him with the heel of my right boot. It hit him in the chest. Then my chair toppled to the floor with me in it. I got up, straightened my blouse, and, laughing—yes, laughing—said, "I'll send you the doctor's bill." The next day he called to say, "Whenever I invite you to my office, you should know it's never to talk about anything literary, but to have some kind of sex. Do you understand this, Jennie? You *do* understand this? Do you not?" For most women that *finally* would have been enough. But it was just a small part of the repertoire of horrors between us. For the rest of the quarter I just went to his class and we barely spoke.

≈ ≈ ≈ ≈ ≈

After Astrid Olson's secretary said she'd check to see if I could come in today and call me back, I called A—a stunning, creative, accomplished, and, of course, difficult man. He told me he might be taking a full-time position at the university next year. Then, A brought up Beck. A had come to the university last spring to teach. He said Beck avoided him. I know Beck is threatened by this man—his great looks, his sophisticated style, the way people gravitate to him. A remarked that Beck "looked like an animal long dead—*road kill.*" I did at the time think A's statement somewhat *overkill* and wondered briefly if A were a bit threatened by Beck. But, it did make me smile.

After we hung up, I checked my messages. Astrid Olson's secretary had left one saying I could come in at 4:30 today. I called back and apologetically said, "I just can't make it."

I then left for the new therapist.

≈ ≈ ≈ ≈ ≈

When I first saw her, all I could think of was the Cheshire Cat—rotund, with a large head, straw-like yellow hair, and an enigmatic smile. She quickly changed positions on her brown couch as if it were the branch of a tree, while grabbing at one of several small blankets next to her and placing them over her midsection. Her right hand, with its too-obviously chipped nail polish, was always exposed, the other frequently hidden under one of those brightly colored patches of wool cloth that were strewn about her office. Once, she even rolled over and sat on the floor next to my leg. It was so curious a scene—I felt as if I'd fallen into *Alice's Adventures in Wonderland.* So much so that I resisted telling her exactly why I had come to see her and only spoke vaguely, saying, "I'm having trouble with a man. It's a strange relationship. It's sexual. It's—" But, before I could say anything more, she interrupted with, "I did research for Kinsey when I was at Indiana University and *anything* is perfectly acceptable, no matter what, if it's between two consenting adults." She then went on, giving me detail after detail about what she had learned about human sexuality as a Kinsey researcher, all this time with her left hand completely concealed.

Her office had a yeasty smell, so much so I felt I might vomit, and when she went an hour over the conventional fifty minutes, I finally said, "I have to leave. I have to be somewhere else." *Anywhere,* I thought. Later at home I wondered if the Cheshire Cat had been masturbating—or at least touching herself—as we spoke. I took a long, hot shower, trying to scrub out that musty, overheated female scent from her and her office. It was then that Beck, once again, rose to the forefront of my thoughts and I remembered all the pungent odors that had permeated *his* clothes and the places he had lived—how I was both drawn to and repelled by them. How A is so clean, his clothes always fresh and perfectly pressed.

If Mandy asks, I'll tell her the truth. But she won't. She's too involved with her own issues—if Sy will or will not leave his wife and that her husband Irv not find out about them, at least not yet. She's probably even forgotten that I went.

Day 5
2:30 a.m.
Ellen Feld, a woman I called earlier this week to ask if she had heard any rumors about what was going on with Beck and me, I now realize, is definitely not a friend. At a poetry function this evening, she came up to me and said, "Beck feels you lied about him, but just *forget it.*" She then added, so flippantly as her right hand fluffed her long, over-dyed black hair, "It's no big deal. These kinds of things happen to everyone."

She also kept smoothing her deep green velvet jacket as we spoke, as if carefully brushing my upset off of it. I saw the cavernous joy she was getting from my anguish. She's a poet, but not a very good one—although she and her husband (an associate provost at the university who teaches a class on the Romantic poets and who, according to Beck, "listens his way into the beds of his female graduate students and prefers them small-breasted— less threatening") are trying desperately to fashion her into one.

It's clear that, beneath that overly made-up, almost embalmed-looking, yet delicate and pretty face, there is flesh rotting with jealousy and frustration, even hate. I must never call her again, no matter what I think I need to know about Beck's behavior. I fear there are pieces of this puzzle that have been thrown out or are forever hidden—hidden, perhaps, in the deep, plush pockets of Ellen Feld's velvet designer jacket.

9:30 p.m.

I keep playing the recording I made of A's and my conversation. And I miss Beck. I wonder what he's doing—if he's completely wiped me from his mind, if maybe this was all *his* setup, if all his kindness (kindness? *I want to watch you get your breasts tattooed with my initials*) over the last couple of weeks was just part of it: take her high, then let her drop. I was supposed to sit in on another class of his, Advanced Poetics, starting Wednesday. I could use that. Sometimes I feel that I don't have the proper language for dealing with such high-powered people as A. Then again, yesterday A seemed most involved with telling me how he wants some distance from his wife and that younger women keep calling him, while I was working so hard trying not to show any signs of my desperation, my disorientation, making a subject like "Advanced Poetics" seem farther away than any planet as yet discovered.

Day 6

12:00 a.m.

Last year, at this time, began the last days of my mother's life. Beck was calling all the time; I'd give him an update on her condition and he'd listen so intently. Now they're both gone. I'll go to bed early tonight, wake Neil, and ask him to rub my head, which he will. Then I'll hope my sleep will be dreamless—*death's sweet dress rehearsal,* a line from one of my poems.

12:30 p.m.

I woke up and played A's tape. Again, he made me smile. He's funny, preposterous, pompous, and seductive on the phone; in person, however, at least last year, he kept a distance from me. He came close, then backed away. "Close" in the sense that when I invited him to dinner, he answered with an enthusiastic "Yes" and then, at the last minute, cancelled. Just said, "I'm tired." It hurt. After that I just came to his class and was pretty quiet. In some strange way I think he respected that—he's so used to having women toss themselves onto him.

≈ ≈ ≈ ≈ ≈

Tonight Neil and I went to a play at the theater that is going to give me a reading of my play. The artistic director was there. I can't figure out if this little man with a big job and lots of power really likes the early version of the play I'd sent him, or not. All his inflated adjectives—his bloated flatterings—seemed to result in what felt like loud, unending flatulence. When I left the theater, it occurred to me that perhaps he just hoped all his puff would result in a large donation.

Day 7
   In three days—a year ago—my mother will be dead. I've begun reliving those last hours. If I'd known when I ran up the stairs to say that second goodbye—*What prompted that?*—that it would be the last time I'd see her alive, I would have stayed and stayed. Maybe it was the memory of John going up *those* stairs. Maybe if I had followed him, grabbed hold of him, talked with him, *everything* would have been different.

≈ ≈ ≈ ≈ ≈

The rumor he heard from his "source" was clearly larger than that I'd told someone he'd tried to suppress the publication of a couple of poems from my fifth book—which in reality were far too vague to suggest him, except in his own blistering paranoia—and that I'd said his phone calls were unwelcome. He *did* mention the attack when I saw him. Could this really have come from Ellen? I don't remember exactly what I told her. Maybe it *is* all his setup. Maybe he wants me to get sick again. When I was struggling to talk with him through his car window, I said, "If you don't talk to me, I'm going to have a breakdown. Do you want this, want this for me *again?*" Then I screamed and added, "I don't care if you run me over with your car, *just talk to me.*" Then, his "Call Me." *Those words*—their slash into me over John, which I've tried for years to push and push out of my mind. All of my efforts, stillborn. *Beck knows that story.*

Day 8

I saw a third therapist. A real hard-ass. I've gone to him on and off through the years, but after a session or two always found him too tough. Tonight, he just said straight out, "Beck is a twisted person and you're twisted, too, for getting yourself locked into his sociopathic behavior." I asked him, "Why would I take such abuse?" He sighed, then said, "It doesn't matter, just *stop it*," adding, "Neil is also a little twisted, for not having put an end to all this the night you came home four years ago, shaking and unable to breathe from Beck's attack—however incomplete it was." I *did* tell Neil much of it and, although he seemed very upset at the time, when I developed pneumonia afterward—couldn't catch my breath for months—he became more focused on helping me get better than with Beck's hurl onto me.

He continued, "You really do have a case against Beck. You *could* go to the university." All I could think of was, why did he pick now to hurt me? It feels so deliberate.

≈ ≈ ≈ ≈ ≈

In just a little over forty-eight hours, she will have been dead for a year. Then, the full circle will have been drawn. *The hospice people were waiting for me, waiting with the body bag to take her away, away from her house, away from me.* The circle will close on the last time I climbed the stairs and said goodbye to what was left of her.

She used to sit on the couch, carefully tearing out her hair. Her head was filled with tiny patches of emptiness. I'd watch. Once, I even brought a tweezers and she let me pull out the new hairs that had begun to grow in—it seemed to calm her. Then, suddenly she cried, "Jennie, Stop It. *Please* Stop It!"—embarrassed.

In the last weeks of her life I'd comb her head—there were no hairs left, only some dead follicles sprinkled over her scalp. I know when I did this, it quieted both of us.

Day 9

I dropped the two therapists, went back to Jason, and listened rather hopelessly as he said, "Beck will call at the very moment you no longer care. But it has to be authentic. Beck will feel it and will panic." Jason has a mystical side to him. He believes in the power of The Furies and in time compression—where past, present, and future converge in unexplainable ways.

Day 10

It's past midnight and now *it is* the day of my mother's death. I've written right into her dying hours. When I awake she'll be gone one year—Joe Silver's cryptic message repetitively playing in my ears, like Beck's bashes.

≈ ≈ ≈ ≈ ≈

Neil and I went to the cemetery this morning. I couldn't find my mother's grave. It had a small temporary marker. It was unlike the others. I got disoriented passing over the familiar names locked in the grass with their dulled-out plaques, my grandfather's name almost erased. I stumbled over John's grave. *Oh, I didn't want to do that.* John was so young . . . And that horrific evening of more than two decades ago jolted my memory as if it were a lightning bolt—with Emily Dickinson's lines following like thunder: "This is the hour of Lead— / Remembered if outlived . . ."

John, weeping over that too-thin letter from Harvard. Joe Silver standing there, furious with Harvard and revolted by the sight of his son. John had been named after the deceased young president—Joe Silver had gotten his "young prince." He was going to create his *own* dynasty, for he viewed himself "no regular Joe," but rather a "Joe" as in "Kennedy"—except Joe Silver got three daughters afterward. Nonetheless, he set John on the path to be the first Jewish president of the United States. My mother told me when I was older, "He *even* wanted to give him the middle name of Fitzgerald! We fought terribly until we finally settled on just the initial 'F.'" Joe Silver's motto in those days was, "If a Catholic can become president, so can a Jew." Then, he'd point at my beautiful brother and say, "You!"

And then, *The Letter*—that snow-sopped, melting letter—arriving one bleak March morning, the hardened ice outside our door so locked in dirt from the impossibly long, frozen winter. And then, John's tears by the end of that day sticking to his cold, flushed face, while Joe Silver's face boiled from red to scarlet to fuchsia as he just stared and stared at John, with John not letting go of that too-thin letter, which by then had made small cuts into his fingertips from his hours of holding it, tracing its edges—its boundaries. And finally, Joe Silver's uncontrollable, searing words to his young, weakened prince. All of us there—even Hedy, two, and Sallie, just turned five—soon to be sealed in that forever moment. "SO WHY DON'T YOU JUST GO KILL YOURSELF?" And then, John's turn at the twilight hour. His silence. His turning his back to all of us and his slow climb up the stairs. *I still see it. That turn. That climb.* The quiet of it. No wave. No hint.

Joe Silver found him hanged on a high hook in that old house. John had put rubber gloves on, soaked the rope in firewater—the marks on his neck and face burning through all layers of skin. *Stigmas of full thickness.* We were never allowed to speak of any of it.

My mother, my sisters, and I were forbidden to ever mention how Joe Silver's eight words sentenced my brother to a short life. In his rock-hard muteness concerning John, he imprisoned all of us to a cinderblock silence on the subject of our lost prince.

≈ ≈ ≈ ≈ ≈

Lazar Sirebro (Americanized from the Russian to "Silver"), Joe Silver's father, used to tell us—as we got older—the same story over and over: "I escaped the pogroms; I was The One. The One my parents sent to survive. And I did! And on my boat were Marc Chagall, Arthur Rubinstein, Golda Meir, Isaac Bashevis Singer, Sholem Aleichem, Jascha Heifetz, and Avigdor Element." (Which, no matter how old John and I were, we knew to be ridiculous.) He'd then sigh and straighten and puff, "Yes, we *all* made it! Me a pawnbroker (here his voice *would* drop) and the rest!" So in Joe Silver's defense, this was the only meal he was served—had grown up on.

Nearly forty and a known womanizer with three broken engagements behind him, Lazar wouldn't allow his son to break the fourth one. He wanted a legacy, and that was how Joe Silver came to marry my mother, who was almost seventeen years younger.

≈ ≈ ≈ ≈ ≈

Both Lazar Silver and his son agreed that from my brother's birth, John was their magnificent deliverance from the boat, from the stink of steerage, from being an outsider, from feeling less—even though they boasted of being more—while Lazar's silent wife, Masha, would just sit there, stout, stiffly corseted and bejeweled with the "borrowed" bracelets, necklaces, and rings from other people's troubles. After John died, both of them quickly followed.

Four days after John's death, Joe Silver was back at work—his old routines more rigid than ever, his talk about himself louder, my mother's rheumy stare at him growing thicker until it slowly seeped down into the rest of her. But that wasn't the worst of it. Not even close. When we arrived home from John's funeral, there was a message left on our answering machine. No one paid attention to it until the next day. What did it matter? What did *anything* matter?

Finally, my father pressed play and we all heard a too-animated voice say: "Hello, Carrington Lowell here, assistant dean of admissions at Harvard." He then paused with a small sigh of what seemed a large embarrassment and continued, "I am calling for John F. Silver. *John*, there's been a mix-up. Letters getting mixed up. A small error. Two John Silvers applied." Then, there was a nervous cough and a clearing of the throat. I'll never forget. "Yes, one rejected, the *other* accepted. And you're The One who's been accepted. Sorry if this has caused you *any* inconvenience. *Call Me*." Carrington Lowell then gave his number twice, as if in doing this he could ensure the undoing of what had been done.

≈ ≈ ≈ ≈ ≈

Ever so slowly, I got emotionally sick. "Survivor's guilt," the doctors said. I felt I was worth less than John and didn't understand why *I* was still alive. And in part because we were not allowed to speak of it, I secretively began writing poems, a few of which ended up—years later—making reference to a man who abused women. Not Joe Silver—the jailer, with his mandated locked-in silence about my brother's death—but Beck.

≈ ≈ ≈ ≈ ≈

I started spinning between the graves. The twirl of disorientation—faster, then faster. *I couldn't find my mother.* Neil came over quickly and pointed to a place just a foot from where I had begun to disintegrate. In fact, my mother no longer had a temporary marker—her flat headstone was in place. She had now become *one of them.* For a year, the two times I had visited here—Mother's Day and her birthday—she, too, felt like a visitor. But this too-heavy, too-bright plaque, reflecting the peaked noonday sun, was just too hard to take. I wouldn't look at it. I averted my eyes from it as I spoke to her, tore apart the bouquet I'd brought, and then carefully laid the flowers down one by one.

Day 11

It's very late and I'm exhausted. Exhausted, yet clear-thinking enough to believe that Beck's insane and so am I for devoting any more of my life's time to concentrating on him. I'll wash my hair and go to sleep. All I need to do is pull myself from this chair and the wall in front of me, which I continually stare at while caressing the bristles of the now enlarged bald patch on my crown, trying so hard not to think about the past—both historic and recent.

Day 12

Bad rejection of my poems from a very good literary magazine. I thought I'd sent them my best work from my latest manuscript. After it happened, I wanted to call Beck. He is very good about helping me with disappointments, or rather, he *was* very good about helping me with them as long as nothing was directed at him. How he'd listen and listen to me talk about John— my grief over the loss of him and my breakdown. Although, if I ever said *he* had disappointed me, he'd fling his fast language back at me and say how filled I was with "reproach." I came to hate that word: *reproach*. Sometimes I'd intentionally start a sentence that seemed like it was going to be a rebuke of him and I could hear him start breathing heavily like a bull, then I'd turn it into some kind of flattery. He'd relax, respond, be happy. Jerk.

Yet, in the end—*this end*—I'm the jerk. The one who sits by the phone, while he's probably in bed with some graduate student.

≈ ≈ ≈ ≈ ≈

Tonight at temple, I hated God. I guess that's not a good thing to write down between Rosh Hashanah and Yom Kippur, when the Books of Life and Death are opened and He's busy recording who will live and who will die in the coming year. I sat next to Joe Silver, while the rabbi read my mother's name, it also being the yahrzeit of her death. Then, I saw a tall, well-dressed woman grin at him. I couldn't see all of her face because of the too-large brim of her hat. Joe Silver looked at her, then looked at me, then nodded at her what seemed like a small "no," and looked down at the floor.

Day 13

Last night before I went to bed, while washing my face, I looked into the mirror and especially focused on my mouth. It was then that it occurred to me that Beck never made me laugh and most certainly could never laugh at himself. He has a terrible fear of gossip about him. He knows he's done damage—breaking up at least two marriages at the university that I know of, and I came upon the "Beck Scene" late. As soon as the women left their husbands, he dropped them. I had been told by Ellen that he married his third wife because he believed she'd be a "good breeder." She was, almost immediately birthing him Maxi. Six years later, he has partial custody, lives alone, and does pretty much what he pleases. Right now it *pleases* him to hang up on me. I had heard so much talk about him and chose to ignore it. Stupid me, *I thought I could change him.* I'm the cliché on the first page of every self-help book, for here I am, trying and trying to talk with him—to get the full rumor, the complete picture, so that he and I can go on. So I can be calm, feel safe again. I suppose if the devil is kind to you, the result is some feeling of safety—temporarily.

Day 14

Slept. Stayed in bed. All emotion—motionless.

Day 15

Jason says forty-three days of *silence* and Beck will call. He's sure. Jason's into numerology—Jewish mysticism, too. This is what I pay for when I go to see him. But he *does* make me laugh—"Forty-three days?" He's adamant—"Forty-three days." I had to look it up. Forty-three is the biblical number of "Contention." So, after forthy-three days of silence, all heated disagreement, all disharmony will be dismissed? Hard to believe. But I counted forty-three days and circled the date on my calendar.

Until then, I'll work on my play and send it back to the theater, take my novella further, and try to come to terms with losing Beck—"Forty-three days" from my last message to him is November 7. On November 7, my sister Sallie will fly in from Florida and, with Hedy, we're supposed to go through my mother's clothes. Thirteen months after her death and finally the final dismantling of all she left that is of this earth. The next day is the unveiling of her headstone—the one I've already stumbled upon.

Days 16–17

I threw up through the night. By morning I laid in bed, crying, shivering, and wanting her. Neil brought me an oversized soft cotton T-shirt. I cradled it in my arms, pressed it against my breasts, and called it *Mother.* Then, I put it on and asked Neil to please hold me to keep me warm. I have to ask Neil to do such things, but he does do them when I ask.

So now losing Beck, coupled with losing her, has made me double up from vomit and lay immobile on the cold bathroom tiles for hours. No matter what Jason says, he won't call. People can reach their limit with you. Isn't that what John did when he turned his back and walked upstairs away from Joe Silver's words—away from Joe Silver?

Days 18–19
When driving down to the university for my class, I thought about Beck and about all the women who've lost Beck. Losing Beck is a major life event in some ways because if you can truly, authentically lose him, you're strengthened. He puts you through so much anguish that if you start studying him and his tactics, you can actually learn some things about a certain type of sadistic behavior. How he uses certain phrases, like: "I really don't want to quarrel with you, but . . ." It's the *quarrel* word that stops you. The more of an emotional mess you become, the more he elevates his language and when you are finally able to compose yourself and become somewhat coherent, he snaps back with: "I can't address this right now." It's the *address* word that is so off-putting. And if you continue to push, to try to stand up for yourself, it's then he tells you: "You are full of *reproach*." And when he goes that awful step further and does not acknowledge your existence, all that's left to you is to collect the thinned, scattered pieces of your impoverished heart and try to paste it back together.

Day 20
Slept. Woke. Slept.

Day 21
The day was bright and the city beautiful as I passed it on my way to the university. The class gets me up fairly early and out of the house quickly at least twice a week—sometimes three, if there's a guest lecturer, or if actors are brought in to read small excerpts from our scripts. Along with working on our own plays, we're reading the Greek tragedies—how too much arrogance (hubris) can so easily lead to an error in judgment, an inescapable mistake (nemesis). How any authority one ever had is lost. I thought of all the politicians in the news, at first denying their fatal career-ending mistakes, then apologizing, then tumbling—bounce by bounce—from their cushiony pedestals of power. I thought of Beck and myself.

Obviously, I said something too casually and it ended up on someone else's tongue—becoming a mint for many to suck on. There's just so far you can swell before The Furies take over and puncture you.

Day 22

It's Yom Kippur and I finally lit the yahrzeit candle for my mother tonight—for the first time—and the one I always do for John. In back of her candle I placed an anemone (*daughter of the wind*) that I saved from the bouquet I took to the cemetery on her birthday. It's dried out beautifully—elegant, the way she was at the end—pruned to almost bonsai dimensions, no excess, just the shape of a pure grace.

Days 23–25

I bumped into Dr. Sam Guttmacher at the university and we went for coffee. He's a retired renowned psychoanalyst on abandonment issues and used to be the head of the Department of Psychiatry. Years ago, he had rented the third floor of his house to the professor Ivan Durmand—until he threw him out for all his womanizing. "Too much traffic up those stairs," he laughed in his elegant English, delicately laced with a Russian accent.

Ivan Durmand was the head of Beck's PhD committee, and years before the world-famous novelist Avigdor Element was the head of Ivan's. Dr. Sam Guttmacher seems to have kept a close, spectator's watch through the decades on these men, so it was easy to talk to him a bit when he asked me about Beck. Finally, it seemed someone said the truth: "Actually, he may never call back. Perhaps you inadvertently hit an old, narcissistic wound—to be seen how he sees himself, but to which he cannot admit. A Brute."

How I wish Dr. Sam Guttmacher weren't retired. I think he could help me. I know he likes me. I know he loves the creative word. I've heard it said that the poet Wilfred Owen found him as a boy of nine lost in the trenches of World War I and saved him. From then on, he looked at Owen as his older brother. Then, I think of John . . .

Day 26

Today when I awoke I found my heart beating too fast. Maybe losing Beck has become too much. Something is going on that my mind cannot contain, so now it's creeping into my body. The body building its tumors on the mind's grief: hardened, knobby pieces of tissue forming that can detour or totally destroy a life. When I got to my class, my heart became more rhythmic and I surprised myself by asking the professor, "Can I speak with you at some future date about something I've been writing?" (I just don't trust the little man with the big theater.) He cheerfully replied, "Of course." I'm hoping he'll read my entire play when the next revision is completed—not just the small portions he's heard in class. His being at the university with Beck—it's a pretty small place—I guess I run the risk that he'll know it's based on Benedict Eck. *Too Bad.* I've had it with being careful. Too filled with care for poisonous people.

Oh, thank you for letting me up, letting me catch my breath—for not completely raping me. I'll keep quiet so as not to offend your current girlfriend.

≈ ≈ ≈ ≈ ≈

Beck has this thick strip of warts near his ass. They look like something I, or for that matter, anyone, could catch. *That day* when he threw off his clothes I saw them, and as he pushed me down and turned his backside to my face, his stink made me gag. It smelled as if he'd never washed. It was the same odor, however subtler, that came from Joe Silver, when I'd sit next to him as a child and he'd get up from the couch.

With these memories, tonight before I go to bed, I'll erase all Beck's messages from my answering machine—a start. He's attempted to tie both my words and my body down. What if I cut all the "knots"—all the "nots"? Maybe losing a mother is somewhat freeing—no more apron strings to cling to—Lose Everything. Big talk in this late hour of the night.

I did not erase him. Just couldn't.

Day 27

Tomorrow it will be a little over three weeks since I left my message. That weak, semi-menacing one—where I do sound like a hormonally unbalanced twelve-year-old. If the play doesn't work out, I will go to the university and file a complaint against him. Although, I'd rather take the creative route. Every night the story staged, with me and my sick ability to listen to words about being permanently marked. I'm beginning to wonder what all of this was *really* about? The complete destruction of the feminine? Is that too much an intellectualization? How *far* I can be pushed down until I become "The Resurrection"? *Is this hubris or nemesis?*

Day 28

Three years ago, in October, Beck suggested I read *Story of O.* The intention of the author was to entice her lover back with a hyper-erotic, masochistic story about a woman and the club of men she allowed to dominate her—allowed into her to hurt her. A "friend" had given it to him, and with a self-satisfied smile he said, "You might like it." Later, he admitted it was one of his graduate students. He pointed her out to me and, unnecessarily, told me that she was on antidepressants. From being with him? Is that what the *Story of O* does to you?

Day 29

Today would have been my parents' forty-fifth wedding anniversary. I awoke to the lyrics clanging in my head of "The Girl That I Marry." They wouldn't stop so I just let them whirl into my every thought, until finally the words got bored with taunting me and left.

≈ ≈ ≈ ≈ ≈

I called Beck. I did. His line was busy. I called him again. It was still busy. I then called Jason at his cottage in France. I asked him if he thought Beck would really call and he said, "Absolutely" and reiterated his forty-three day theory. He then added, "If he doesn't, it will be the best thing for you, but I'm sure he will"—although Jason also believes that if Beck's line hadn't been busy and I'd gotten through, he would have hung up. "He's not ready. He has to start to feel you're really not there. That you've let go."

Yet, I know if he ever did talk with me again, he'd demand I never write about him. And I'd agree. And then there'll be the play (yes, it's far from finished, but with my new revision I'll soon have an even better draft). And the novella, with Idy Cometh always searching for the right composition to grab on to for a full explanation of what happened to her and how to exact a just retribution. And now, this diary—in which I write at least a few lines almost every night.

Day 30

The written word is a weapon—a witness, a record of what's happened. Whether it sits in a room forever or gets published. It still exists. Beck is lost to me. Words are not. Neil said tonight, "I'd die without you." Yet, his words get lost, dissolve from their lack of concreteness. Neil and Beck are mirror images of each other and I live within the cracks of their unique emptiness.

My father "owned" my mother for almost forty-four years and toward the end he sometimes carried her like a doll downstairs for a little light—out of that bedroom where the shades were always drawn. I belong to no one and nowhere except in this chair with my pen and paper—these I own.

Day 31

I got a rejection of a few poems from an important magazine—what's going on? A few years ago I would have taken to my bed in tears. In the letter the editor asks about having lunch next week—is he kidding? No. And I'm sure he expects me to pay. I always do.

When I was little, my father would bring home silver dollars for me from a currency exchange where he audited the books. The coins felt so solid in my small hands. I loved their endless shape. When I was nine I gave myself my own bald spot—it was the size of a dime. After John's suicide, it became the size of one of those silver dollars.

My mother would pay me with one each week if I hadn't touched the spot for seven days. Sometimes it worked, sometimes not. After I earned a few, I'd go to school with them. Then I'd drop the coins one by one into the charity tin or sometimes give them away to my friends.

Eventually, my teacher called my mother. Maybe she thought I was stealing my parents' money—a little Robin Hood, taking from the rich to give to the poor. Although at the time we, too, were poor—six adults, if you counted Uncle Meyer's drop-ins, and two children in a two-bedroom apartment, Sallie and Hedy not yet born. Joe Silver, my mother's sister Gladys, and I are the ones now left above the ground from that place of unending unhappiness. Someday and soon, all memories of the constant hollering from that place will be sealed into the earth, as it is eventually with all crazy families. Can you imagine the possible racket beneath the ground? Probably worse than all the noise up here—the awful tinnitus of *this* world.

After I opened the envelope from the editor today and saw the rejection, I picked up the phone and called the theater that has the play. It was a risk, but I felt what more could I lose? Actually a lot, but I wasn't thinking very straight. At least I didn't dial Beck's number. The end result was I found out I *am* getting a reading of my revised play, probably in February. The artistic director is going to invite his "patrons." Ultimately, he'll decide if the theater will produce it—with his most important (affluent) patrons' feedback. I just hope he's not just "playing" with me, thinking in the end he'll get me to become not a playwright, but just another well-managed patron.

The phone call has temporarily enriched me, filled me up, made me feel healthier. Right now, the rejection of the poems seems superfluous. I feel the precious weight and shape of silver in my pocket. At this moment I feel how brightly polished my name *is:* Jennie *Silver.*

Day 32

The last time we met, aside from telling me of his fantasy of watching me get his initials tattooed on my breasts, he asked me if I'd like to be bitten—that he'd like to bite me. I had forgotten about *that* request. I told him, being as measured and unflappable as I could manage, "Being bitten isn't real high on my list." Understatement does, sometimes, prove to be a good prophylactic. Then, I remembered his parting words that day: "Jennie, I think about you all the time." That sentence and how he said it with such fervent yearning—seemingly so impossibly romantic . . .

If it is true, that he does think about me all the time, how can he so suddenly force me out of his life, out of his mind? *Me, out of mine?*

Days 33–34

Tonight at 10:15 p.m. it will be a little over a month since we last spoke on the phone. The conversation prefaced with his rhetorical, professorial, "Have I Not Been A Good Friend To You?" Then, All Accusation, All Assassination. Aside from my one, pathetic running down there and calling him after his own awful "Call Me," and my one inept effort to leave a menacing message, my calls have been "anonymous" attempts to just hear his recorded voice—technology becoming the firewall for all longings.

Day 35

I saw him. I saw him from a block away. I could tell it was him from two things: his thick ash blond hair and the slight paunch of his belly. I crossed the street and walked onto the wet grass. My car was on the other side. It made no sense—no logical sense—to cross the street, but when I saw him coming, I suddenly got frightened. Almost five weeks before, I'd thrown my body against his car, begging him to speak to me. I was the pathetic female lead in a badly scripted B movie.

As I crossed the street the concrete became wavy, and when I reached the other side the grass felt like worms grabbing at my sandaled toes and ankles. I had taken a short walk with the professor who may, or may not, be Benedict Eck's friend. Suddenly, I asked him if he'd read my full play—"The play I'm working on in class." He said yes with such an ease I was shocked. I told him it wasn't ready, but was very grateful, adding, "Perhaps at the beginning of spring." Yes, spring, that gives me time. Time with further revisions, time with hearing the theater reading, time to find out if the director is authentic with his gush. Yes, he said *Yes,* he'd read the full play, and with that *Yes* I smiled and swallowed it whole. It sounded like song and it sang inside my body for half a block—that's when I turned the corner and saw him.

≈ ≈ ≈ ≈ ≈

Tonight Neil said we spend too much money on therapists. I *am* making progress. Aren't I? I *did* cross the street today so that truck of a man couldn't, at least then, roll over me. Jason's back tomorrow. Of course, I'll slip and ask if he thinks Beck will ever call again and he'll say yes, and that will be another $150 for his time and *his* "Yes."

Day 36

Jason said, "You should deal less with people—detach from them and contemplate the sun, the moon, the stars. In France, that's what I did—and drank lots of wine."

He does stand by his belief that Beck will call, although he hopes he won't. That I did the right thing by getting out of his way. Then he added, "You should get out of Beck's way for the rest of your life. But I'm worried one day soon the phone will ring and there he'll be, and just that will make you far too happy." I told Jason how I'd hit a "narcissistic wound"—repeating Dr. Sam Guttmacher's words. He just continued by saying, "It wasn't so much the part that he tried to suppress some of your work—that probably inflated him a bit—but rather the part about his calling and calling you and that you're married and his advances were unwanted. Now, *that* made him feel so utterly small." I thought to myself, well isn't *that* a narcissistic wound? I said again what I'd already told him, about Beck telling me that I looked so much like his mother and that he wanted to "fuck me." How I'd replied, half-joking, "So, you want to fuck your mother?" How he quietly and with an almost melodic melancholy answered, "Yes, yes."

I then added Dr. Sam Guttmacher's analysis of this: "In his mind, that's just too much. His desire for some attention, however perverse, from both you and his deceased mother has come to torment, haunt him." He seemed so wistful—actually sad—when he said this.

Jason just laughed, then sighed, "Too much Freudian regurgitation."

≈ ≈ ≈ ≈ ≈

Only writing helps: sitting in this worn chair, so marked with ink—an abstract painting of my years of writing nights. Here, it feels so safe. As safe as a place can be in this world of unending frights:

The image of the cab driver reappears: At first it's just the back of his head. Then I look at the picture of his face on his license, clipped onto the right visor. A year and a half later, I THINK I see him again—his photograph—on television.

Neil and I are in Boston. After one of my readings we have just left a long dinner too heavy with food and drink and writers. The driver's talk, too, seems thick with drool. "Where are you from? Chicago! So Beautiful! Yes, A Beautiful City, Chicago. I've seen pictures of your tall buildings. Soon I plan to visit there. Have you been in the John Hancock?"

Were we that close to such pure rage? Such pure undoing? I'd been so used to just microscopic terrorists: Joe Silver, Beck . . .

Day 37

Hedy's birthday. I ignored it, and that felt right—just the way she and Ed, the difficult, demanding man she lives with, ignored the fact of my fifth book of poems. Actually, all my books of poetry. My mother once asked, *"Why* does she stay with *him?"* I replied, "Do you really want the answer?" She came back with a staunch, "Yes." "It's the sex," I said. Then, I added, "Haven't you noticed how 'Ed' fits so easily into the center of Hedy?" We couldn't stop laughing even though she was in bed and nearing the end of her long journey toward death.

Sallie has sex, but says she'll never take any man seriously—"Too many Joe Silvers out there."

Day 38

After my first book came out, Hedy decided to become a poet. I have a strange effect on people—they think anything I do is easy and want to show me they can do it, too. Just today Mandy told me she and Sy are going to write a play. *Just like that.* I stay quiet when people talk this way. It's hopeless to do much else. I hope I don't sound the way they sound when I'm around people who are more accomplished than I am. It's easy to fall into that abysmal pit of insecurity and then overstretch to try to become someone's equal. I know I can take to jabbering, when I want to impress the impressive.

Day 39

A special appointment with Jason, because I truly want to die—to go and be with my mother. Maybe together we can find John, if she hasn't already. Jason, in his low-key way, suggested instead, "Use some of the money she left you and take a trip to a faraway place—a place with few people, a place you've never been. Then, you'll see how small your world is and the problems with Beck will shrink to a new perspective."

Days 40–41

More sleep. More just wanting to sleep.

Day 42

Coming back from the university I had a panic attack in the car. The road began to undulate, like the day I crossed the street to get out of Beck's way—except this was worse and I felt short of breath. My eyes could barely focus on the pavement, the grass, the buildings, the sky. Everything tilted—my attachment to this planet became so tenuous.

I had left the university feeling so empty. I wanted to look for Beck. Too much the opposite of the day I crossed the street. I knew his class was just ending, but I also knew it was something I shouldn't do. Anyway, I didn't look that great. Looking great is important when you go looking for Beck.

Days 43–44

This is the loss that conjures up all the rest.

I've decided that the only way to get through losing Beck is to believe it's not over, that he *could* just call at any time, that I *could* call him at any time and maybe he wouldn't hang up. I tell myself it's not over, certainly not in the way it's over with my mother and with John.

≈ ≈ ≈ ≈ ≈

As she became sicker she sometimes seemed to inhabit a different space, especially when we were all together. She'd quietly concentrate on us as if we were characters like the ones she'd watch on television. She created a distance. We were the situation comedy so involved with our daily lives and she was the independent observer of our comings and goings—our small troubles and even smaller resolutions. She became the traveler in that bed. We were the townspeople and she, near the end, was just passing through.

≈ ≈ ≈ ≈ ≈

She told Hedy she wasn't afraid and was ready. But oh, how she shined those six weeks when she went into her final remission. How she loved the way she looked in her two new size 6 dresses that she bought for the fall and never wore. She even bought eyeshadow. Not a sign of someone preparing to die. The never-used eyeshadow is probably still in that soft cloth purse she always carried with her those last months—never letting it out of her sight. I'll claim the purse next week. My sisters won't care about a cheap cotton bag and what's left inside it.

≈ ≈ ≈ ≈ ≈

Sometimes I think she's "up there" messing up the relationship now that she has the whole picture—an overview from above. Right at the point I was close to doing whatever he wanted, some crazy rumor appeared, as if dropped from the sky, plummeting to Earth at a major intersection, creating a crater between us. All action, all talk—stopped. *Mother?*

Day 45
It was very cold in our room last night. I awoke to it and woke Neil. He got up and raised the thermostat and then came back to bed and fell asleep. I lay there still cold and shivering and I missed Beck's aggressive desire more than ever—even its hurts, its risks. When I'd come home all marked from Beck, Neil would be asleep. I'd scour my body, appalled by how I looked in the mirror—my skin sometimes broken to blood. I'd wash my hair—the stink of Beck on me everywhere—then I'd put on one of Neil's long, clean white T-shirts. It would wrap around me like gauze. I'd

rarely wake him to rub my head. Just lay there confused. For a few days—
sometimes weeks—I'd have enough of Beck's appetites and could live with
and appreciate Neil's reserve and distance. I'd make up excuses when Beck
called. I needed time to heal and rest—not just my body, but my mind.
Sometimes I'd even decide never to see him again. Then the loneliness
would rear its head and, of course, Beck would be there waiting...

≈ ≈ ≈ ≈ ≈

One day this past summer, I fled a class on the lives of great playwrights
because the professor wouldn't stop talking about Beckett's breakdown
after the death of his mother. I called Beck and ran to his apartment. He
opened the door and there I was, all blotched up from crying. He put on
some soft music and we danced. If I had just left after that, what he'd giv-
en me would have been a gift. But then he pulled up my shirt, unsnapped
my bra, pulled out my breasts, and sucked them to blood, telling me how
beautiful I was. When I left, my body felt burnt from his heat, the opposite of the ice in Neil's and my bed last night.

Day 46

Each time I see Joe Silver he appears smaller. He doesn't seem to be sick,
just old and stressed, and this week won't help—even though he won't
involve himself in sorting through her things, just as he didn't with John's.
That day Joe Silver left the house and went to work. My mother and I silently packed John's clothes, but couldn't give them away. They still sit in
the basement of our old house. In his room, on a high shelf—almost hidden—we found Kennedy's book, *Profiles in Courage*, that Joe Silver had
given my brother for Hanukkah when John was just ten—too young—
and commanded him to "Read It!" We also found the iconic poster of
Marilyn Monroe in her white pleated dress, skirt flung up, with a large
note scrawled on it that read: "Happy 13th, Son! Enjoy it! Enjoy her! Your
Father, Joe Silver." As if, in signing it that way, he, too, would become part
of a collector's item to be placed someday in a museum. We found that in
the back of John's closet, tightly rolled up. My mother, who didn't know

about it, was flushed with rage, and it was then she screamed, "*Nothing, no nothing, can ever be put back together,*" as she tore and tore at the poster and quickly threw the pieces away.

We also found a couple of magazines under John's pillow about playing poker and how to make a "bluff and win." These we were sure were from Uncle Meyer, whom John worshipped. After John's death he, too, left. "Gone to Las Vegas to make millions," Joe Silver would say. There Uncle Meyer became "My Sky" (Meyer Shershevsky was not "cool" enough, but certainly a name one could work with) and for several years Uncle Meyer was a "big shot"—until he, too, disappeared. After that, no one talked about him either.

≈ ≈ ≈ ≈ ≈

Going to the cemetery this weekend for the unveiling of the permanent stone on her grave, to the right of John's, won't be as difficult for me because I've already seen it, or enough of it, and experienced the shock of its permanency and how mother and son now lie side by side in their concrete conclusions. It's the handling of her clothes—giving them away—that I dread, dividing everything that was hers in that room where, over the endless months, she went from diminutive flesh to porcelain figurine.

≈ ≈ ≈ ≈ ≈

Tonight, Neil and I had dinner with Joe Silver. The man talks endlessly about himself. It's only when we drop him off that he turns and asks me what's going on in my life. Only when there's no time left, he asks. Of course, by then I'm so grateful for any attention that I rush, gabbing away (grabbing at the couple of minutes he's allotted me), trying to get everything in—sounding agitated and foolish. I've noticed I also do this with other people when they turn their focus toward me. I talk too fast and become repetitive. I want so much for them to get a full picture of what I'm saying and don't know how much time I'll have, so I talk—speed dial—in what seems too loud a voice, saying things not once, but twice. With Beck, so much of the time, *I could speak slowly about myself, about my mother, about John.* Yes, he, too, like the associate provost, was a good listener.

Day 47

Neil bought me a beautiful scarf today. It was very uncharacteristic, given all his complaints about expenditures on therapists. Maybe because he knew it was the last day of Jason's "He'll Call In Forty-Three Days" theory. He said, "The gift is part of a new beginning, a fresh start to being happy." I wish I could believe him, but he's said this too often. Beck never gave me anything. I have no possession from him, but I am possessed by every move he makes toward me or away. The worst inversion of what a gift is.

≈ ≈ ≈ ≈ ≈

What my mother left in her dresser and her closet—what I choose to take away with me—are the embodiments of when her physical being and soul resided together, craving harmony. She was a woman who was desperate for balance and peace. Years after John's death, she befriended a Catholic nun and she seemed to help. The nun worked in a church where my mother took an exercise class three times a week. She would talk about Sister Teresa Marie only to me. My father had no idea of their friendship and the solace her words brought to a middle-aged Jewish woman's bottomless sorrow. She'd repeat to me what Sister Teresa Marie had told her: "In the fullness of time, all will be revealed." I don't think my mother understood that meant the second coming of Christ, because one day, she took my hand and with a soft command said, "Jennie, *you* write of it. *You write of all of it.*" Her palm was warm and healthy—although it was close to the end of her nine-year remission—and I agreed with a nod of my head, although I didn't know exactly what she meant or how to do it.

≈ ≈ ≈ ≈ ≈

The day is over. Jason *was* wrong.

Day 48

Slept, then ate. Then slept again. Escape.

Day 49

After class I drove twice around the block where I'd seen him two weeks ago. Too much of a change from when I crossed the street. So, two days past Jason's pronouncement that Beck would call, I was driving around the block like a forlorn, lovesick schoolgirl. I wonder how I'll be two weeks from now. *Banging on his door? Saying, I'll write anything you want—a disclaimer you can carry around inside your worn, tweedy blazer that you never attacked Jennie Silver. That nothing you ever did to her drew blood.* Sure, I'll sign it. What does it matter? I'll burn the play. I'll burn the novella. I'll burn *this*. (The thing is, I won't.)

I couldn't help it; I just wanted to see him. Maybe some of it's from the pressure of this coming weekend. I just wanted to tell him, "Beck, we're dividing up her clothes—it's hard. Let me come over." *Hold me, hit me, I don't care. Just make me feel that I'm still here.*

Day 50

Awful night—kept waking from dreams only to lose the memories of their frights.

Day 51

Late today I took a knife to my bald spot, tried to cut it open. I truly believed if I could draw blood from it, I'd feel some release of tension. Also, I thought if I injured it, caused myself unbearable pain, I would stop touching it.

I couldn't cut through my thick scalp. I used a serrated knife. I even dug in with the tip of it. Then I sat down and cried for her. I thought about her head filled with all those sad, small sores. All the troubles she had with her mother, her sister, my father, and her heartbreaking grief over John were expressed in those hidden diggings. I'd comb the healthy hairs to one side and read the script of her whole life right there on her bent head as if it were a long, confessional poem she'd written in another language and I'd been given the privilege to translate it.

That apartment: my grandmother lashing out at Uncle Meyer for his wild ways, then hugging him with her large, gnarled hands, you could see his arch, his strain to get away; my mother's sister high, then low—manic-depressive; my father physically unavailable or if there, just trying to push through the chaos, to tell one of his unending business glory stories with my mother forcing a half-smile, her downcast eyes a contradiction; Grandfather Moses sitting in a corner, continuously smoking—smoking his poor heart out; John on the back porch, repetitively slamming a ball against the brick wall, then agilely catching it. We never knew what emotions would be expressed from one minute to the next. Hit Or Kiss. Kiss Or Hit. Beck.

Day 52

I think I'm going to weaken and call him next week. Maybe because tomorrow—thirteen months after her final wave to me, that beautifully composed last arc in the air—I'm returning to that room to choose to take from what's left.

Day 53

Silenced.

Day 54

The phone rang last night as we entered the kitchen with heavy shopping bags, which felt like weighted cavities of emptiness. Saturday night at 8:00 p.m. It was A calling. He needed an address, or so he said. We talked for about fifteen minutes. He told me there's a very good chance he'll be moving here.

Walking into the kitchen with those bags overloaded with so little, and then hearing A's voice on the phone, felt like a large gift. The timing otherworldly.

≈ ≈ ≈ ≈ ≈

I found a lock of her hair from her first haircut—a strawberry blond curl from my mother's soft baby head. It was in an old, yellowed, thick envelope that felt like parchment. On the front was my grandfather Moses's handwriting in Yiddish: *A Grayzi Fun Beybi Lettie's Kop*. Too Hard. Then there were the clothes she wore those final days when the two of us whipped up and down the road along the lake, drinking black coffee. Pretending to be tough. Pretending to be Thelma and Louise. And her last purse—the soft cloth one, the one she wouldn't let out of her sight when the remissions got shorter and shorter, when she got so finally sick. It's still filled with her lipstick and makeup. I also found John's baby book—its cover, blue silk. It was hidden in the deepest part of the largest drawer in her dresser. I didn't open it—just couldn't—but let my hands caress its smoothness and then placed it carefully in one of the bags next to me.

I discovered two needlepoint mats with the titles of my books in different stages of unfinished . . . And I remembered how pulling those brightly colored silk threads through the canvas would sometimes settle her hands away from her head.

≈ ≈ ≈ ≈ ≈

At the unveiling of her plaque Joe Silver stood on one side of me and Neil on the other. Gladys wouldn't stop talking about how wonderful a sister my mother had been to her. She never told my mother this when she was alive, would just demand things from her and criticize.

I tried hard not to listen and mostly looked up at the sky and watched a small bird fly high above us.

Day 55
I want to fly away like that bird—my birthday wish for tomorrow.

Day 56
Neil and I went out for dinner to a small, quiet place—my choice. He gave me the earrings I had pointed out to him in a store a couple of weeks before. They're nice. All day I hoped that the phone would ring with

Beck's voice wishing me "Happy birthday." Of course he didn't call, and neither did Joe Silver.

Day 57

Mandy, Jason, and Neil are surprised Beck still hasn't called. Now, Jason's taken on Dr. Sam Guttmacher's language, saying, "Yes, a narcissistic wound *has* been reopened." *Irritating.*

≈ ≈ ≈ ≈ ≈

After the class today I asked the playwriting professor if I could give the play to him at the start of Christmas break instead of in the spring. Once again, his Yes came so easily. For some reason—the reappearance of A?— I'm more willing now to take the risk that he might be a friend of Beck than I was a couple of weeks ago. Although I truly hope his reaction to the work isn't contaminated by any relationship he might have with him. Well, I guess it would be okay if he hates him.

Awful, how with all the trouble he's caused me, I still can't get over him—keep wanting to give him another chance. He's tapped into that old chaos—my grandmother screaming at Gladys, Uncle Meyer, Grandfather Moses, then suddenly acting as if nothing were wrong. When my father was around, she'd try harder to behave better. She did try to be careful with me, too—less so with John. She was always warning him, "Do not touch *that*, you could break it." Even though I was three years younger, as I grew older I tried so hard to protect him. But he was already becoming a too-quiet child—all outer pressures repositioned to an inner turmoil. Although he'd always brighten when Uncle Meyer was around. He'd appear so suddenly and sometimes stay for weeks. Always perfectly dressed in a suit—black pinstriped in the colder months, white linen in the summer. He'd make lots of quick phone calls, speaking only in a whisper. He'd let John stand next to him, and John's face would light up with the grandest smile. *I'll tell you how the sun rose . . .*

I was my grandmother's little doll that she'd take around to show off. She'd forcefully say to anyone she knew, "Look. Look at her. Isn't she beautiful?" I lived in fear that someone might say, "No, not really." When everyone would agree, inside I felt that I grew uglier. Sometimes I'd look in the mirror and be surprised that I *wasn't* ugly. Beck never found me ugly, but he did seem to want to destroy whatever beauty he saw in me. Wound my flesh. Somehow that felt right for both of us.

Days 58–59

First snow over my mother's permanent headstone. It buries her even deeper—puts her farther from me. Last year when it snowed and she was so new to the ground, I'd feel I couldn't breathe. A heavy, white claustrophobia covered and froze my body.

I wish he'd call. His voice could lift some of the weight of the snow that falls over her grave, over her body, over me.

Days 60–63

Saw *Dear Liar* today. After Stella Campbell published Shaw's letters to her, he didn't speak to her for sixteen months. Then he wrote her a letter and they got back together—on and off through the rest of their lives.

But Beck's not Shaw. He's not a creative genius, although I'm sure he's as prideful, if not more so, than Shaw was. And crueler in a more base way, maybe *because* no genius resides in him. But maybe not. History is full of genius male artists who were brutes. I think of Avigdor Element. Anyway, all this leads me to the fact that Shaw wanted Stella Campbell back enough to make a move toward her, even though he thought she had betrayed him. Beck won't.

Haven't heard from A again.

Tomorrow is my day. No people. Doing some research for a long poem: purses—womblike, vaginal, sexual containers we women carry around with all our little junk inside to beautify ourselves. Make ourselves look good. Good enough for an A—or a B.

Last night in bed I needed to be held, but vowed never again to ask Neil for affection. If rubbing the top of my head is all he can do, so be it. Beck was the "buffer" even though he used the coarsest sandpaper.

≈ ≈ ≈ ≈ ≈

Mandy says she's going back into therapy. Could she be going to the Cheshire Cat? I didn't ask, but hope not. Anyway, she usually lasts for only one session, then she and Sy have a reconciliation.

Day 64

A poem today about my mother: how soft the skin around her skull was toward the end, how I saw the face of her good father pushing through— their same wide, bright smiles. *I'll tell you how the sun rose* . . . I had never seen the resemblance before. Their same sweet temperament was always there. But this was something different. She was *becoming* his face—each day more so—and soon he was going to take her completely back to him.

Day 65

Tomorrow, I'm being videotaped for a television show (small cable channel) about my poetry. That's nice. That's good. I told Mandy and she didn't know what to make of it. Always the competitor, she replied, "Oh, yes, my son is being videotaped today." She didn't ask me what it was about—she didn't ask me ANYTHING, just started talking about how she and Sy got back together and were now going to write a book and make "millions." (I wondered what happened to the play.) Sy, who yesterday took her to the gambling boats. Then, she admitted with a giggle, "We really went to a 'posh' hotel—day rates." I envision: gambling boats; posh hotels; day rates for sex, and become Shiva, with his third eye, possessing the vision of the essential nullity of all forms. (Jason would like me doing more of this.)

Now, because she has some time tomorrow—no one to screw around with—"Let's get together." I say, "No, I can't. I have to get ready for a taping of a TV show." Normally, I wouldn't have told her, stayed quiet about it and just continued to play the underdog—a scrawny, balding poodle to her overly coiffed collie.

≈ ≈ ≈ ≈ ≈

I keep asking myself exactly what is it one *should* do to live an honorable life—one where, at the end, a person can truly feel good. I know it's cliché, but I think about this a lot. I feel so much cleaner not seeing Beck, but the "Slutty Pumped-Up Mandy Collie Dog" can so suddenly reappear, and it's then I want to pick up the phone and call Beck. *See Beck. Be with Beck.*

Day 66

I called him. I called him at 11:55 a.m. from my car. I didn't know I was going to do this until I did it and I was pretty sure he wouldn't be there anyway. I called him and after two rings, he answered. He said, "Hello?" I said, "Hello." HE DIDN'T HANG UP. He actually seemed glad to hear my voice. Am I making this up? However, I then asked, "Will you talk to me?" He answered "No." Just *No.* The "sick feeling" reentered my body and I couldn't believe I was having this conversation—if you could call it that—*while* driving. I should have been arrested for driving under the influence of insanity. I asked, "Will you talk to me sometime?" He replied, "I don't foresee it now." Shaken, I said, "Okay, goodbye." I sounded pitiful. He just said, "Bye." That was it. I play the call over and over in my mind. The key is the *foresee* word. When I get home I'll look it up in both my dictionary and thesaurus. I *know* I'm splitting hairs—those shredded fibers disintegrating between my thumb and forefinger.

Note: The TV thing went okay. I forgot they were filming, but when it's aired, I won't watch.

Day 67

I played a "nice" tape tonight of a phone call I had with Beck from last March—way before this recent chaos. It's not a tape where he's yelling at me. I got the idea a couple of years ago of taping our conversations because his words would leave me so confused—the way he could twist language so articulately. There was probably nothing he couldn't invert, convert, or knot.

I thought if I had tapes of our conversations I could play them and figure out later what was really being said, what was really going on with him, and better understand the dynamics between the two of us. I have, I'm sure, over a hundred tapes—over a hundred hours of "Beck Talk." Sometimes playing them would keep me away from him for almost a couple of months. The way he'd scream at me never to call his office. It was when he got really vehement over this that I'd know he was having sex there with one of his students.

If calling him yesterday was a mistake, mistake it was, it hasn't prompted me to do anything more bizarre. The fact that he didn't hang up means something—doesn't it? *God, I sound pathetic. Pathetic*, too, on too many of the tapes.

Day 68

My mother's last surviving first cousin died this week. Joe Silver told me this at dinner tonight. After that it became difficult to speak. I spent the rest of the meal just trying to swallow—the death of Rosie and my mother. The image of these two women locked in their vaults got lodged in the small space of my throat. I couldn't eat. I wanted to scream, "*Do you ever think of John? What you did to him? WHAT YOU DID TO YOUR SON?*" It's not the first time. In fact, it's always there, just quieter.

Day 69

I think more and more about what it means to be a good person. I'd like to be remembered as someone who had a positive impact and was capable of love, but I don't think I'm on that path. Wanting to scream at Joe Silver and wanting Beck—brutish, humorless, ungiving, unforgiving Beck—to call has nothing to do with being a good person, and obsessing on his sentence, *I don't foresee it now*, is such a waste of myself. Yet, those words these last days are what I ruminate on the most, leaving little room for any generosity or goodness toward others.

≈ ≈ ≈ ≈ ≈

Four years ago, right before Christmas, Beck's first cousin, whom he idolized, was killed in a motorcycle accident. Drunk, he smashed into a utility pole. Beck packed up and flew off. Called me after the funeral. I thought about my own awful grief over John and I felt terrible.

He asked me to meet him at the airport between flights on his way back from the funeral to the Modern Language Association Convention in Washington. I met him. I sat with him. I was *good* to him. Neil gave me his card to the Red Carpet Club.

He showed me family pictures and talked about the service. Months later, he told me what he was really thinking when I met him. How dominant he felt. How he fantasized about asking me to go into the men's bathroom with him and suck his penis. He thought if he had just asked, I would have done it. When he finally told me this, at first I thought it was about how loss can make a person feel more sexual—an affirmation of one's own life, an "I'm still here" assertion. But now, as I write this, I realize it had more to do with his insatiable need to control me in order to soothe himself.

When Joe Silver told me about Rosie's death and it felt like I was going to choke, I was in "The Men's Room" again and someone was forcing life's foulness down my throat. I was being given no choice. Joe Silver was using me one more time to take *his* grief and swallow it.

Day 70

I got a strange letter in the mail today, from that third therapist. The one I had characterized as a real "hard-ass." In the envelope was a photocopied statement about his impending retirement. But folded around it was a letter—a personal letter to me. I was stunned that he took the time to write it, and somewhat intrigued by what he wrote:

> *Dear Jennie Silver,*
> *I am sorry any further sessions with you did not happen. Therefore, after much consideration, I am sending you this letter. I believe your attachment to Beck could best be termed "Fragmented Mental Life." It is not transference as some of your past therapists have characterized it. It is NOT coming from a repressed UNCONSCIOUS attachment to your father.*

I suggest this is the original, unmodulated, unattenuated, untransformed "three-year-old" infatuated attachment to your father, which by age four was thwarted, ignored, and set aside—i.e., postponed, sequestered until one "greater man" restored you to it and you regained that blissful state of childhood importance, glory, splendor in the eyes of "The Father."

"Smart, Cruel, Demonstrative" Beck replaces "Stupid, Cruel, Undemonstrative" Father. Except neither your father NOR Beck wants to help you grow, expand, mature, and be a blessing to this world . . .

Fill in the blanks.

Best regards,
Dr. Solomon Teich

I've tucked the letter away between the covers of my daily calendar. I am not offended by it. In fact, it's quite the opposite. Dr. Solomon Teich must have felt guilty about being so abrupt with me and therefore took the time to write. I just don't know how much truth about my relationship with Beck is imbedded in such jargon, and right now I don't feel like attempting to tweeze any of it out, if some does exist. Even if it does, what am I to do with it? Dr. Solomon Teich *was* mean and now is retiring to some cloistered island where he can drift on his analytical raft until his death.

Day 71

Dinner with Hedy tonight. We were to take each other out. Birthday presents to each other. I ended up paying. Guilt, I guess, for ignoring her birthday. She won't read my books, but likes to listen to my troubles—similar to Mandy, but Hedy gives me more time to talk. For my birthday she called and sent me a card, which made me reach for the check.

Hedy thinks Beck set me up, because of what I wrote. Being *that* nice: talking about inviting our father to a boxing match in late September, saying I could sit in on his class, telling me he thinks about me all the time. Then that phone call at 10:15 p.m.—his voice shouting, "Have I Not Been A Good Friend To You?" Then his slamming and slamming of the phone. "Was all of this a calculated setup?" I ask. Hedy answers, "Yes."

I guess the devil wouldn't be the devil—everyone would just steer clear of him—if he weren't filled with charm at least half of the time and initially quite nice. Maybe half's too much—just enough to pull you in and drag you down

> ... to his futon
> on the soiled hardwood floor.
> His child had napped there
> earlier. I could smell
> the urine ...

More lines from my fifth book he wanted me to delete. I didn't.

Day 72

Called A. He's coming to town for final interviews on the 11th. He'll be in a hotel off campus on the 12th. I said, "I hope we can meet for coffee." He enthusiastically replied, "I hope we can, too. Call me at my hotel the morning of the 12th." A's "Call Me" slid me into memory—Beck. And even further back to Carrington Lowell's "Call Me" message to John of Harvard's mistake. John barely an hour in the ground. I felt so suddenly sick. I threw up.

≈ ≈ ≈ ≈ ≈

When I first met Neil, he reminded me so much of John. I have never made this admission to anyone, not even Jason. I can just hear Beck's reaction, if I had told him this. "So you want to fuck your brother?" I would have said quietly, "No, I just want my brother back." And with Neil I do get some of this. Perhaps, therein lies the great flaw in Neil's and my relationship. Neil *can't* be my "brother, lover"—we're not characters in some Greek myth.

Days 73–75

The artistic director left a message. He now says the only way his theater can give me a higher-level reading is if I *pay* for the space and the actors that evening. I know this isn't how things are done. All my suspicions about him have been realized. He'll never allow me to get beyond the category of "patron" whom he will patronize with one night of play, if I pay.

Neil was too quiet tonight when he came home to this news. We then went out for a drink to dull my pain, but at the restaurant and in the car coming home he became mute. I felt like I was going to suffocate. And with all this, any comparisons to John *did* evaporate. Lately especially, he brings with him no solace, just an increasing reticence—his behavior becoming a burgeoning series of hyphens, dashes, and long pauses.

What the artistic director said really offended me. Listening to his overly worded message of what he could do for me, my first impulse was to again—*yes, again*—call Astrid Olson's office. Have the university confront Beck directly. Let them be his jurors. After all, this *is* truth, not theater, not fiction. I said out loud to myself, "It's just your crummy little life, no more terrible than all the other crummy little lives surrounding you—Neil's, Hedy's, and Gladys's included." I thought, too, of my Grandpa Moses's, of my mother's, and of John's.

≈ ≈ ≈ ≈ ≈

Mandy's broken-hearted again; for the twentieth time she realizes Sy will never leave his wife. His money is more important than Mandy. I met her at the House of Pies. Her face looked like a pie—a sad pie face—and she looked wide, no getting around it, she looked well into middle age. The affair has worn her down and spread her out.

Talking with A makes me feel young. I've marked the 12th on my calendar—cleared the day. Mandy said, "He'd be a bigger mistake than Beck." But what do I have to lose? So what if eventually it will be another rejection. They come in the mail (male) or over the phone more frequently these days.

Day 76

Thanksgiving. Although I still finger my spot, I haven't attacked it again and I'm thankful for this. The chance of seeing A has filled me with some amount of happiness. I *know* I'm outclassed, out of my league, putting myself out on a limb, and borderline out of my mind with my anticipation of the possibility of seeing him. But it's Thanksgiving and for now I'm grateful he's come along. When I go to bed I think of him. I need to lose at least five pounds in a week and a half. I'm thinking "small" again. I guess I should be thankful, too, that it's well over two months that Beck—more metaphorically than physically—cut me. It could have come to the actual. And now A is riding in on his white horse to *save me*—he and his stallion melded into one. At least that's what I'll almost believe for the next days. Sure, the 12th could come and go and he could—at least in my life—be a "no show." *Fairy tale canceled.*

Days 77–78
   Tonight Neil told me again that he's truly "in love" with me, but I don't believe he knows what that means. He pays no attention to what I tell him I need. I can say it loud or say it soft—it just doesn't have any effect. I've given up and await A's gallop.
   A random therapist once said, "You have a high tolerance for abuse." He was right, but it was hardly revelatory and hardly worth $200.
   Familiar Old Abuse. One human being verbally destroying another. Sometimes I yell and yell at Neil for what he lacks. It's at these moments I feel I've become Joe Silver, or worse, that I'm so furious with John that he could ever leave me, abandon me, that I want to yell and yell at him.
   I wish he had taken me with . . .

Days 79–81
   Tomorrow I give the latest version of my play to the drama professor. Does he know Beck? Are they best friends? I doubt it. But who knows? In a way the giving over of the play helps solidify the end of my relationship with Beck. My mind's a yo-yo, I'm back to thinking this *is* better than reporting him to Astrid Olson. To write a play seems much more effective. *He attacked me on university property. Told me whenever he invites me to his office, it's never to talk, but just for sex.* Stupid me, I actually thought we'd talk about poetry, but for Beck it was just another place to expose his penis.

≈ ≈ ≈ ≈ ≈

Tonight Jason reiterated, "You're too much with people—too much with humans. Nature is safer, a garden is more predictable and rewarding." Although, he does like the idea of my giving the play to a possible friend of Beck. "In and of itself, it is its own play." We laughed. He's quite a strange therapist—not "sick-strange" like the Cheshire Cat.

He added, "Watch how humans 'play' with each other—join in, then step away. Go tend a garden." For now my garden is what I've written. Better than therapy, better than running to Astrid Olson and the sexual harassment committee at the university, I hope. More worthy eventually of a larger audience? Is there a message here that needs to be heard by many? Sometimes I doubt this with all the talk shows, tabloids, and self-help books.

≈ ≈ ≈ ≈ ≈

The professor was perfunctorily polite when I handed him the play. I told Neil that *today* for sure I'd bump into Beck after class. *After* I'd handed over the play. And, of course, I did see him. A heightened kinetic energy surrounds me—not making me feel more special, just more crazy.

He was crossing a street just beyond the campus's reach. He was with Maxi. He was smiling. I thought, *see*, he can smile without me in his life. Then, he noticed my car and looked at the license plate, and as he began to look up, I turned away. Turned my face to the left. To the playground where I first met Maxi. The playground was deserted today. I looked at its emptiness. I kept driving and, unlike Lot's wife, I did not look back. However, since I saw him I can't stop wondering what he felt when he saw my car. I think about how badly he's behaved with me, how my impoverishment of physical intimacy drew me into his life and kept me on that street where he was crossing, where he was smiling, his little girl skipping. They're fine.

I don't regret giving the play to the professor. But I did want to stop the car and pop out and ask, "Can I come play?" No pun here. I had fun with them. I *did* want to look back. Yet, being with Beck and Maxi wasn't always fun. He'd make promises to her so she would behave in a certain way and when she did, he'd rarely follow through. She'd ask, "*Now* can I have ice cream?" and he'd say, "It's too late, time for bed." Maxi was forever saying, "But you said . . ." And so many times I'd run home to scrub away the smells from Beck, after Maxi was asleep. I'd climb into bed next to Neil and toss my damp mop of hair on his just-washed T-shirt. And that sterile bed where I placed myself next to Neil, I'd bless.

Days 82–83
Today, after class, I delivered my sixth book of poems to my press. So much of my life revolves around that damn place. I'm worried this book won't be taken. Kane—the series editor—is indebted to Beck for positive reviews of his own books and some mid-level awards. So there are reasons to worry.

When I expressed this to Neil, he just gave me a blank look and we started to fight—or rather, I did. Nothing affects him. He just gets this weird grin on his face the angrier I become, which I guess is some kind of protection he painted on his face when he was four to defend himself against his mother. Now he's turned me into *that* bitch woman. More than ever, all he brings to any conversation is an unrelentingly litany of redundant, generalized statements and questions.

I've gained more weight—with Neil around I seem to always need something sweet. The two days this week he was out of town, I lost two pounds. How much more alone could I be if I were actually alone? But how to get from "here to there"? When he realizes I mean it—that I have to get away, away from our relationship—he starts to choke (literally). That "hard-ass" therapist once said, "So what. So he'll choke. That's not your problem." It's then I think of John and wish so much I could have saved *him*. So I save Neil instead, by not leaving.

Days 84–85
I'm eating a lot of ice cream with hot fudge. No way to slim down for A—but seeing him seems so slim, so why not "fudge" a bit. Sure, I'll wash

my hair next Thursday and the worst that will happen is that I'll wait for a call that won't come, but I'll have clean hair throughout the weekend. However, I fear if he ignores me, it will make of my mind a dishevelment and send me flying back to Beck thoughts and *to* Beck. Not that he's ready to grant me mercy.

How old does one have to get before one stops playing this role? The Waiting Part: "*Sorry madam, but the only role we have left is the 'Waiting Part.' Would you like to play it? No need to audition—your reviews have been [pause] let's say, more than adequate.*"

Even in our best times, I'd wait for Beck to call and I still sometimes hope (wait) for Neil to change.

Day 86

We are moving toward the shortest day of light, and when I can sleep late there are only a few hours left of haze, then a thick blur of gray, until the world again shuts to black. My mother sleeps deep in the cold, dark ground. Instead of missing her less as time has passed, I miss her more. In a way, this makes sense—it's the longest I've been without her in my life.

≈ ≈ ≈ ≈ ≈

I'm guessing Beck leaves soon for California to visit his younger brother. I'm still living in his days—the patterns of his life. I, too, will be in California in two weeks. At the end of the trip—give or take a few miles—I could be so near Beck. By then, will he *foresee* things differently?

Day 87

The class is over for the quarter. When I awoke I stayed in bed for over two hours, anticipating A's arrival . . .

Day 88

I turned my answering machine off through the night just in case he called and set my alarm for 9:00 a.m. This morning at 8:30 a.m. the phone rang. Startled and happy, I picked it up—it was a friend wanting to leave me a message. She asked why my answering machine wasn't on and I mumbled that I was waiting for a repairman. Not too far off base—A, the perfect "repairman."

I tried to go back to sleep, but at 8:45 I got out of bed and called him. He answered. Pleasant enough, but I could tell we weren't going to see each other. He had a cold. He coughed. He was going to see places with the realtor I had suggested, Joyce Levy (Mandy wasn't interested—"too busy"—and *thank goodness,* for she really isn't bright enough), and afterward he was having drinks with students from last spring and then dinner with a friend.

Give me a chance, I was silently screaming, *let me leave my small room, leave my small life, it's getting late.* "Are you busy tomorrow afternoon? Tomorrow night?" I asked, calmly. He said, "Yes." Then, he added that there would be more trips, because he had accepted the job and would return after Christmas *after* his five weeks in Europe, which included a ski trip in the Swiss Alps. Perhaps he'd be back in six or seven. I was pleasant. I sounded happy, even blithe—my voice filled with falseness of full life.

Joyce called at 9:00 p.m., leaving a euphoric message: "I can't thank you enough for putting me in touch with such a *fantastic* man. I had a *wonderful* time and I think he did too. We're going to look at more places tomorrow."

Day 89

Early this morning I played the message from Joyce again. She had added at the end, "Thank you for *introducing* us." As if it were a date and the date had spawned a romance. They were supposed to be looking at lofts—not a fairy tale cottage.

Aside from the possibility of their having had sex and any future whatnot, Joyce does know the business and for this and only this, he should have called to thank me.

Day 90

I met Mandy for coffee late this afternoon. The world had begun to slope again, with me on the sharp edge of falling off, and sometimes she does make me smile. She kept telling me how good I looked. With my hair a little shorter, it looks fluffier. I told her, "I had it trimmed for A and it's being wasted on you." We laughed. Then she told me about her quick trip to Miami. "My mother refuses to be buried next to my father—'the philanderer.' Says, 'I've spent enough time with him in this life and I want a different cemetery.'" Mandy then told her mother that *she* had promised to be buried next to him. Her mother's reply was only, "Well, you always were *daddy's girl*." "It's true," she said to me, "'Mandy, the philanderer.'" It's the closest I've ever heard her get to any self-awareness. We laughed more and for some minutes I forgot about Beck as I listened to Mandy talk about her tour of cemetery plots, when all she wanted to do was eat— adding with a giggle that, "Sy has named my breasts Stella and Dora, after Stella D'Oro, *that old cookie!*"

Days 91–92
It's almost three months from the hysteria of throwing myself in front of Beck's car—he and his car overheating in the dying Indian summer sun. The day was so high-pitched with blazing color—me in that *red* sweater— and then came the dead time, the emptiness, the heading into the lack of light, into the now charcoal of darkness. *Emotions on wet roads on autumn nights . . .* Poetry from her funeral.

The shortest day of the year is hours away—a thickening frost sepa-rates us.

≈ ≈ ≈ ≈ ≈

Last night I finished a book on purses and started another one on combs. About all the turtles that have to be killed to get a tortoise shell one, so some woman can play with it, place it in her hair in front of her mirror, make her-self more beautiful while she waits for an A or B to show up—or just call. My fascination with containers grows larger. *About being contained. About being a container:* "You can't write about me. I want to fuck you."

Day 93
   Tonight I wrote:

Her Purse, at the Winter Solstice

The needled red tea roses were distorted
by the quilt in the fabric of the cheap cotton
bag she carried through the filth
of snow to the transfusions

and back again to her bed
where she fanned herself
into the soft pink blankets and then closed
into them like a small item,
lost. Sometimes I couldn't find her—

a swansdown powder puff,
misplaced. All night
I'd dream of black taffeta, locked inside
a day bag of white painted metal plaques
or an evening clutch of lacquered brass
covered with ash, ribbed silk. Her purse

had too deep a background
where blossoms were pinned down
—stitch to stitch—
with never a hope they could climb off
and into the coming spring air, join

the others. I'd dream of a framed
French carryall, pale blue silk
and silver thread worked into
a pattern of a spiderweb, finished

with a tassel of carved steel
beads, my fingers constantly being cut
by handles decorated with flowered urns
and the cold heads of the sphinxes.

Then, I slept.

Day 94

Neil came home from work and we went out to a nearby delicatessen.
After the soup and before the sandwiches, a woman started screaming
from the kitchen—running from the back of the place to the front. The
Munch painting "The Scream"—That Shriek Of Pain—flashed before my
eyes. Then, I heard her words, "*They've killed my baby. Abe, they've killed
my baby.*" I started to cry. The world leaned in on me, but had just rolled
over this poor woman, crushing her forever. And there the waitress stood,
holding the rest of our order—stunned. Neil offered to pay her, but she
just whispered as best she could, "No, just go. It's okay. Just go."

We left, but that woman's large, amorphous grief follows me. Her
world fell out of its orbit. I heard it. It was loud and awful and quick. I
think of my mother's shrieks when John was found . . .

Day 95

I called him this morning. I guess the gods of small minds were looking
out for me—his line was busy. Still, I thought maybe it's just a phone call
coming in for him or he's checking his messages from a distance. Although
it seemed more likely that he was home and on the phone. I called Mandy
and she called him from her cellular phone, using *67. He answered—or
some man did "with a very nice voice." She asked for "Brian" and he responded quite politely that she had the wrong number. So he sounds fine.
Remembers his manners. Is polite to strangers with wrong numbers.

Tomorrow we fly to California. Everyone says, "Go, get away." Away
from Beck's hangups of a few months ago, away from my "hangups" about
Beck. Even Neil, but why shouldn't he? We're using some of the money my
mother left me.

Although, how do I get away from this creature that is me?

Days 96–97

Early yesterday morning, as the plane broke through the clouds, the sky on the right became a soft rose red, and on the left a twinkle of light blue. Then, suddenly from the right a slender beam of yellow lit the cabin. It was the sun. *Far from any human.* I thought, this *is* what Jason's been saying about making a space between myself and people—letting in a little of the natural world. And I thought, again, about Dickinson's lines: *I'll tell you how the sun rose,— /A ribbon at a time.* And my added one—*Her smile was that to us.*

When the landscape inside the airplane and outside its windows came together with intricate kaleidoscopic light, I felt closer to her—both of us bold beams drifting.

Day 98

Big Sur. Carmel. Finally everyone seems so far away. I could stay here forever. This is *truly* what Jason meant. Then, we made the mistake of watching two pornographic movies in this gorgeous, nurturing, natural space. (Strange, how we've never done this before. But the hotel offered them for free.) The first we had to turn off. There was a woman naked on a swing, her legs apart, and a man standing in front of her with a very large knife in his hand—too cruel an image, even if it were just a toy.

The male lead in the other reminded me of Beck—not so much in how he looked, but his moves, as if Beck had made a study of how to behave from watching these movies. How the man physically manipulated each woman, spreading their legs with the strength of his knees—moving his mouth and hands from breasts to vagina to backside. How quick, yet mannered his motions were, as if having sex required a certain procedure, like boning a fish. In this movie there was only one woman the man hit. The ugliest.

I'm not ugly, but because of my girlish voice—in its way not so dissimilar from the star-crossed Jacqueline Kennedy and Marilyn Monroe—I guess people think I'm easy to dominate. That they can take whatever they want from me. I *have* allowed myself to be trampled on, before I rise up. My stubbornness when Beck pushed me to his futon reared its head and strengthened my pen. Telling me I couldn't write about anyone who resembled him made me cower in a corner, my third eye watching there. But my third eye *can't* stop me from missing him. Not Beck "the porno star," but Beck with his voice on the phone, listening... The rumor—or part of it—that his calls were unwelcome wasn't true. "The Caller," when I was in his presence, was, at best, problematic.

Day 99

The ride down Highway 1 seemed to clear a path in my mind. We stopped at a Vista Point where we got out of the car. The sky was almost too bright—cloudless—with the purest California promise of unending success. The green mountains shaded from forest to lime, the ocean all periwinkle.

I went to the edge of the cliff and balanced myself there. One more step and I would have fallen off. Neil tried to pull me back, but I needed to do this. I saw my shadow on the opposite mountain and raised my arms as if I were about to fly—*unsubdued / Elations when the forest blooms*... Then I turned toward Neil and he said, "You look like a small bird." I replied, "No, a female eagle." We laughed and life at that moment—far from Beck—felt good.

Yet, as we got closer to Los Angeles I thought more and more about him. He was born in Las Vegas. His father was a frustrated ballad singer who got no further than being the lounge act at the Sands, Sahara, and Riviera hotels, while Frank Sinatra's, Perry Como's, and Tony Bennett's voices filled the main stages with huge audiences and loud applause. His mother was an aspiring showgirl who never made it to the final round— her breasts *too* large, *too* round. They bounced too much. Eventually, his family left for Los Angeles where his father barely supported the four of them, crooning sad love songs at inexpensive supper clubs with bad acoustics that sprung up along Sunset Strip, only to eventually go bankrupt.

Day 100

The Getty Museum. Statues of Greek gods. Especially Hercules. The legs. Beck's are as good. I've never seen legs like his except on a statue. A figure to be idealized. All day I tell myself I can't reconnect with someone just because of an outer perfection. Sometimes he'd tell me he couldn't help his cruelty toward me—he actually "enjoyed it, didn't understand it." How can I consider turning back to *that*?

At the museum I thought I saw him everywhere—the Greek god statues and tall male visitors with thick, ash blonde hair. Neil grows heavier, his speech slower, and he's always thirsty—a metaphor for nothing, just worry about some weighty, unquenchable illness. The second week in January he has an appointment with his doctor.

≈ ≈ ≈ ≈ ≈

The Greek gods had many sides to them and were the best teachers of retribution, I wrote of Beck. However, these days when I write of him it's not from a place of vengefulness, but more from that quiet place of loss.

Day 101

Los Angeles. Newport Beach. Los Angeles. Night rides over the twelve-lane highways. White headlights blazing, racing toward me. Red taillights racing away, past me. The *possibilities* in the white lights—the not yet mistakes—the endings, the leavings of the red ones. *She wore a red suit . . .*

Right now, this hotel room seems the only place I belong. We've extended our stay by a couple of days. I don't want to go back to where I live. Who would? There's nothing there but unhappiness—Beck's silence, her headstone flashing before me, the letters of her name an alphabet of sadness anchored in the late December ice and old snow. The last time I saw her alive, she waved. We were in the middle of nowhere. The highway nearby was filled with the comings and goings of other lives.

Day 102

Mandy said, "He'll call after the first of the year." I don't think so. Nor do I think A will call again, even when he moves here. If I were prettier I think they'd both be calling. Although three miles from where we are now and many, many years ago, Marilyn Monroe was found dead. Dead in Brentwood. And, once again, I am reminded of the poster of her that Joe Silver gave John on the occasion of his thirteenth birthday with his large, oafish message and signature scrawled on it, and feel sick. When I learned more about her, it was the first time in my young life that I was struck by the concept that *pretty, prettier, prettiest* was not necessarily the best.

Day 103

We're leaving tomorrow. Leaving the statue of Hercules. Again, we went to the Getty Museum and I re-entered the room where the statue was centered. I couldn't help but return to it. His legs and hips, my eyes kept being drawn to them—*to him.*

Day 104

Today, my mother spoke to me as we boarded the plane. She told me our flight would be fine. "Another plane. Somewhere another plane would have trouble." Tonight at home, when I turned on the late news, I found out she was right.

Who is it that sends me these messages, over my right shoulder—whispers in my right ear? In the skies over Colorado, after the air finally quieted, she said, "You'll get home safely, but never again have anything to do with Beck. You can be polite, but *that's it.*" My mother's voice? Or just what I know she would now say? Among the violent winds, my mother blew in strong and willful. Not the quiet woman of this earth, baking butter cookies in her kitchen, but a force now merged with the erratic atmosphere, jostling the universe.

Day 105

Snowy day here. Okay if one stays inside. I read in the sunroom—not in the room I usually work in, with my chair cornered by shades. It was snowing lightly, and what had already landed on trees outside my windows lay thick and quiet on the branches. Sun lit the room. Alone with myself like a satisfied angora cat, getting fatter with each flake—the phone off the hook—I felt so safe.

Then my thoughts traveled back to Beck. That tomorrow he, too, would probably be back, if he went anywhere. Beck back, me back, a new year in forty-eight hours—and I thought, so what, what can I possibly do with any of this?

Day 106

Neil says 40 percent of my spot is very much better. The rest is pretty bald, with only two or three damaged nubs pushing through. Maybe 40 percent of me is better, too, with the rest still abraded and empty.

Tomorrow we take Joe Silver with us for New Year's Eve. I can hear my mother telling him, "After I'm gone, Joseph, please don't talk so much about business; be more interested in your daughters." But he's just not. He just lost a huge amount of money on a bad decision so he'll jabber even more. His excitements and griefs are always about cash flow and ego. His investments always about paper, not people—*not ever* since John let go. And I do think grief makes most people extra chatty—a huge need to reconnect to what has been lost. That's why I write every night. When it's dark outside I feel so many vacancies, and like a vagrant I visit each—sit inside each shed, think too much, and pick my head.

Day 107

Tonight people think they have a chance to start over, and inarticulate C-list celebrities with no scripts in front of them will overspeak with too much flutter in their voices about the promise of the forthcoming year. *We are all so unimportant.* Things will or will not happen. Individually we will be lucky or unlucky—temporarily. Then not. Beck will or will not reappear and that will be *both* lucky and unlucky—temporarily. For now, with the cusp of the new year, I, too, have some small hopes. The very poems that lost me Beck became a play, or rather are *becoming* a play—revised, then revised again. His large and small tortures of my being, becoming *this* record. Then, there is my sixth book of poems, delivered to my publisher. While my novella waits patiently for me to return to it—with Idy Cometh growing sicker and Avigdor Element's protégé, Christiane Juul, becoming quieter . . .

I do feel so uncertain as to what will happen—as to what *I want* to happen—but the one thing I know for sure is that I need Neil to be here, with my hair sprawled on his stomach, and me curled up against him like the gnarled, ingrown hair that I am. He can't possibly be sick, I keep telling myself.

Day 108

I dreamt of Beck the first night of the new year. Neil and I were in a restaurant across from Beck's apartment. I had just woken up and was a mess. Our hotel was on the opposite corner from the restaurant. A triangle: the restaurant, Beck's place, the hotel. Beck walked in with Maxi and another man—A? I tried to get back to the hotel to wash my face, fix my hair, but some party was going on in the street and I couldn't get through the crowd. I walked back into the restaurant barefoot with Neil's long T-shirt on and my eyes all smudged from old mascara, thereby proving to Beck I wasn't very attractive.

Beck looked beautiful in the dream. Fit and happy. I, on the other hand, looked at best disheveled and felt unsafe.

≈ ≈ ≈ ≈ ≈

Sometimes it feels like there's nowhere to go on the surface of this planet that's safe (not even my writing room or the sunroom). It's at these moments in particular I remember that cab driver's oily words, his photograph on the visor, with Neil and me listening from the back seat as he extolled the grandeur of this country, of Chicago, the John Hancock building, and I wonder: *How does one protect oneself against that?*

We run around doing our small tasks as if they're huge urgencies, when in fact they're not. Yet, it's only when realizing that they're *not*, that the panic sets in: *Where to go, what to do? How to be of any value during our short stay?* Writing a poem? A play? A novel? Writing *this*? I doubt it.

In the moments of creation, when self-awareness is swept away by the pen, the panic *can* calm, but what good is it for "some paltry eternity that's called posterity?" Not my words; I copied them a while ago onto a Post-it and stuck it to the radiator cover next to where I write.

I think the quote is by Camus. Jason gave me the book, *The Myth of Sisyphus and Other Essays*. My therapist gives me books about "why live?" and they are *not* exactly self-help ones. They're the classics from the brilliant depressed types and it does help me to know that some smart people have been forever nagged by "why live?"—have felt the claustrophobia of wandering between earth and sky.

Maybe some amount of pleasure would help. Beck didn't understand why I chose such loneliness. Neither does Mandy, who is at the other end of the spectrum, with two men, two birthday presents, two anniversaries. Essentially, two husbands. Two lives. She doesn't question her existence; she's too busy living it.

Day 109

Went into the city. Had lunch with Neil near his office. He needed to catch up on some work. Seven years ago, he moved from a large, established architectural firm on LaSalle Street to a smaller one where they not only offered him more control over designs for buildings, but more money. His office is *now* in the John Hancock. "*I hope to visit it soon.*" How those words slithered on that cab driver's too-moist, too-talkative tongue.

≈ ≈ ≈ ≈ ≈

The world wakes up next Monday. Everyone gets back to where they were. Some will take a step forward, some back. Some forward steps will really be backward ones. I think of Beck when I write this. To see him—what a fix that would be. Then a fall back—a crash.

Day 110

A has a girlfriend, a girlfriend in Washington and a wife in Boston—the marriage breaking up. This was told to me by Joyce. I called her today to find out what happened when she showed him more places. I was very casual. "How are you? How did it go?" She sounded awful. The second day of their outing he brought along a woman. I could still hear the pain and surprise of this in her voice. As she spoke, I got the sick feeling in my gut. A has a thirty-five-year-old son with his soon-to-be ex-wife, and his recently divorced new girlfriend has four-year-old twins. Didn't he *tell* me he's very popular with younger women?

She told me how affectionate they were in front of her. Her voice all strain—saying, "Maybe it won't last." I felt sorry for her, and for me. Embarrassed, too, for both of us. And as she spoke Beck rose up like a phoenix pushing through my body.

A arrives at the end of March and already he's gone. Even if they do break up as Joyce prays, he could never be relied upon. Too many women for too well-known a man.

My shame about waiting for A, I keep to myself. These days I feel like keeping everything to myself. What business is my life to anyone? Mandy once said, "People don't really care what you do—so they'll gossip about you for a little while, then they'll go back to their own lives. Big deal."

≈ ≈ ≈ ≈ ≈

Beck would talk about pleasure for pleasure's sake. I should have taken the pleasure and kept it. Kept *everything* to myself. From this day on, no one will really know me. So they'll think me vague. But they'll have nothing to repeat. "'Garbo' with all her scars covered," I say out loud as I mock myself and think of Yeats's line:

Only that which does not explain itself is irresistible.

Then, I write it on a Post-it and stick it onto my overheated radiator cover.

Day 111

I wanted to call Beck less today, which was very good, although I wish I understood what governs my erratic emotions. The desperateness and then the quiet. Neil and I watched TV. He had brought home a familiar dinner of thick bean soup from our favorite nearby restaurant. That seemed like enough, that seemed like *a lot*. I never have to worry if he wants someone else—he just wants me, in his own way. I am his eternal

"virgin" on a pedestal. To Beck I was the mother/whore in a large bras-
siere whom he fantasized he could ravage, leave on the floor, and return to
when he wanted more.

We watched a movie on the "woman's channel" that was easy to follow.
A generational saga, which made me miss not only my mother, but my
grandmother—her parents sending her small self to cousins in America
before the Holocaust sank its jaws into the Jews, never to see her mother,
father, brother, twin sisters again. It made her more than cling to us; her
thick fingers clenched too tightly around our wrists—handcuffs.

The image of my grandmother doesn't fluctuate, she's always old. The
picture of my mother won't stabilize. Some days she's bird brittle—a delicate sculpture of bones—and some days she's full-fleshed and healthy.
That's the mother the child reaches for to feel safe; near the end I was her
protector. The last time we went out I encircled her with my arms and
hands and fingers—made a lattice cage around her—so no one could push
her, hurt her. A month before, when she was out with Joe Silver, they were
going through a revolving door and a child of eight—infinity's number—
twirled through it and she fell to the ground. I wasn't there, but felt the
shatter when I learned of it. No one got near her that last time. They saw
the fire and the terror in my eyes. That day our desperateness was respected.

Now, alone, it was good to have Neil in the room.

Day 112

Tomorrow the playwriting class begins again and I'll be down there
even more often because we'll officially meet three times a week. Will the
professor have read the play? Will he say, "Get out of here, Benedict Eck's
my best friend"? Or will he say, "We need to talk and soon; I really like
your work."

Day 113

The professor perfunctorily taught the class, then left. I didn't see Beck
anywhere. I looked. I remembered how taken he'd been with me at the
beginning, how he thought me so beautiful, how he lost control of himself—his tackle. Then his begging for forgiveness. Then my cough. The

pneumonia—the wind knocked out of me for months. Then the writing of the poems, the beginnings of a play, then the novella about the man I looked and looked for today.

Day 114

Mandy's husband gave her a beaver coat and a lynx jacket (or so she says) for the holidays. Sy gave her a gold Gucci necklace.

Nothing ever from Beck. It still astonishes me that for the five years I've known him, I can't find a note, a rubber band, a paperclip he left behind. Nothing to hold on to except the tapes.

Day 115

Skipped the class and just slept. When I awoke I looked for the envelope with my mother's curl inside it. I couldn't find it. It was then I started hitting my head with a cheap, heavy bracelet. When I finally remembered where I'd put it—to keep it safe—I grabbed it and screamed, "THIS IS MINE." A huge relief overtook me—*as if I'd beaten the design of our lives.*

I fell asleep for about twenty minutes. Then, in the quick moment after the nap—that snap to awake—the large empty truth rose up that she *is* intrinsically lost.

Day 116

More Valium. More sleep. More trying to forget.

Day 117

"Madame Butterfly." Toward the end of the second act I think I stopped breathing when she sings "Un bel di vedremo." I felt Cio-Cio-San and I were the only two women left on the planet.

I began to think about how Beck had driven me to obsession. About the day I went to see him after I got over my pneumonia and how he said to me, "I'm involved with another woman. We can have some kind of sex, but then you go back to your husband." He liked the power of those words: *"But Then You Go Back To Your Husband."* I now know if I'd just left, he would have been on the phone to me within hours. Instead, I fell to my knees (O Cio-Cio-San) and begged him to love me. The more I begged, the more dismissive he was. Weeks later, when I threatened suicide, he stopped calling—for a while.

One morning during this time, when I'd been up all night upset, Neil turned to me and asked, "What would make you feel better?" I just looked at him. He then added, "How about some kind of *revenge*?" I remember how the word made me smile—not like the sun in the Dickinson poem, but the sun that can singe the skin, do malignant damage to it. My head was on my pillow facing him and then he said *revenge*. But when I mentioned his "revenge" idea a few days later, he just said, "I think not. We—you—could be caught. No, it's not for us." I thought he had a plan and was very disappointed—then I just let it drop, like the sun's seeming abandonment of us each night.

Day 118

The bash of the phone in my ear. And now I'm one of them—Madame Butterfly, Madame Bovary, Anna Karenina (wonderful Anna, passionate, elegant, tortured), Blanche dragged off to the asylum, Frida Kahlo painting knives into her body, always because of Diego—Diego, in and out of her life, in and out of her. *I love you today, then tomorrow the slam—that crack of goodbye—and then a crack of light—of hope—in the* "foresee" *word from a cracked mind.*

Day 119

Again, just slept. Dreamless. The balm of it. The calm of it.

Day 120

The professor said he'll have my play back to me in a week. For some reason, out of my mouth came something like, "You're probably hating it," or "Do you hate it?" Maybe it was just a quick manipulative way to get a little reaction—or maybe it was some variation of the horrid insecurity I carry around about myself. He just looked at me enigmatically, which made me worry.

Day 121

A weird thing arrived today: a huge box with no return address. Inside was a wrapped gift that looked like a bouquet of flowers—or a bomb. Then I decided *who cares* and ripped off the paper. There, I found a handmade rag doll—strange and interesting fabrics finely sewn together. The name of the doll was "Spirit Lady" and a little card was attached to her. It read, "We are each of us angels with only one wing, and we can fly only by embracing each other." I was confused. At first I thought of Beck and then I thought, *Beck?* Not possible. I couldn't find any identifying card until I reached deeper into the paper that it was wrapped in. It was tiny and was just signed, "Hedy." Everything about this felt creepy, and for all the handiwork that made up the doll, she was almost grotesque. I was confused as to Hedy's intention and ignored my first inclination, which was to throw it away. Instead, I took the doll upstairs with me.

Day 122

Neil lost his job today. Ralph told him, "Because the architectural firm is basically a family business and, as you know, business lately hasn't been that great . . . and there's my nephew . . ." He gave him a year to find another job. My brilliant, impotent, soon-to-be-jobless husband reports all this to me so passively. Ever since Neil's arrival, Ralph's been looking over his shoulder—apprentice-like—as if trying to learn everything about the artistry of Neil's work: his unique inventions, interpretations, and modernizations of balustrades, parapets, and cantilevers . . . Now it's over. He'll be moving out of the Hancock building—still standing in all its strength. Although others as strong have fallen since that thick, excessive drip of words out of that cab driver's mouth—now a forever taunt.

≈ ≈ ≈ ≈ ≈

I look at Neil and our life together and wonder, where's the pleasure? I look at Neil and wonder what will happen to this man who draws like an angel—and to me, who at this moment has become a devil-woman. "Neil Grace promises to be one of the most innovative architects of our day.

He's married to the accomplished poet, Jennie Silver [Grace]."—*Chicago Magazine*. By all definitions there was no "grace" in this house tonight. With Beck, there was so much pain, but with him there was *also* pleasure—sometimes. He spent little money on me, but there were occasions when he paid me good attention that felt so rich with life. Attention like that never given from the absent, narcissistic Joe Silver. Is Dr. Solomon Teich right?

Day 123
Neil's great expressions of himself, his precise drafts—the eaves of a roof, an entrance recess, facades, the placement of the lighting, the pavilions of glass—are, for now, of little worth. He took such a risk going with that small firm, but they gave him much more money and carte blanche to do whatever he wanted—it was such a seduction. Sure, until he finds another job they'll lean on his creativity, while inside his body cells might be working overtime creating their own designs.

Days 124–125
These last two days in the middle of the night I've awakened with alarm. There's a confusion as to what is going on, then questions arrive and with them awful answers and more questions. The sequence surrounds Neil. At first there's the disorientation as to what is going on, then a more focused query followed by a quick realization that he *is* being let go. Then, another question: *Being let go in life, too?* I curl tighter into a ball, cradling a small pillow as if it were a precious doll—a beautiful baby girl yet untouched by the world.

≈ ≈ ≈ ≈ ≈

When I was six, I saw a baby doll wrapped in a pink blanket at Sears. It was the time my mother, grandmother, and I had come to visit my grandfather at work—the only time. There we were in the shipping department and I saw a decisive, beaming—*I'll tell you how the sun rose . . .*—man, giving directions to everyone as to where to load and unload boxes of all sizes.

Moses Shershevsky was where he belonged—his voice so strong, like one imagines Moses's was as he descended from the mountain. Yes, *my* grandpa Moses with *his* commandments.

The dolls on display came wrapped in pink or blue blankets. We passed about thirty of them on our way to see my grandfather. The dolls and the blankets looked so soft. I wanted one. I asked. My grandmother said a quick, "No. It's between Rosh Hashanah and Yom Kippur and during this time it's a sin against God to make purchases." What she said made me feel so guilty because of how much my six-year-old self wanted a doll *right now.*

For my birthday that year I was presented with a "walking" doll made of hard plastic. When I took her to bed and held her against my body, she'd leave huge indentations on my skin because of her rigid structure. I hated her. Except for her hair. I really liked twisting and pulling it out. I was fascinated by the small holes doing this left in her head. Did she feel better afterward? Soon my doll had tiny bald spots like my mother's.

Now, I sleep—have for years—with a soft pillow next to my heart. I hold it as I would have held the soft doll I had craved. I can still see that display of pinks and blues when I close my eyes. My grandmother told me, "All those dolls had been sold and, anyway, the 'walking' doll was more expensive." No one seemed to care that I was ruining her. No one seemed to care that my mother had all those sores.

When I turned nine and gave myself my own "tonsure," my mother was the only one it bothered. It was then she started bribing me to stop with those silver dollars. How I loved the shape and feel of them—so round and solid. I'd caress one before sleep.

≈ ≈ ≈ ≈ ≈

Gladys slept in the dining room. She'd roll a cot out for herself from the coat closet each night. We'd hear her swear and swear as she struggled to open it. It was then I'd think about her name—how "Gladys" was the inflammation of the GLAD, the *ys* really *tis* as in laryngi*tis* or appendici*tis*.

John and I slept in the living room. A chair that unfolded into a bed was for me. Even with a clean sheet placed over its wooly fabric, I could smell the odors left from when people had sat on it. John slept on one of the plastic-covered couches with bedding for him placed over it. I loved being there with John—his breathing seemed so calm. I'd listen to his breaths and they would help me fall asleep. Sometimes, in the mornings, we'd find Uncle Meyer, still impeccably dressed, just his tie loosened, passed out on the other couch. I could tell he was there even before I opened my eyes if the air was soaked with cigar smoke and the heavy scents of liquor and Shalimar. How excited John and I would become when we'd find our handsome, mysterious uncle sleeping there.

≈ ≈ ≈ ≈ ≈

After John died, I vowed I would never have children. I had to let go of the longed-for hope of a pink or blue softly blanketed baby. I was terrified that I would become Joe Silver. *What if one day something awful—inadvertent or intended—slipped out of my mouth and the child went upstairs . . . ?*

Day 126

Neil says my spot looks like the face of a tiny clock no bigger than the size of the fingernail on his left thumb. Sometimes he traces the edge of it with the first tooth of a small plastic comb. He'll say, "I am going to start at twelve o'clock"; then he names the hours of the day. Tells me—in hours—where the clock is the emptiest. "Right now it is between ten and midnight. Between seven and ten, that's where the most growth has been." Beck rarely called between seven and ten; he knew Neil would be home and not yet asleep.

Day 127

Neil has far too much calcium in his blood. We don't know what this means and we don't ask. The doctor says he's not very concerned and we let it go at that. He will, however, have Neil take a second blood test to reconfirm it's not a laboratory mistake and, if it isn't, talk to us about referring him to a specialist. Joe Silver has a more blatant symptom. The hospital needs more samples of his stool. *Blood and bowels.* That's what today was about.

Day 128

Though he said he would, he didn't bring the play. I took five milligrams of Valium before the class and arrived a half-hour early. He walked in late. Except for the course anthology, his arms were empty. Afterward, he got up and left. Stupid me to expect him to keep to a few casual words he probably doesn't remember. Or maybe he *does* know B. Eck, knows him well, and now doesn't know what to do—call Astrid Olson's office, call Beck, call me about it? *Calm down,* I said to myself, and wait . . . *All* that waiting to get out of class. When it was over, I bolted out the door and through the halls to get to my car. Then, I saw a flash of paper. I don't know why it caught my eye. Maybe it was the color—sunflower, like what I'd left on her grave that day last November when they sealed her in the most final way with that impenetrable bronze plaque. On top of that weight that so heavily acknowledged her death, I left a single sunflower. The bright of the sun reflected on it, and a single bird flew overhead. *Remember.*

It was *that* yellow on the paper that stopped me. An announcement of a poetry reading—Thursday. Beck controls the fund of money at the university to bring in poets—the announcement was for a reading of a friend of mine who I'd brought to Beck's attention. Suki hadn't called to tell me she'd be in town. I wonder if Beck told her, "I don't want *her* here." I actually called her a few weeks ago to wish her Happy New Year. I spoke to her answering machine. I'd go to hear her anyway, even though she hasn't called back, didn't tell me she was coming to town. Except for Beck, I hesitate.

Day 129

I've decided to go to the reading. I owe it to Suki to be there—she's gone out of her way for me. Came to my book signing party when my fifth book was published. Flew in from another state. Soon she'll be light years beyond me. No one important hates her yet.

Neil is coming with me. I don't know how Beck will react when I intrude on *his* territory. (God, this sounds like *West Side Story*—except the knives are pens.) I figure with Neil there, Beck will have to act properly—which just means he won't throw me out. The worst scenario will be if he ignores me. But in reality, I know this is the only scenario.

I pedantically say to myself out loud, "Remember the road of warts just above his buttocks. Envision those when he turns his back on you tomorrow."

Day 130

He walked into the room a few minutes before the reading, saw me, and walked out. When it was time to begin, he stammered when he introduced Suki—unusual for him. He looked awful, as if all the boxing—all the working out—was for naught. His shoulders looked narrow and he slouched. He had on a black long-sleeved T-shirt that looked rumpled. Had he slept in it? But I have to say, at the time I didn't think of the warts—only now, as I write. His hair was all chopped up—an attempt at a crew cut? On the street this fall he looked handsome and, but for the small paunch, almost sleek. Now I wonder if my desires hallucinate.

During the reading, he sat on the side, so it was hard to see him. At the end, when people were socializing with Suki, he left the room. She was delighted to see Neil and me.

I left the room a few seconds after Neil. Beck was standing right there in the hall. I was surprised. I put my sunglasses on and turned my face away from his. I met Neil at the bottom of the stairs.

After we left the building, Neil became animated—this had all proved to be a great distraction for him—and said, "Beck looks like a high school math teacher—you know, the ones who always wear tiny-checked, cotton short-sleeved shirts no matter what the weather, their pens stuffed into their left pocket, forever stained with ink. You're a 9.9. Beck, *maybe* a 4.5. Why have you placed yourself so low? He's an unattractive jerk standing in a small mud puddle." Then, he sighed and almost inaudibly whispered, "Who am I to criticize someone else at this point in *my* life?"

Frankly, I didn't know exactly what I was feeling and also didn't know how to react to what Neil had said. I'm not sure I know the man who stood up there today. I have this *other man* in my mind, whom I still think cares for me and I for him. If I realize he doesn't exist in the man I just saw, it leaves me too empty. And I still have my rage toward *whomever* it was I saw today and now even more toward myself: *Why All This Time Over That Guy?*

Day 131
Things fall apart; the centre cannot hold;
                    —Yeats

I stood in the driveway today with a knife in my hand. My bathrobe was open—my breasts exposed. It was freezing and there was snow on the ground.

≈ ≈ ≈ ≈ ≈

Seeing Beck really upset me. Too many memories of a warm body—someone who had responded so strongly to me. I didn't care how terrible he looked. I was feeling beyond insult—frozen in the Ninth Circle of Hell's uncontainable frostbitten pain.

The first thing out of Neil's mouth when he arrived home was to tell me which books were nominated for a national literary prize. Mine was not among them. I didn't need to know this. *I'm in a hole; I'll stick you in one.* The room we were in got so suffocatingly small. I pushed at him to go away and his glasses fell off. He pushed me back, called me a "sicko," and left the house. I fled to the sunroom, took the sash off my robe, and tried to choke myself with it. I tried harder. For a moment everything went black except for a bright yellow circle that flashed in front of my eyes. I thought, was this what John felt before he . . . ? Then I thought—the sun? The sunflower? *Mother?* I dropped to the floor, loosened the sash from around my neck, and started coughing. Couldn't stop. I wanted to die, but didn't know how to do it—*wasn't I capable of it?*

Neil came back and that's how I got to standing in the driveway—my robe open, with a knife and screaming at him to just go away. Then I ran inside and threw a pot through the kitchen window. I saw cause, I saw effect, and I liked that. If I couldn't kill myself, I could at least break something.

Day 132

Neil threw out the doll Hedy sent. It was too strange. The day after it arrived was the day he was told to look for another job. And today while talking to Hedy, she eagerly relayed to me, "Father told Ed and me that Neil had been fired." I could feel the electricity in her voice, the voltage of her joy. Then she asked, "Does he now just sit home?" Adding, "Is he *very* depressed?" After I didn't answer, she continued, "Maybe it's the doll," and she laughed—Hedy, forever incapable of subtext, subtlety, or tact. It's clear Joe Silver's youngest has become a good student of his insensitivity, his inappropriateness.

≈ ≈ ≈ ≈ ≈

Recently, Joe Silver told Neil and me about how to seduce a woman. "First you take her to dinner, then you say, 'Let's go back to your place.' And, when she's not looking, you turn up the heat. Soon she'll feel hot because the heat is up and maybe you'll 'get lucky' and she'll take off her clothes. And, at eighty-four, if you're still able to have sex, you 'go for it!'" *Great.*

Neil tried to call him tonight to find out who told him about the job and ask him to *please* not tell anyone else. But he's been gone all evening— probably having sex right now with some "overheated" woman, while Neil sleeps.

Day 133

Tomorrow I see a new therapist.

Day 134

Getting out of the cab to see the therapist this afternoon, I misstepped and lost my balance, or the little I had left of it. Right before, I had been staring at the photograph of the driver on the visor—now a ritual. I became transfixed by it. His smile a replica of John's—the shape of their mouths exactly the same. *I'll tell you how the sun rose . . .*

While falling I heard something rip and then I hit the street. I had tried with my left hand to grab on to the cab's door handle, but was not successful. Lying there on the street, I imagined a bus coming along and just running over me, finishing me off. That would be that. No more worrying about losing Beck or about Neil losing his job or being sick. *Road kill.*

≈ ≈ ≈ ≈ ≈

After the fall, I was stunned. I couldn't adjust my mind and body to what had just happened. I sat in the therapist's office in terrible physical pain and cried and cried about my mother and Neil and Beck and John—his smile on the cab driver's visor. I seemed like a joke, a character in a Woody Allen movie—falling out of a cab, then rushing up an elevator to some unknown therapist to sob and sob.

"Physical pain is a curious thing." I told this to him between my sobs. "It supersedes the psychological, makes it corporeal. I can now point to my arm and say *this* is how much it hurts. See my sling. My being is half-broken and this is how I carry it. Pressed against my heart is this excruciating pain." (At the time it seemed like a sling would be a good thing.)

He didn't even help me with my coat when I left. My right arm and hand had to do all the work. I told him that I didn't feel right. He suggested an antidepressant and another appointment. If he had *just* helped me with my coat, I would have considered coming back.

≈ ≈ ≈ ≈ ≈

I guess when Neil threw out Hedy's doll he didn't throw it far enough. It must still be somewhere on our property. So strange. She sent me an "angel with only one wing" and since then there's been a compression of time in which things have gone terribly wrong. Neil's left again. He said,

"This time to make sure it's completely off our property." He's now taking all this quite seriously—I hope. I hurt too much to interrogate him as to exactly where he was going—what he was planning to do with it.

Days 135–137
I can't lift my left arm. All upper muscle strength is gone. I try, but I can't. I can't make my arm work and the pain is getting worse. A tear in the rotator cuff—that's what the emergency room doctor guessed last night. I'll have to see an orthopedic surgeon.

Stayed home. Too hard to get dressed and impossible to comb my hair. I'm not able to think about too much, except how much pain I'm in and how amazing the uninjured body is. When I started getting ready for bed last night, I had to wake Neil so he could pull my hair back and put my shower cap on my head. While showering, I screamed and screamed from the pain of instinctively trying to use my unusable left arm. Afterward, I crawled into bed sobbing and said to Neil, "Tomorrow my mother will come to comb my hair, help me dress and sit and talk." I almost believed it and he softly responded, "*Yes, maybe yes.*"

≈ ≈ ≈ ≈ ≈

I missed my class and lunch with Kane's assistant at my press. He didn't call back when I left him the message that I had fallen and probably ripped a muscle in my left shoulder. I take this as a bad sign. How could he *not* call back? I'm supposed to know in March about the manuscript, but I feel I already know . . .

I must be a little better because I'm worrying about my manuscript and not my body. Just my body of work, not the body that forty-eight hours ago I could slip a fitted turtleneck sweater over so easily. My arms just popped up over my head. Now, just being able to raise them in sync and pull my hair into a rubber band would be impossible to accomplish.

Hurt. Tomorrow, the orthopedic surgeon. Scared. All is tumbling down since losing Beck, or maybe since my mother began her final descent toward the unforgiving ground. For the second night when I maneuvered into bed, into the worst of the pain, I told Neil, "Tomorrow my mother will come to comb my hair." Again, he responded with a quiet, compassionate, "*yes.*"

≈ ≈ ≈ ≈ ≈

Neil got the day of the appointment wrong. The office was empty when we arrived. The doctor was in surgery. Everything's off these days, especially with Neil and me. We got coffee, then he drove me to my class at the university. The professor said he had brought the play on Tuesday. He seemed snappish, but I was wearing a sling (yes, a sling *was* a good thing) and when he noticed it, he became kinder.

I'm thinking that all he's going to do is return it to me, possibly with some written comments on it, which I guess will be better than nothing. But at this point I want so much more. Time is running, while I'm stopped—*trying to grab on to a handle I couldn't quite reach to break my fall.* That probably says it all.

Day 138

Mandy called, hysterical: "Sy's wife says she has evidence of our affair." I listened even though she pretty much ignored what had happened to me—the pain I'm now experiencing. Just quickly said, "Oh, that's too bad." I thought maybe the distraction of listening to Mandy would help, but all I could think about while she was yapping was how lucky she was to have the use of both of her arms.

She continued, "Arlene has tapes of our conversations from the last three weeks. She's threatened to give the tapes to Irv, if we continue to see each other." Arlene told Mandy (I wondered whether Arlene was taping *that* conversation), "You can't have any more business deals with my husband. Nothing." I thought, yes, no more *joint sales in cheap strip malls.* (I like the not-so-subtle double meanings here and the monosyllables of the words. Am I feeling a little better?)

Day 139

Missteps. A few words spoken. Then an inflammation of troubles. The rumor that got back to Beck and suddenly it's "all over"—meaning both *everywhere* and *done*. I've become all swell and fever. The doctor ordered an MRI on my arm for Monday to determine how torn up I am—but it won't work, unless they include slices of my brain.

Day 140

Sy's wife called Mandy again with more rage and threats if she doesn't stay away from her husband. Mandy is shaken and frightened. Mostly, that Irv will find out and her "perfect" marriage will be ruined. Arlene said Sy admitted to the affair. He told Mandy he did this while being sick with the flu, chest pains and a red, swollen eye. That he was on huge doses of Codeine to help him sleep and probably would have admitted to anything "just to get Arlene to shut up."

≈ ≈ ≈ ≈ ≈

Tonight I thought I'd just go out to my mother's grave, spread myself over it, and let the icy rain glaze me to her. It seemed a poetic, graceful ending to all the losing—my black coat, its lining ripped from my fall, glued to her grave. I freeze frame myself against that flat stone—her raised name an imprint on my face.

≈ ≈ ≈ ≈ ≈

One misplaced step can tear a huge muscle and an arm can no longer support itself, deaf to all the messages the brain is sending it. How many times can you be repaired? How many remissions? My mother had one long one, then a short one, and then a nothing one. Even then, she became hopeful—that was when she bought eyeshadow. *Eyeshadow.* Sad, shadowed, watery eyes were upon her while she primped that lived moment in front of the magnifying mirror at the department store. Moment of sad splendor, as the salespeople watched how the dying

woman tried and tried to triumph over her despair. We couldn't see the
great tear yet, although any MRI would have caught it. Those slices of
pictures—gray gloom clouds—would have showed us what was going
to happen next, what was imminent.

Day 141

They asked before the MRI if I was prone to seizures. I'm not, at least
not the kind they meant. But tonight at dinner my eyes blurred and my
face felt as if a mask were being tightened over it. I became faint and raced
out of the house without my coat. I needed to reestablish myself with the
hard slap of winter. I wondered if it was a panic attack or an aftershock
from the MRI, which in actuality, wasn't bad at all.

Neil sat next to me and read from a slick local magazine about an opera
star—about her fame and family. Someone could do a puff piece on me
and I, too, could sound good. *Believe Nothing.*

Day 142

Each morning when I awake I vow never to touch the spot again. It
seems so reasonable to just let the hair that's still there *be*—exist. Any
twisted patch of growth would be better than what is. And each morning it also seems so reasonable to never go near Beck again—images of
the warts, his semen-eaten blanket, the festering sponge in the kitchen,
which he used to wipe up all waste, make me sick. Yet, by afternoon I'm
tearing (with my right hand) at my head again and trying to figure out
how to reconnect with him. By nightfall my appetites grow more bold,
more bald. I become so obvious. All parts spread to a red emptiness. *She
lies in a red emptiness.*

Day 143

The muscle isn't torn, just inflamed—inflamed like everything else inside me. The deep ache will last from one to two months. Jason said Beck
would call in forty-three days—then the deep ache will be over. I think
about how Beck could calm the inflammation down, when he'd listen to
me talk about my mother and John.

Day 144

Neil may be quite sick. Tumors, perhaps. The symptom of too much calcium in his blood means something serious. It's Neil, not me, who may need surgery. Our small joke of a life together is getting larger. We deny his "perhaps tumors." I think about calling A, which is more hapless. Even though he's moving here, I clearly won't be an important ensemble member of the theater he'll create—my part, if any, will be very small. *At this late hour my worry swells as to how large a part is left to Neil . . .*

Day 145

The playwriting professor wouldn't look at me today. Didn't bring the manuscript. I won't push at it. Just try to get it back when the quarter is over. I've decided not to attend the spring class. He *must* know Beck is Benedict Eck. Suddenly, the panic hits, not over this, but over Neil, and stops my pen. I'll shower and go to bed, curl next to him. Take in the fragrance of our clean sheets and listen to Neil breathe.

Day 146

Tomorrow I go back to Jason. Neil will drive. At least there's no potential to slip and fall out of a cab to see an unknown therapist. I'll talk to Jason about Neil. What can we expect? The odds of a good result? I'll tell him about the professor going silent on my manuscript. Right now that seems a small loss given Neil's illness.

Day 147

I didn't wash my hair from the moment I touched the frame of her body—the carapace that she left—until after the funeral. My hair glistened with dirt. I didn't care how I looked. I was thin and knotted with grief. Today, I'm hippy and flushed with loss—a slender layer of fat coats my body. Will it thicken and quickly grow me into an old woman? I both fight it and don't. Any youthfulness is in limbo. "Limbo" is that special place in hell where the poets wander. (Dante wrote that.) Their index fin-

gers rubbing out patches of their hair—small craters created to get to the
bottom of thought. (This last sentence I made up.)

Note: Jason said he's sure Neil is going to be all right. He seemed to
whitewash all the details I gave him of Neil's illness. Maybe he's forgotten all of medicine. Just sits in his chair and listens—or half-listens—as
he "detaches."

Days 148–149

I needed more diversion from Neil's uncertain future, so I picked up
the phone when I heard Mandy's voice on my answering machine. Sy
wouldn't take "No" when she told him she never wanted to see him again;
he ran down to her condominium and insisted she talk to him. He told
her, "After my son's wedding in June, I'll do *something*—I'll move out of
my house and start *today* to hide some money." Beck and I are stopped.
Mandy and Sy will take this further. Arlene will orchestrate the crash. She
has already set this in motion with her tapes.

Mandy says, "I never want to hurt another woman." Arlene has the
tapes where Mandy and Sy talk about sex. Arlene is very hurt. MANDY
DOESN'T GET IT. (Although Beck never met her, his characterization
of her as "the tart who isn't very smart" is apt.)

She then told me, "Irv helped me hook up my computer in a way that I
can begin writing—you know—creative stuff." I stayed quiet.

Day 150

Last night I had an awful nightmare. Fifty roosters were locked in the
trunk of a car. It was very hot outside, which made the trunk even hotter.
Finally, someone opened the lid and the roosters just lay there, I guess
dead. The fronts of their bodies had been picked clean of their feathers
and huge red sores marked their flesh. It was painful to look at.

My left arm hurt while I slept, but not enough to warrant such a night
terror. True, Neil is far from 100 percent and probably will need surgery,
but now it doesn't *seem* like it will be a major thing. At least that's what the
specialist phoned to say last night—we were his last call. I guess he wanted

to end his day with the most hopeful message he had. Neil and I went to bed peacefully and at the same time. *So, why that dream?*

Day 151

Neil interviewed for a job last week, but was told today he didn't get it. "Too much experience. Overqualified." *Why can't we just be happy that he's probably not going to be so terribly sick, not going to die—at least not yet?* Neither of us has handled this news well. We fought. Then he went downstairs to sulk.

After a while, he came upstairs and sheepishly asked if I wanted to go out for dinner. At the restaurant he said that he had something to tell me. Then, ever-so-shakily, he admitted Hedy's cursed doll was "not *quite* off our property." It's clear to me *now* he is truly spooked by it and he swore that when we came home he would throw it far, far away.

At home, I just sat in my chair and stared at the wall. That's when the phone rang. I wasn't surprised it was A. I don't know why, but I wasn't. He said I could sit in on his class this spring. I'm confused about what he's thinking. He does have a girlfriend "of sorts," but he backs away from admitting, at least to me, that it's serious. As for Joyce, he really likes her— but beyond that, "no way." No matter what he feels about me, he made me smile. When Neil finally came home, we spoke civilly to each other right up to the time he went to sleep.

Days 152–153

Monday he finds out more about what needs to be done to get him physically well. His condition was probably birthed by too much stress and now most likely has to be killed with a knife. Perhaps living with Jennie Silver is just too much. It is for me.

≈ ≈ ≈ ≈ ≈

Joe Silver wore his tie of hearts. The one my mother gave him many years ago on Valentine's Day. The one he wore the day we buried her. The one he wore the day her name was officially locked into the ground with that plaque.

≈ ≈ ≈ ≈ ≈

On this day of hearts, she'd buy us each a small gift with a little personalized note attached about how much she loved us.

≈ ≈ ≈ ≈ ≈

Driving home from dinner Joe Silver talked and talked again about his boxing days, when he was "Boy Thunder" and made it to the finals of a citywide tournament only to have his eyelids split, nose broken, and lip badly cut by Walter Karpinski. When he came home that night—all of fifteen years old—his mother said, "If you show up one more time looking like this, *I'll* beat you up." As he went on and on with this story, which I've heard dozens of times, any beginnings of tender feelings I felt toward him, inspired by his wearing the tie of hearts, thinned. I concluded it must just be part of how he puts himself together on specific occasions.

During dinner I thought a lot about A. It's quieter here because of A. I've lost a pound since we talked. My "candied" heart is a bit lighter. I want to lie next to A and kiss his high cheekbones, just like every other woman wants to do. I want to have him say, "You're so special, so beautiful," just like every other woman wants him to say to her. With him I may have met the champion of heartbreakers. In the ring, out of the ring, wearing the ring, taking the ring off, he wins. He's the heavyweight champ. I'm just one of the chumps.

Day 154

Monte Grazer, a frequent nominee but never a winner of the Pulitzer Prize, gave a reading a few miles from here tonight. (I'm not supposed to know he's a reader for my sixth book of poems, but I do.) I thought it best that I attend. Afterward, he turned away from me as I brushed his face and gave him a miss of a kiss. I then stood next to him for a couple of minutes while he talked on and on with another poet. It felt longer than my entire life above the ground, until I said, "Bye." His reply: "See ya." How should I hang myself on that? Whatever is or is not going on, to him I've become nonexistent. Tonight I decided I'm going to circle a date and if things aren't better, kill myself. (I wonder if John had a date circled in his head [we found no such circle on his calendar] when he figured the letter of acceptance or rejection would arrive from Harvard and he had a secret plan if rejected. Or was it *all* because of Joe Silver's eight words? In my sad, listening heart I believe it was the latter.)

Day 155

I sit on the couch with Neil. I'm at one end, he's at the other, in the dazed TV light. Existing in this nonexistence, I've circled a date.

Day 156

Because of Monte's behavior, I called Kane this morning. I could hear the indifference in his voice: *He's been busy, too busy to get to my book; it's on the floor of his office—unopened.* CAN'T YOU JUST PICK IT UP AND PUT IT ON YOUR DESK, I wanted to scream, but didn't. I just said, "That's fine. Thank you." (THANK YOU?)

Dinner with Neil. We eat too much. Some days it seems all that's left is the gift of chocolate.

Then, the phone rang. *More* tests for Neil. "Why?" we ask. The specialist's response, "Just checking; there's still a little inconsistency in the results." Neither of us takes this further. Neither of us wants to look at the big picture, perhaps because it feels like it might be disappearing fast. I don't push Neil anymore about his behavior—the *why* of it. I know if I stay in the present moment I can get through and, also, it's a relief to have a circled date. No problems of this world left. *Left.* You're just some name that passed through—too late to do anything special enough to get a street christened after you or the quintessential memorial: a day when there's no mail. No one will study you in school. Just a bunch of bones positioned in a casket—with a Star of David carved onto it for an extra $1,000—then locked in a vault.

Day 157

Sy denies that Arlene is still taping their conversations, but Mandy tells me, "When he talks to me from his house, what he says is so matter-of-fact." *Everyone,* it seems, in recent years, has sex tapes—from the White House to Sy's house to my house.

Day 158

Mandy started writing her book today. Again, I stayed quiet. She's even printed out the first pages of *Sandra Dee and Me* and hidden them in the drawer where she keeps her "raggedy" underwear. So Mandy stayed home and wrote. *How she loves to write.* The last few times we've spoken, I now realize, she's let me talk more and more about myself, which is odd. Bad idea. I don't want to end up in a book entitled *Sandra Dee and Me,* even if it only sees the light of day when Mandy opens her drawer to put on some old underwear.

I've told her too much about Neil, Beck, and A. I shouldn't have. About four weeks until he arrives. And then most likely nothing will happen. I'll polish his ego by dragging myself to his early morning class and there I'll wait for some small attentions. A man like A *could* change one's life. Yet, at almost sixty, he has, I'm sure, a long line of long-legged women thinking about him and waiting... My legs are not long enough, although Beck loved my body—all the parts. But A, I can tell, covets idealized perfection. That's why he's so captivated with himself. So perhaps he really *doesn't* want any competition? Nonetheless, it won't be long legs that draw him in, and my too-round body feels squashed. Why not? *A stinking hippo stepped on it and then stepped back.* A is more like a panther, sleek with perfect teeth (are they false?) that could easily take a squashed heart, make a meal of it, then ever-so-gracefully leap up and out the nearest exit. I believe that's what he did with Joyce.

Day 159

Mandy saw Sy. She forgives him. Then, they had coffee, or at least that's what she told me. She used to tell me of their "trips to the zoo" (good metaphor) when all the while they were having sex. She sounds so much better. Someone loves her, or at least says he does and is demonstrative.

Days 160–161

Everyone continues to be surprised that Beck's never called. Everyone is beginning to think that maybe he won't. I obsess on it less, just want to sleep more so as to forget.

I went back to bed three times today before I got dressed and left the house. I think about Neil and am frightened. Today another place told him how fabulous his résumé was: "We'll be in touch." This is the pattern. First the superlatives—the buildup—then the not calling back for days—weeks—followed by the drop.

I think about the coming spring—that erratic season that sometimes arrives so late.

Day 162

I still feel the coldness in Kane's voice—the perfect ice cube of it. I'd like to withdraw the book before he says, "A reader"—Monte—"didn't think it quite good enough." If Kane were treated like this, he'd go nuts. I want to get out from under Kane by taking the manuscript away from him. But Neil and Jason say, "Just be patient, in the end he'll take the book."

≈ ≈ ≈ ≈ ≈

Joe Silver told me this evening that he's going on a cruise to South America and will be sharing a cabin—"It's cheaper."—with a woman. "She's a close friend I've know for many years. A widow." *I've never met this close friend he's known for many years.* Is *she* the woman from temple in the hat with the too-large brim and the too-large grin?

My mother is dropped, dropped into the ground. Gone. *Everyone* is running around, trying and trying to hold on. No one can stand being dropped.

Is it because it feels like the rehearsal for the final one?

Day 163

Last night I couldn't sleep at all. Being upset kept me up, thinking about what Kane is going to do or not do—the way he's left me hanging...

≈ ≈ ≈ ≈ ≈

This is the Hour of Lead –
Remembered, if outlived,
　　—Emily Dickinson

We have been in our suburban house four years. It is now snowing heavily outside. Joe Silver calls my brother to the table for dinner. After fifteen minutes he climbs the old stairs...

Hedy, two, in her highchair, and Sallie, five, in her booster seat, don't understand what is happening. In their eyes is startled, generalized terror.

They will not let me go up there. My screams won't quit...

A neighbor comes and carries the now kicking and wailing Hedy and Sallie away. My mother holds on to me so tightly, both to keep me from the stairs and to make sure I'm still here. Her trembling hands press against my head like a soft vice. She covers my face with kisses. Our tears mix together.

THERE ARE TOO MANY PEOPLE IN THIS HOUSE. THERE ARE TOO MANY PEOPLE HERE WITH WET, BEWILDERED, GRIEF-FLUSHED FACES...

Day 164

This morning, if I had had the time with my upset and anger growing more high-pitched, I would have called Kane to withdraw my book. But I was late leaving for my playwriting class.

Aside from listening to revisions of short scenes, we are now reading Brecht: *The Good Person of Szechwan*. I'm halfway through it and can't put it down. I love what it's about. The fine line between goodness and self-protection. A shrewdness to one's goodness must be developed, else everything one has can be stolen. The news is filled with stories every day about those who were blindsided, weren't prepared and had so much—if not everything—snatched from them.

Brecht has a line in the play that haunts me: *Show interest in her goodness—for no one can be good for long if goodness is not in demand.*

I've tried to be good all of my life, but I am always at the precipice of that unrelenting scream at Joe Silver over John, and how I loved the idea of getting revenge against Beck when Neil suggested it and was so disappointed when he decided against it.

For the moment I feel clean with wisdom that it is best to stay away from him. I'm very lonely, but right now I'm also glad I'm not Mandy, however stuffed she is with sex.

Days 165–166

A peculiar day for February—50 degrees out with sunbeams oozing from the sky instead of the usual sleet. It was spring, or so it felt, and with it powerful memories came to mind—how I'd run to the hospital, starting in April two years ago. The running lasted on and off through August. Driving too fast, pushing too hard on the elevator button to get to the fourth floor, and then hurrying down that awful corridor permeated with the odors of decay. In each room lay a desperate human being. She was there, too. Many times just sleeping. I'd sit down and just listen to the two of us breathing. *Remember this,* I'd say to myself, *remember the sound of her breaths.* And as that spring arrived, flower by flower, leaf by leaf, it felt as if each were struggling with their own breath, fearing it might be their last.

Today, alone in a coffee shop, I looked out the window at what seemed at first to be a dead tree. Instead, on its branches were the beginnings of buds—they looked like miniscule tumors, and even their color looked like *hurt,* that swell of deep purple. *Neil?*

≈ ≈ ≈ ≈ ≈

I went to my physical therapy session, knowing that my arm was better, but after exercising it, I again began to doubt it would ever be completely right. When I came home I was more tired than I'd ever been at the twilight hour. When Neil arrived, I told him I had to go to bed. Even though everything is now out of the ordinary, he could barely handle this—maybe *because* we have lost so much order to our lives.

I cut him short and lay in bed for almost an hour. Immobile. Fixed on the fact that she's gone; that I'll never see her again and that no matter how old we get, so many of us still need our mothers.

Day 167

Tonight the baldest place on the clock is between 9 and 12 a.m.—is "the hour" of baldness getting earlier because of no call from Beck? Neil circled the inflamed tenderness and I felt my soul was being touched—that the essence of myself was rising up and I *could* easily travel the road from flesh to dust. In my play "Lissa" talks about *her* spot. On stage, she twists her hair into a large knot and then untangles it to expose it.

I like the sound of the name I've given her—how it feels so smooth on the tongue—and its two meanings: "sweet" and "intoxicating." Then I wonder if such a combination is possible without causing some amount of trouble.

Day 168

A comes to town this month. I'm capable of just jumping into bed with him. What do I have to lose? A? I'll never have him anyway, nor will any other woman for very long. I think again that maybe Beck was right about pleasure for pleasure's sake.

Day 169

Kane's assistant at the press called. Left me a message: "Kane says it's your best book yet. You should call him in a week or so; he has a few minor suggestions." My paranoia about Beck's power over Kane or Monte Grazer's behavior *was* off. Now, I wonder how many people are *really* out there trying to hurt me. Did the toxins that spat out of those slams into my ear sicken the synapses that create good thoughts? All healthy chemistry polluted and weakened by just *one* sociopath?

The call makes me feel more healthy, so perhaps all infections can begin to dry up and I can strengthen. *Five and a half months I've been broken.* Maybe now I can glue myself back together. In physical therapy today the therapist said, "You're healing quickly—you've almost regained full range of motion." I asked, "But, what about the sometimes awful pain?" She replied, "That will take more time."

Day 170

Jason's back from Portugal. He travels a lot on my money. He looks good and it was good to see him. He said, "Beck is loaded with passion for you. But right now, it's heavy with hate. People just don't bash the phone down on *anyone,* try so hard to get them 'slapdash' out of their life." He thinks Beck's feelings eventually will shift—probably suddenly. Jason really believes Beck thinks of me *more* than I do of him. Frankly, I don't see how that's possible. How could he possibly function? How could he get *anything* done? I barely can. Even when I think of A, it's mostly to contrast him with B.

Jason, I can tell, envies A—his casualness with the opposite sex, his lightheartedness, the women waiting. Jason tells me: "A's not weighted down into darkness like Beck is. He will not be as heavy with obsession for you." I do understand this, that his fascination will be thin as the spray of rain on a sunny summer's day—so quick to dry. *"A" take it or leave it attitude from a rarified altitude.*

Day 171

I'm tired of writing about losing Beck. I'm tired of how I think I'm getting better, but then slip back to worse, like with my weight and the spot—which I haven't touched since Kane's assistant's message of two days ago. However, I still don't quite feel all is right with the book.

Day 172

Worry or not, I want to call my mother and tell her, "Kane thinks it's my best book yet." I want to show my mother *this* book of how I experienced her wave goodbye. I *know* this makes no sense. She used to say to me, "Someday I won't be here, Jennie, and you'll just have to accept it." I'd reply, "No. No. You have to be here always." She'd respond, "Oh, Jennie, it doesn't work that way—just doesn't." Then, she'd go quiet.

Day 173

Tonight hail hits the windows—it's winter again—but I'm housed and protected. Beck is so far away from here in this kind of weather, as is my mother, as it seems to be getting more so with Neil. His face is so pale and bloated and he grows ever more passive. It's clear he's quite sick, but the specialist's been vacationing. We wait for his return from a warm island— tanned, sunny man with a secure profession, unlike Neil, who seems to be slowly slipping off this planet, his face becoming a sallow moon.

Day 174

When my mother found out she was so sick again, that *this* cancer af- ter nine years had reared its reptilian grin again, she was understandably terrified and furious and I do believe sometimes the sight of me angered her, because I was the future without her. I brought her the front cover for my fifth book and she barely looked. I brought the photograph of my- self that the press was putting on the back cover and she said, "Oh, I've seen it before." It wasn't true, but I didn't argue. Yet, three days before she died, when I told her I was going to stop writing poems, she emphatically responded, "No, they are your babies." Shivering, all wrapped up—she couldn't get warm enough—transfusion bags dripping from her broken veins, she said those words from a place I've not yet been. Her voice all strength and guttural—an insistence rising from the essence of herself, beyond her fragile body, as if she were the messenger in advance of the soul/self she would become.

Days 175–178

Slept. When Neil finally woke me, he uncharacteristically said with a smile, "I *won't* be sick. I *will* get a new job." Then he handed me a bowl of thick bean soup and told me, "A called; he left the message that he'll be here soon."

≈ ≈ ≈ ≈ ≈

I dreamt my mother talked to me. I don't remember anything she said, but it *was her voice. I heard it.* She hasn't completely disappeared from me—from my life.

She talked to me. She did. And before that, A called and Beck grew so small and Neil's words stayed and grew large.

I slept more.

Days 179–182

When A arrives is what supersedes all thoughts of calling Beck while Neil is gone the next three days. He'll be running around on job interviews, while I silently worry about how he looks—that his pallor and his weight will work against him. How can it not? And the jerk that's letting him go keeps asking him to lunch to get even more ideas for future designs—pulling on Neil's long, shiny strands of thought.

Neil says, "I'll get revenge on Ralph." I think, *no you won't; you never did with Beck, you'll never do it with Ralph.* However, I also keep these thoughts to myself.

≈ ≈ ≈ ≈ ≈

Mandy's lover Sy is still around—in her life, in her. Today they celebrated her birthday. She and Irv were in California for her actual one. Sy gave her a gold ring today. She says it looks like a wedding band. She wears it on her right hand. She told Irv, "My mother gave it to me when I was in Miami." Mandy is all frivolity and frivolousness and these days it's hard for me to find her anything but ridiculous.

Day 183

From my view it looks like a too-heavy cloud has been dropped onto our planet:

The image of the back of the cab driver's head—the one in Boston—the picture of his face on his visor and his words still haunt me. I don't know where to put it. This manuscript of loss can't contain it. The damage of the dissolute, the damned—so much pollution—both colossal and minute.

Days 184–185

Neil *is* quite sick and needs surgery. Cancer cells were mentioned as unlikely, *but* a possibility—"something's not quite right, but of course everything *should* be all right." So much doctor doublespeak to protect just himself.

Last night before I put my head on Neil's stomach, *I saw my mother in the room.* "Mother," I said, and then she was gone. I wonder, has she come for Neil? At first I was comforted by the sight of her, but now with what the doctor said, I'm really worried.

Day 186

Ralph told Neil this morning that Neil's most recent designs are the best he's ever seen. When Neil arrived home with Ralph's words, I went crazy. "Why didn't you seize this moment to make the large, sharp point of your great value?" I shouldn't have yelled at Neil. I went to bed early— same time as him. But, the guilt of what I said to Neil kept me awake. I watched him sleep. *Neil. Breathe.* Then, I got up and wrote this.

Day 187

A few days over six months of writing about losing Beck. Pages upon pages of yellow legal paper inked up. In six months the loss of him *has* to be less. At least I'm not calling Astrid Olson's office twice a day making and breaking appointments. But the ache can reawaken itself so quickly. (Even the image of the warts above his buttocks can't stop it.) It's then that my hand reaches for the phone. Now I just press half his number and hang up. *Half a year, half his number.*

In six months my mother will be dead almost two years. Every morning I awaken to the fact of her death. With Beck it's different. He *could* come back and explain it. My mother's appearance in my room two nights ago—unexplainable. Her shadow follows me and I fear it has come for Neil.

Days 188–189

Nothing's final about my book of poems yet, except Kane said today, "It's a remarkable accomplishment—especially the poems about your mother." (Here, I cannot help but think about Ralph's flatteries to Neil.) Then came what felt like a too-long pause, after which he continued, "However, I'm worried that the love/sex poems are about Beck and you must take out any reference to alcohol, for Beck could construe it as reference to his mother." I don't know if Kane's worried about *me* or *Beck*. My guess is Beck. He doesn't want Beck's rage. Beck *is* a critic—however minor. "Minor" is Kane's characterization. I agreed to take out the word "gin" from the poem he's most concerned with, but I'm upset by this—it has such a surprising next line that ends with skin: "gin always on her kissy lips/ poisoning your shining child skin."

It is kind *if* he's trying to protect me from Beck's wrath, which at gut level, I think not. Beck and Kane are old friends from way back, even though Kane has voiced disgust quite openly about him—from his crude manners to his intellect.

At the end of the conversation, he said, "You'll have to wait a few more weeks for the other reader's report, even though *I* think it's your best book yet and a remarkable achievement." I hung up the phone just worried about replacing "gin." The closest I could come was "sin," but that puts a completely different intention on what I want to say.

I'd like to just lock the door and work on my play day after day. Another angle on Beck. More theatrical, yet maybe more the lifeblood of what happened than some poems. Or, is *this* manuscript the final truth? Or is the novella—with its many more references to the rogue Avigdor Element and his ruthless legacy—the right approach? *How many genres will it take?* All I know is that I am the reporter, the recorder of it—the obituary of the relationship.

≈ ≈ ≈ ≈ ≈

Note: I politely asked the playwriting professor on the second to last day of class for the return of my manuscript. He then, surprisingly, pulled it out of his briefcase and handed it to me. I said thank you with a facetious half-curtsy—an almost indifference. This is where Jason would like me to get with Beck.

Day 190
Tomorrow is Neil's and my anniversary. We will give each other token presents and go out for a nice dinner. We will peck each other's lips and late into the night when the anniversary is over, I will go to bed and lay my head onto his stomach. His body grows so large. His surgery is at the beginning of May.

Day 191
We went to a fancy restaurant for dinner that we used to frequent. When Neil asked me yesterday what I wanted for a present, from nowhere I immediately said "peach lotion." I want to be covered with the juice of a peach, like in T. S. Eliot's poem "The Love Song of J. Alfred Prufrock." Prufrock, obsessed with old age and death: "Do I dare to eat a peach?" *Yes, Permission For Pleasure, No Matter How Sloppy.*

Day 192
Two days until A arrives. The female population of the city—at least the portion who reads serious fiction, which now includes the realtor, Joyce—awaits the quixotic A.

Day 193
          Will she ever get clean of the burnt-
          out center of others' lives? Hit me,

          she whispered last night
          to her lover. There, pointing
          to the wiry pit. How it fascinates—
          the way the two of them mix

up love with hate . . .
　　　　Jennie Silver

Tonight Neil and I went to the university to see "The Cherry Orchard." We parked right next to the second of Beck's apartments—the apartment where the hitting started. That's when he became utterly drawn back to me again. The force of that arousal fastened him to me for much of those last two years. At the theater, the man in front of us and the man to my left both put their arms around the women they were with, while Neil nodded off. I watched the fleshy bob of his head. I was so agitated that we left at the intermission.

My own loneliness hung heavy and silent over me. I missed what I had lost—the grab of him on to me, his need that could cover me with both dirt and stardust. Where have I gone in his mind's heart? A arrives tomorrow. Can he keep me away from B—the wart back, virus sponge, and the stardust—that energy that ignored what once were the planetary boundaries of my locked body?

Day 194

I said mean things to Neil. He barely reacted. It was a good way of getting back at me, because I then felt even more the monster. I hated the things that came out of my mouth. They made me hate myself even more than I already do. How I acted pointed me in the direction of my death, made me feel that was the only way to silence myself. I became Joe Silver, spewing out his furious, final, fatal sentence to John.

The images from last night of *those* men's arms around *their* women had returned to plague me—so I taunted Neil in my misery.

The only thing that calmed me down was going with Neil to his office to revise and type the play. And a heightened state of mental activity in Neil's office *did*, at least for a short time, make me forget the loneliness and my words to Neil—their awfulness.

The day passed and with it A's arrival with smaller pomp in my head than I would have guessed. Most of the focus on Beck and Neil—the convergence of anguish past and anguish present.

Day 195

The weather, again, is unusually warm for this time of year, and I think Spring Fever is a real disease. The last time we walked along the lake in mid-September the air was like today. So clear, and the day infinite with positive, forceful, wild, frightening words all looped together. Then, nothing, like an awful winter blizzard that shuts down the city and seals everything in ice or like a death, when the person you've been standing next to *goes* upstairs or you *leave* them upstairs—either way they just disappear into the empty, unending atmosphere.

Day 196

Neil's tumors—now a 50 percent probability they're malignant. Tomorrow he has an important breakfast meeting about a job and has to pretend he's perfect, although it's so obvious just from how he looks, he's just not.

Day 197

All Fools' Day. And it was. Saw A. Sat in on his class. Sat in on another, which he also sat in on. He said, "Hello, I'm tired"—he looked old, but not awful, his bones too good for awful, but he's more wrinkled than I remembered. Still, I wanted more attention. At least more attention than just the acknowledgment that I existed for that minute. My life makes no sense—a midday panic attack over Neil's health (he took the late afternoon off to calm *me* down) and still in the underbelly of myself the foul need is still so alive to get in touch with Beck, to be touched by Beck. This day was named for me—thinking A could be a person in my life, that he could be a person *at all*, that Beck is whom I need.

Day 198

I keep losing slips of paper with phone numbers I need, page revisions for the play. I hear her say, "Neil is going to die." That's why losing things drives me crazy. What I'm looking for right now I had in my hand in *this* room ten minutes ago. Disappeared. I've trashed the room and I can't find it. Neil sleeps in the next room. I can go in there and easily find him, like when I'd go to the fourth floor, go into her room, and find her.

Day 199
The weather has cooled and with it the fevered spring that further singed my mind. Let A distance himself upon his arrival—it's disappointing, but right now it's okay, as is whatever is going on with Beck. With Neil sick, some distance is best. It will, I predict, be harder if Neil heals well and the weather heats up not to call him, ask if "the wait" is over. What does he *foresee* with the rising temperatures?

Day 200
Worked again with Neil all day on the play. I forgot about the fizzle of A's arrival—a defective firecracker slowly sizzling into itself. Anyway, he looked waxy, his pallor reminding me of my mother's—my *dying* mother. Is this just my sour, sorry self reacting to his indifference? Is that what drives me back to Beck—to Beck thoughts? Instead, I rewrite and refine the play. Love. Rape. Hate. I look at these words and wonder about their ordering on the page—in my life? Would another juggler be more adept? Would a proper therapist have been better than this unending filling up of language on paper? Where's the cure? In the pen? In some doctor's den? In calling *him*?

Days 201–202
All day again with the play. I've reshaped its opening to be more similar to this diary. I've increased the mother's part, giving "Lettie" (the name of one of my grandmother's lost sisters and the name she gave my mother) more words. She keeps telling Lissa she has to accept what's happening. Also, Beck's, A's, Gladys's, and Mandy's names remain unchanged—at least for now—but Neil's and Joyce's names are different. I've added more ballet—given Nijinsky much more stage presence. I even tried to call the father of the deceased poet Cecilia Slaughter to ask if I could use Cecilia's poem "Nijinsky's Dog" for the play, but I couldn't find his number. I then called her cousin Celie who told me he, too, was deceased, but even

if he were alive there would be no problem. Her exact words were, "In life he could not have cared less about Cecilia's poetry, so he most definitely would not care in death." Her voice was fragile and nervous, and her laugh, after she said this, bitter. Then she calmed and told me she was Cecilia's literary executor and she looked forward to my play with her cousin's poem in it. I thought of Joe Silver as she spoke and his indifference to my work.

Neil cried when he typed the new ending into the computer. Next week he leaves for three weeks—a proposal for a large building in another city. His design, but one he'll never get to build—even if he recovers completely. Mournings are getting more impossible. I mean, *mornings*. They stretch to 3 p.m. By 12 a.m., again, I'm more comfortable with the world, because everyone's asleep. I write and write. I write Lissa's mother an even larger part. Mine stands over my right shoulder, moving my pen.

Day 203

The anniversary of the day my sweet grandfather died. Moses Shershevsky knew, just like his daughter did, exactly what was happening. Both so quiet in their leaving. Their faces blending together in the earthly atmosphere. *I'll tell you how the sun rose . . .*

≈ ≈ ≈ ≈ ≈

Tomorrow I'll not go to A's class. It bores me, but I will try to take the highway to the city and past it to the afternoon class—to master it. Proust. *Swann's Way.* Marcel's obsessions: his "madeleines"—the exquisite delight he took in their taste—his mother's kiss, his Gilberte, Swann's Odette. Attempting to master the highway is worth it.

Day 204

A smiled a lot at me today in class. (The Proust class, where he, too, appeared again.) I wasn't going to go. I woke up rigid, almost immobile—all emotion so tightly locked in the physical. Neil called as I was trying to get dressed. I told him, "I'm not sure I can make it there." He said, "I'll meet you in the city and drive you the rest of the way."

It was raining. The highway makes me too shaky. I keep focusing on the possibility that someone's going to smash into me—*I wonder why.* He designated a place and said, "Jennie, you can do this."

I liked A's smiles—his acknowledgment that I exist. (How can I have gotten to such a place—that A's smiles are enough?) I like the class. I love the book. Even if A weren't there, it's where I'd want to be. Reading Proust. Reading *Swann's Way.* All passions gone awry—the machinations of elegant and base obsessions written in the most artful of ways.

≈ ≈ ≈ ≈ ≈

After the Proust class, A showed me his office and as I sat down to enjoy it and him, he put on his coat. Where he is psychologically in relation to me was perfectly realized in that gesture. Posture. *Poseur.* Anyway, Neil was waiting a couple of buildings away. What an odd relationship I have with A: over the phone relaxed and intimate, in person almost *mime*—most definitely not mine.

Day 205

Almost 4:30 a.m. I've been working on the play again. Small, but seemingly important revisions. Tomorrow I'll sleep until I wake and when I wake I'll want to die. At that moment of wakefulness the litany floods in: *She's dead. Neil is leaving, leaving on a business trip to present his designs for a firm where he'll soon be gone. What designs lurk inside his body—malignant or benign?*

Day 206

It's a thick dark outside. I miss Beck's smile. How his face hung over me—a ripe apple, a lust to bite into, to chew and swallow—fat, without the calories, yet foreboding—the setup in Eden? In Ellen?

Day 207

Neil leaves tomorrow. Now it seems I'll be alone for only two weeks. He has fully stocked the refrigerator and he's made me stickers; he's placed them on the radiator cover next to where I write. They're funny. "Emergency Scum Protector—Valid for 1 hour," "Extra Strength Scum Protector—Valid for 24 hours." Of course, they're meant for when I want to pick up the phone and call Beck.

Day 208

Neil left. A quick kiss on each cheek. Tears in his eyes. I felt sick. Mandy came over and we went to a movie. A romantic comedy—*her* life, not mine. Now, I sit and stare at one of Neil's Post-its: Extra Strength Scum Protector—Valid for 24 hours.

Days 209–212

The day was clear and I got myself to class. I was pleased with that. Before the class, I entered a small lounge and there A was—I sat next to him on the hassock. He probably felt crowded. He told me he called Joyce to take her out to dinner, but she wasn't there. He'll call her later. Poor her—she'll get all excited and then nothing, or they'll have sex and *then* nothing. I tried to make conversation, asked where he'd be this summer. "The South of France." Then another woman came in and all his attention went to her. I got up and left on cue.

≈ ≈ ≈ ≈ ≈

Tonight I went to a "literary event"—too many people wanting me to help them get their manuscripts to my publisher. They pushed their fingers into my back, pulled on my hair as if it were the cord of a drape that would open to a view of their future success. (How shocked they'd be to see my reality—that scoured, sour patch of bald.)

I wondered if that's how I am with A. Then my thoughts turned to Beck. Beck of the lost heart—Beck of the last heart to touch me. Tonight there were people there who are friends of Ellen Feld and friends of Beck. They stared at me—a scarlet "A" somewhere on my body? I would have liked that . . .

≈ ≈ ≈ ≈ ≈

Neil's coming home tomorrow night for the weekend. He misses me, he misses home. He told Ralph and the others that he has an important doctor's appointment and they'll never know it's a lie, because the secret of the surgery will be out—everything will fall into place so seamlessly. "I'll be home earlier than I thought and this weekend, too! Everything's going very well," he reported. *With whom?*

Days 213–215
  I thought Neil might be more passionate when he came back—it *was* a passionate act. But he wasn't. Just Neil, filling the car up, washing towels, buying groceries—making sure the practical was taken care of, while I wandered around my room for three days going from play to novella to this manuscript.

Day 216
  I punched in all but the last digit of Beck's number today. I was 90 percent sure that I'd stop and I did. I just wanted to hear his voice. How far he's gone away from me. How little I've gotten away from him. One more digit and we *could* have reconnected. At least for a split second.

Day 217

> *This is the Hour of Lead –*
> *Remembered, if outlived,*
> —Emily Dickinson

  Hitler's birthday. Kane called this morning. He left me a message on my answering machine like Joe Silver did the day my mother died. I awoke to it. Kane's message, however, just said, "Call Me." *Carrington Lowell's words to my dead brother. Beck's words from last September.* I called Kane. He told me the "other reader" (Monte Grazer) didn't like my book and, although he said again, "I think it's your best book yet and a remarkable achievement," he added, "I've got these pressures." *From Beck? From Monte?* Anyway, it's over. I've lost my publisher after five books, *just like that.* My "best book yet"!? He continued, "We met last night at midnight on the phone." WHO? A CABAL? No names given. It was never going to happen. That was always Kane's intention. My pen has been "put down"— the euphemism used when they kill a sick animal.

I called Neil. He said, "I'll come home." I wept, "You can't. You have to stay there and try to look as if you're okay." Then, I added, "Just stay on the phone." Which he did for a very long while. Much of the time we didn't talk and I just listened—listened to Neil breathe, while he listened to me cry.

Day 218

I'm numb. Kane, Beck, and Monte, a Greek chorus of hate and assault, have spoken. Once upon a time each blanketed me with varying degrees of interest. Now, they are all lost. Jason has inverted it; said tonight, "Now you are *free* of them." A patch of me—a square inch of flushed skin (my face still so blotched from all my tears)—can almost feel this. But, inside and out, I *am* so ripped and raw and red. *The color she wore, that she requested we bury her in . . .*

Day 219

"Best book"—*What?* Every mistake I've ever made slaps me in the face and then into my brain's already sick soft tissue, creating more thought-lesions. As with Beck, I don't know what really happened. Every room I inhabit spins. I've taken two Meclizines to keep the walls from crashing into me and now just hope for dreamless sleep.

Day 220

The reminder flyer's come out for my reading next week three blocks from Beck's house—it's sponsored by my "former" press. On the phone Kane had said, "Forget the reading, just forget it"—that's how much and how fast he wanted to get rid of me. I'm going to go anyway and I'm going to read *all* the poems that would offend.

I keep looking at my lost poetry manuscript—not reading it, just looking at it. I keep thinking that Kane will call and *take it back* (both the negative of what he said and the actual manuscript). "Best Book Yet?" The sick, dead feelings are piling up.

Days 221–223

I made some calls and two publishers said they'd like to see the book. I'm beginning to feel a little better. Yet, I wonder if what *they* did to me will ever really fade. I go into Beck's territory—yes, it *is* like *West Side Story*—in two days. I'll read for my "no longer" publisher. I'll possibly read in front of the sadist-keeper of my affections. I wonder about A—will he come or be "too tired"?

≈ ≈ ≈ ≈ ≈

Taken more Valium and Meclizine than ever and now await unending, blank sleep.

Day 224

Neil's birthday. Nothing to celebrate. Surgery ahead. Job prospects not quite dead, just on life support. We'll go to my reading and then stop for scoops of ice cream.

Note: Beck wasn't there. Nor A. *Last reading for the press.* Sad. They're good people to work with—a home that I've lost. The associate director was there and apologized for what Kane had done. Ellen Feld was there, wearing her thick mask of makeup and a fixed, false look of concern for me—all of it so easily washed away, as she, too, will be someday.

≈ ≈ ≈ ≈ ≈

Another burial. I *am* Joe Silver, who said seven years ago at my grandmother's funeral, "I'm so sick of looking into *that* hole." Yet, unlike him, I want to crawl in.

Day 225

Tomorrow I go to a writers' conference where people think I'm successful. They don't know. And all I want to do is call Beck and tell him all the
detailed, evil things Kane said about him. I'm free. And I'm no one. They
think they've silenced this "no one" woman. I'm not sure that the future
will prove them wrong.

Days 226–229

Two and a half days of performance at the conference. All weekend I
eat the small yellow and blue pills—Valium—as if they are M&M's. My
mother seems so far away, sometimes I wonder if she really ever did exist.
Maybe I was hatched from some neurotic hen that just got up and waddled
off into her own oblivion. *Maybe the roosters in the car trunk were hens?*

Days 230–231

I've worked all night on the play. Soon it will be ready to give to another theater. Neil and I are trying to complete it before his surgery next
Monday. We'll throw another piece of hope into the atmosphere. Yet, I
can't stop worrying that my book of poetry is already "damaged goods."
The image of John reappears: standing there holding his rejection letter . . .

≈ ≈ ≈ ≈ ≈

Neil says, "Tomorrow evening we can revise the play again." Does Neil
know that's the day I've circled?

Day 232

Writing about losing Beck in the Proust class. A's not here. Would I
still be in this class reading Proust if A weren't sitting in? I question all my
actions these days.

≈ ≈ ≈ ≈ ≈

How peculiar the professor's words. His random over-intellectualizations, the too-many empty adjectives he uses about exquisite, psychological pain. A not being in this room allows me to write this. If he were here I'd be distracted by him and have to cover it up, look more intent on what now seems the professor's total immersion in himself—he sighs, he coughs, he gasps, as if he's drowning in a whirlpool of his own personal thoughts and can't seem to pull himself out. Maybe *he's* distracted by something else— an A or a B? Or worse: maybe *he's* just lost his publisher.

Trying to focus more on the professor's words—what *exactly* is he saying? I look around and know I do not belong. On this day I'd circled to disappear, I'm in this room, half-listening to some professor's suddenly ditzy spin on Proust's angst, writing about losing Beck and A-less. And the more I write, the more I want to get out of here. *Here* being everywhere. However, if I keep writing, it helps me stay.

Neil's presence doesn't anchor me, yet he drove me here to keep me in the world. (He *must* have seen the circle.) This world where two blocks away Beck crushed me into his mattress. This world where four blocks away I counted on my next book being published. This weighted world of heaped-on circumlocution, an over-seductive intelligence with a too-sweet, lethal fragrance that drew me in, then turned its back caked with warts and stink.

Day 233

Had a phone conference with the director of the press. Neil listened from his office. He sometimes joined in, in a meek way. But he's sick, so I can't ask him for much. The guy mostly sided with Kane—"Kane has the final word." Although I felt from what he said that Kane would be reprimanded. Big deal. He said, "'*Call Me*' in six months to give me an update on what's happening with the book." There they were again, those two words—*John so newly planted in the ground*. Those two words to get me away from Beck's car, return Kane's call, off the phone with the director of the press.

≈ ≈ ≈ ≈ ≈

Neil and I did work on the play last night. I'm getting closer to the draft that I can give to the person in charge of new play development at a theater in the city. The deadline is in a little over two weeks. Working on Beck's attempted censorship in a theatrical way seems a larger project—that *it is* more than something that just happened to me—and it distracts me from my homeless book. I've known of people who've had breakdowns, become suicidal, after losing their publisher. I imagine Kane, Beck, and Monte Grazer—forever nipping at the Pulitzer—dancing around a fire; my bones are in the center. A tired image for sure, but I'm tired. It must have been a good release for their own burgeoning insecurities over insufficient success. *So why not a gang bang? Yes, a good release.*

Day 234
   All night I've worked on the play. Monday, Neil goes into surgery and by then the play should be finished. Yes, the play saves me.

Day 235
   Tomorrow's Mother's Day. A visit to the cemetery with flowers, then out to dinner. Point. Counterpoint. Did someone once say, "Let's create this holiday and make some money?"

≈ ≈ ≈ ≈ ≈

We're on the sidewalk in front of our old apartment building, all puffed up in new spring coats and hats, my mother, me, my grandmother, and Gladys. Joe Silver takes the picture. Click. Then, my grandfather moves to one side of Joe Silver; John and Uncle Meyer are on the other. They're swelled up, too, in their new lightweight suits. Uncle Meyer has his arm around a beaming John—everyone's a spring flower bursting forth, pushing up from the ground. My mother takes the picture. Click. We are all smiles for these minutes. But, nothing can hold it, recreate it—not even old photographs.

≈ ≈ ≈ ≈ ≈

We'll go to the graves, bring flowers, leave them there to die in the quiet.
No click or wish can fix this.

Day 236

Neil. Surgery tomorrow. Cemetery today.

Day 246

Ten days later. Neil has cancer. "We think we got it all. But it's the type
that *could* come back." They tell me its name—what they call it—it ends
with an "a" and if I didn't know better, I'd think it was a spring flower. I
just stare at them as they tell me this. I just stare at them as they drink
black coffee and chat casually with each other.

He's out of the hospital. Has been for almost a week. He can't be left
alone. The knife of free-floating anxiety stabs at him frequently. We go everywhere together. I even took him to a poetry reading at the university
three days after he got out of the hospital. The woman who got what was to
be my poetry book publication slot at my former press read from her work.
I wanted to hear her. I couldn't help it. It proved to be the most boring
reading I've ever attended. I worried Neil might keel over from the linger-
ing effects of the anesthesia and the tedium of it.

Beck introduced her. But before that came *The Shock*. He introduced
Me, saying, "I am so pleased to say that the very talented poet, Jennie Silver,
is here today." Then he clapped his hands together and the audience, like
ducklings, followed his lead. I sat stunned. The man who bashed away
at my existence—banished me from his life—in September was, in May,
announcing my presence with such celebration.

A was at the reading, too. He took another look at me. In other words,
I turned his head (literally). He said, "Let's have dinner." I said, "Fine. Will
I see you in the Proust class this week?" He said, "Yes." I said, "We can
make a plan then." He said, "Fine." He gave me a big hug and a kiss. Beck
watched. This was *after* the reading, *after* the introduction, *after* Beck said
my name *Out Loud*. I became Odette in *Swann's Way*. The mysterious
Odette. The woman with the indecipherable past. I was no longer Anna
about to throw herself onto the train tracks.

A didn't show up to the Proust class.

Day 247

Jason now feels that Beck did sabotage my book and given that, he can be more generous. *A Sad, Astute Interpretation.*

I think about calling Beck. If it was a vengeful trick to say my name so as to try to put himself so positively smack back in the middle of my mind, it worked. Did he do it because we are now even: I wrote of *him*; he made me lose my *publisher*?

Day 248

Neil went on an experimental medication today. He won't be having conventional therapy—at least not for a while. In six months he'll have another scan with a *"We'll see then"* tacked on.

Day 249

Late last night, actually in the early morning hours of today, I took a safety pin, opened it, put some alcohol on the needle tip, and punctured the skin that's bald atop my head. At first nothing happened—just a pin stuck in my too-hard scalp. I pushed deeper and finally some blood trickled out—a tiny puddle of red—leaching all the toxins from my life, or so I hoped. Mostly what I felt was the hurt of it. And I enjoyed it. It was a large relief that the pain was so utterly focused.

At some level, too, I was disgusted. In the bright hour of full dawn I had reduced myself to such unsavory, sick behavior. I stood before the birth of a flawless summer's day—nature's overabundant gift—florid with disease. True, I've picked my head since I was nine, taken a serrated knife to it, waxed off the hairs on the spot—made a little brush of the stubs with hot wax that I would rub instead of my head—but I've never tried so hard as I did this early morning to draw blood. Never have I felt the need to enact the fantasy so intensely of trying to drain all poisons out of me—and out of Neil—as if in doing such a thing, that were possible. Never have I felt more pressure building inside me as Neil slept with the fifty-fifty chance of more sick cells, just dormant; my mother and John slept dead; my ex-publisher slept well without me—while I had never missed Beck more.

When the blood became visible, there was a second where I felt that I had conquered my head. *A war had been won against thought.* Then the revulsion set in—same as I'd sometimes feel after I'd be with Beck.

Day 250

A interviewed a famous writer tonight, but mostly talked in a not-so-indirect way about himself. How did he get so far—on his fabulous cheekbones, great voice? Afterward, during the reception, he yelled at someone who was on a panel for a large fiction prize—actually screamed, "I *know* you voted against me. I'll *leave* the dinner if you're there. So don't be!" I stood there appalled. I truly don't know A. I thought, *let him go—go into summer's overheated oblivion.*

Before all this, in the afternoon, I called Beck. I did. I didn't expect him to answer. Just wanted to hear his voice on the recorded message. But there he was. He didn't bash the phone in my ear. We talked. We did. He was arrogant, I pathetic. I did, however, get to tell him his "best friend" Kane had written a cruel, revealing poem about him (he knew of the poem; he didn't know Kane had talked about it, was proud of it) and the details about how Kane doesn't speak well of him.

I said, "I want to meet with you and talk." He replied, "We will, but first I want you to tell me who was your main source of bad information about me." It was then that I told him about Kane and after that, of Ellen Feld. I was glad to tell him. I asked him, "What exactly was the rumor you heard and who started it?" He was vague, but guessed it came from Ellen to the wife of one of his graduate students. Then, he said, far too casually for me, "I've mostly forgotten exactly what it was and want to get on with my life." He paused, then followed with, "I have to pick up Maxi. Let's talk again and soon," thereby reneging on making a plan after he got any information. I said, "Thank you." (Again, a THANK YOU?) But I think he meant it— that we should talk soon. I meekly asked, "Can we start over?" He slowly and pedantically answered, "I don't think so, there would have to be *certain rules.*" I knew what he meant, at least in part—that I could never have any details in my poems that suggested him. It was only after we hung up that I wondered if Beck's "certain rules" also included his "tagging" me as the owner of my body. He does treat me like a dog—a dog in need of obedience training—and if he really pushed me down entirely to the animal level, I'd never be able to write again, because *Animals Can't Write*.

Tomorrow, I deliver my latest draft of the play—about Beck and me.

Days 251–252

The play is delivered. I should have some feedback in about two and a half weeks. In the meantime, I play the tape with Beck's and my conversation on it. SIT. FETCH. LIE DOWN. BARK. SHUT UP.

≈ ≈ ≈ ≈ ≈

Mornings I still want to die. It's in the deep, fallen night I play his most recent words—over and over. I like his voice. Yes, I awake world-sick. But as light gives in to dark I think how seeing him would be so nice. A walk. A handhold. Except it never stopped at this. All of it becoming too high-pitched—escalating toward the violent. I am still far too ambivalent.

Days 253–263

I continue to play the most recent tape of Beck. I don't seem to be able not to do this. Life is so bleak with Neil. He is getting stronger and that is very good, but it also means he's becoming more himself and that self is still a dulled out, sad man, even with the tumors cut out and the medication ingested. We both push the thought of the "We'll See Scan" as far out of our minds as we can. I sit with him more and more. Once again, we watch a lot of television.

Days 264–267

No entries. Have I just given myself up to the mindlessness of TV—all creativity slowly being sucked away?

Days 268–275

This week I'm supposed to hear about my play and I'm supposed to hear from the two publishers about my orphaned book in the "next several months—or so."

I touch my head less since my vicious attack on it and read more about decorative combs. The kind that can almost conceal a torn-up head, a buckled mind. The few new poems I've written seem to be healing me better than this manuscript of loss.

My mother told me to keep writing poems—with or without her. Now it's without her and also without a publisher. I'm a high-wire artist working with no net. The crowd has vanished. Mother. Publisher. It's pure. However, I still awake in the late morning to a world that smells so sour from its own foul breath and it's then I recall the fecal smell from the small of his back. But the poems are no longer about him. They're of elegant combs—of placing them on my mother's crown.

≈ ≈ ≈ ≈ ≈

Joe Silver called to say, "Howareyou? and by the way Hedy had emergency surgery—her appendix." (Did Neil bring the doll back to *her* house?) Then he added, "My sister (eighty-nine years old) has discovered a lump on her breast." I'm too tired to care much about Hedy's almost burst of an obsolete organ and I've had enough of wild cells trying to destroy a body. His howareyou? again his prelude to get rid of his junk. Almost silent, I just add it to the ruins.

I do think about calling Beck. What stops me is my growing certainty he was the prime force as to why I lost my publisher. Kane so insistent that I change the word "gin" so there'd be no chance Beck might think it referred to his mother—his sad, alcoholic mother—and of all Kane told me about her. *Romanticism and sadomasochism—its conjoined twin—battled within her*—words that I just added to my novella, and might add to my play, which came back to me from the woman I'd given it to two and a half weeks ago. She kept to her promise. Her long letter was filled with much praise and some suggestions I can work on—save one. She ended by writing: "This is a very serious project, so give it all you've got. I only insist on one thing, that Lissa must not die. She has to live. You can do it! I'll get back to you soon to schedule a reading of it in the fall." All I could focus on when I read her letter was—*Lissa live?* Oh no, I thought. That changes everything. I just don't see it.

≈ ≈ ≈ ≈ ≈

I keep trying to figure out how to let Lissa live. I don't seem to know how to do it and for some reason allowing this makes me panic about the possibility of reinvolving myself with Beck. Maybe because I feel it's the only way for me to live—to feel alive. But, why would I want a man who claims he has no money and most definitely has no generosity of spirit? Because he *desires* me? Because he'll grab at me in public? Because he fantasizes about executing intrusive acts upon my body? A pulsating nausea overtakes me—both about not knowing how to let Lissa live and any possible reinvolvement with Beck.

The feeling escalated when I couldn't find a certain blouse. Then, I thought about Neil. He's not a pig. He doesn't want to physically hurt me. Why lose Neil to refind Beck? And the more I couldn't find the blouse, I relived that I'd lost my mother. How I'll never *find* her. My thoughts, however disconnected, had a strange emotional logic. All around me were bags lined up reminding me of her—the stuff I'd brought home from her house last November and have never put away.

The more I couldn't find the blouse, the more I went nuts and the more I couldn't stand looking at *those* bags—filled with the material memories of her—*the more* I knew I had to stay away from Beck.

I've been living in an indecipherable clutter.

Finally, I asked Neil to take everything I'd dropped here to a place where I can't see it. I gave up on finding the blouse; if it shows up, great, if not, it just doesn't.

Day 276

I read tonight about petit point—research for a poem. My life a patch of minute stitches—the picture constructed always unfinished on the canvas. The threads I use are frayed hairs. I can tell before its written "Petit Point" will be a good poem.

Day 277

The poem is written and I see a trilogy of them—*a petit point of hunger, a petit point of pleasure, a petit point of terror.*

I do still think about calling Beck (hunger, pleasure, terror). And how impossible it seems to let Lissa live.

Days 278–280

Mandy's husband is getting calls saying she's a whore. Mandy says it really doesn't bother him—he feels he has in her "such a prize." Irv tells her how to dress when they go out, which body part she should expose that night so other men will want her. Like a doll—*A doll I can carry, the girl that I marry.* She goes along with this all wound up like that awful walking doll I got, except by day she does fuck Sy and "gambles" with him. They go "to the boats" and drift along in the River Styx. Afterward she goes home to cook Irv brisket.

A comes back to the city in ten days. It was weeks ago when he said, "Let's have dinner in late June." True, he never showed up in class for an exact arrangement, but when I saw him after the interview, after he finished screaming at that guy, he said it again.

Days 281–287

Last night I had two drinks and got so sick. My scalp once again became an inflammation—all infected thoughts rose to the surface. Nothing could put out the fire except 20 milligrams of Valium. I've grown allergic to liquor. The only "sugar" to appease me is Valium for calm or Meclizine for balance and, of course, the rubbing of my spot as if it were a genie lamp that would make Neil be okay and eliminate our continual worry, make a publisher appear, make A look at me longingly, instill in Beck "true" love. How strange that I still believe in my fool heart someone will come along and save me—help me live beyond the need of knowing that pills are just an arm's reach away as is my designated soul-spot. Lissa can't live. I simply don't know how to write it.

The phone didn't ring all week, then Mandy called twice this morning. "I have some time and can fit you in tomorrow. I'm trying to break up with

Sy." On the second message, she quickly remembered to ask how Neil was doing. *I have to stay away from her more.* She lives at the least satisfying end of the friendship spectrum, creating large pockets of emptiness for me, while she hungrily gobbles everything up for herself and gets chubby. I wonder if A fits into this category, just the mirror image of Mandy—a tall, handsome stick of flesh who eats you up, then spits you out.

Days 288–299

Neil and I had a terrible fight—about sex. I brought up the topic because I've come to equate sex with life and I wanted him to show some interest. But the conversation went on to a too-familiar worn-out path. After he left to get some air, I called Beck and A. Both had their answering machines on. Saturday night, what did I expect? They're out having fun—hugs, a kiss, maybe even sex. I called each of them twice. It was a beautiful summer's night. The sad wanting, the desperation, the answering machines playing in my ear. *Leave a message. Leave a message.* The loneliness almost appeased by recorded voices.

When I finally reached A, he actually seemed very pleased to hear my voice and said he was available for dinner Thursday. So for an hour or two I'll have A's full attention. Thursday is my mother's birthday, I wonder if this was her plan—a gift to her daughter on her birthday. A little life sprinkled among the losses.

≈ ≈ ≈ ≈ ≈

Dinner with A was low-key. He told me rather unemotionally that he and his girlfriend will be broken up by the fall. Then he straight out said, "I'm looking for a rich woman who's beautiful with a brain. Someone I can travel with." I wondered sitting there if he thought me "rich and beautiful and with a brain." He doesn't look at me the way Beck did—so filled with an overweighted lust. A is sleek. A is clean. He invited me to sit in on his class in the fall, which pleased me. I didn't mention the reading of my play, which the director of new play development now wants to schedule for early October. However, I did tell him that Neil's been sick, but not about him losing his job. Then suddenly, unexpectedly, I said, "When Neil is stronger we're going to take some time away from each other." As we left the restaurant, he gave me a long, soft kiss on the mouth. I liked his lips, the cool smoothness of his cheek. Then, he quickly left. I don't know if he became aroused or bored or scared that I possibly wanted more. For now I'll pick aroused—it will help me not call Beck. A life with A would be so different than what I have. A life with Beck would in weeks—days? hours?—become too much of a degradation and I can't get out of my mind that he most probably did say to Kane, "Cut her—cut her sliced lines."

I'll hold tight to that soft mouth kiss.

≈ ≈ ≈ ≈ ≈

Neil and I brought flowers to my mother's grave the day after her birthday. The cemetery was too hot—the air thick and immobile.

I want to fly away with the exotic A. So I'll pretend for now he finds me desirable and is playing it a bit distant. Or maybe I just confused him because I'm so confused. I hope he finds me beautiful. I look in the mirror and it's filled with ridicule and riddle.

Days 300–308
    With A away until the end of August I am left with Neil and Joe Silver. Again, we are down to talking about Joe Silver's bowels—everything reduced to shit. It used to be mostly about his business deals. It's *always* been too hard to digest. The only reason I could stand it was that today Neil had his first complete check-up since his surgery. The doctor was so positive. No mention of the "We'll See Scan" and we didn't ask.

    For months the fantasies about A mostly kept me away from Beck. Now I'm closer than ever, if I can wait another seven weeks, to knowing what is possible. Why not leave Neil who, with the help of his examination today, I've decided will stay well—*he has to*—and try for some strange chance for a strange happiness with the strange A?

Days 309–310
My wanting wanders more away from Beck. What would I do with him? Let him kiss me? Touch me? *Tattoo me? Bite me?* All conversation on my part would be dishonest. ME: "I promise never to write about you again." (EXCEPT: There's *this* diary *and* a play *and* a novella.) HIM: "I can do anything I want with you." (ACCEPT: And keep quiet.)
The staged reading of the play is now scheduled for October 5. "GIVE IT UP," he'd scream. For him? Not possible. I've grown past that. He's already either directly or indirectly taken away my publisher. Neil and Jason are sure it was a direct hit. *Hit Me.*

Day 311–314
Neil reiterates, "I'd die if you left me." I say, "Didn't you hear the doctor? You're going to be okay." He sleeps quietly; he breathes better. He looks peaceful. He looks healthier. I'm no longer the sadist in his life. In mine, Beck is *or was*, while A just fades in and out—an exquisite lace of hope like the play or like the silent publishers who still have my book of poems. No ties that yet bind, just lovely, long, loose silky threads—*healthy hairs still on my head with new ones that are starting to grow in.*

Days 315–318
Two nights ago I spoke to another poet in The Series and he was *shocked*, or so he seemed, by what had happened. He said, "If it could happen to you after five successful books, it could happen to anyone." After I hung up the phone I realized I had sweated right through everything I was wearing from reliving my upset.
Then quite unexpectedly, after changing clothes and sitting in my chair to calm myself down, I saw a new title for my rejected book of poems and how I could expand it. The poems I wanted to write for it. I remembered a chair at East Haven Rise that my mother sat in when I was three, four, and five and she so young. How John and I would dance around her in the full glory of those summers. And today, I wrote a new beginning poem for my suddenly reinvented book:

Mother in Summer

Here, the Hardy Gladioli with their delicate
butterfly florets surround her
as do the Blue Ribbon Dutch Iris bulbs
that live and multiply for years,
their cuttings lasting so long in the vase—
just like forever becomes her face.
She borders my life,
dependable as the garden
lilies. I listen to the trumpets
of their sweet yellow throats—the music
of their silent voice.
We are in the heat of deep summer
and she sits so young and quiet
in the painted pastel
lawn chair, while Green Magic
hybrids with their pure white petals
assert themselves against the shade.
Their perfection protects us,
while I poke

my small fingers through
the cutout design in the steel seat
I've crawled under to touch her.
My back is to the ground.
She jumps. We laugh.
We are not yet old:
Golden Splendor, Rose Fire, Sterling Star,
Enchantment, cluster near us
in this extravagance of color.
She wears a crimson chemise
and her hair flames
equal to the sun.

I wrinkle my pink pinafore
as I lie in the fleshy
grass, turn over, tickle my face
against the weeds. We are surreal
in this light. We are surreal
with all this bright.

Day 319

Neil and I drove up to East Haven Rise today to find the cabins that
my family and several aunts, uncles, and cousins fled to during the summers so many years ago. All that was left was one—the one my mother,
grandmother, John, and I stayed in—Gladys at home. It was everyone's
rest from her and hers from my grandmother. Uncle Meyer always said
he'd come up, but never did. Joe Silver and sometimes my grandfather
made the trip on the weekends as did the other fathers.

I jumped out of the car before it came to a complete stop and ran past
the now horribly dilapidated cabin to the bluff where a single, cream colored aluminum lawn chair stood strong—the exact one I'd written about
last night. It faced the lake as if someone were seated in it watching the
flow of the water. I felt like I had broken through the barrier that death
creates and found my mother waiting and watching in her chair—watching me from across the lake, across all the months since she left.

≈ ≈ ≈ ≈ ≈

Neil grew more inexpressive the more excited I got, until he became completely silent. It seems he just can't participate in too much happiness—
life? When we arrived home, an incantation of "Go Away" pushed up
from my acidic heart, until he did. He packed and left.

He knew I didn't care what he did—felt no guilt—and for him that's
always been a hook so I wasn't surprised when he returned in fifteen
minutes. He said, "I forgot my medicine. Let's go for a pizza"—all in one
breath. He promised that he'd let me leave in the fall for a while. Won't
bother me at all. I don't believe it for a moment.

Days 320–337

The phone *is* off the hook through the nights into the morning, so now if Beck called all he'd find is a busy tone, or none. I need to sleep. When I finally pull myself from my bed, even then, I often keep it off the hook. To keep it on and just wait and wait for Beck to call would be stupid—too many months of doing this has had a severe depressing effect.

More and more, days skipped.

The date for the staged reading of the play continues to be October 5. But I still don't see the path as to how to let Lissa live. It goes against all my impulses. *She has to die. SOMEONE HAS TO . . .*

≈ ≈ ≈ ≈ ≈

Four more weeks and it will be a year since that bash in my ear. Now, maybe three months since "Let's talk again and soon." Does it end like this? A more quiet silence? Is that all I really *did* want? A kinder ending so I can try to keep my sanity and have my play? Beck traded for "art"? Is art better than sex? Can I write the untouched life onto the page and call it a day and a night? Shut the vault. Seal it. *Close Her. Clothe Her. Closure.*

Neil looks at my body as if it doesn't exist. Then, when I am fully dressed, tells me again how beautiful I am, says, "You could have most any man." Does that include A? When I call him I'll know immediately from his voice if he cares to *know me* better.

Days 338–341

Two days ago someone came to my house and just shoved his poetry collection with a note attached through the mail slot. "Would you *just please* pass this along to your publisher?" *Doesn't he know?* I can't stand it. And I can't stand spending any more time with Joe Silver. All he does is repeat himself as to how busy and important he is—now, eighty-five years of hardened ego. He has his monologues and after two hours, when he finally asks how I'm doing, I just say, "Fine." It's easier than telling him I'm having trouble getting out of bed, getting dressed, getting out of the house, staying in this life—*Not Able To Understand How To Let Lissa Live*. The urge is now almost uncontrollable to say, "Quite frankly, Daddy, I want to die like John. *Remember Him—Your Son?*"

Days 342–363
These days I just sit in my chair staring at a wall, sometimes writing, sometimes not, still struggling with how to let Lissa live. Once in a while, I watch an old movie on our upstairs TV with Neil downstairs watching whatever . . .

Day 364
Tomorrow begins the fall season. I think about calling A. I've started putting some of my things together for my small move into the city—a furnished studio apartment with a monthly rate. Away to A. Away from Neil. It's fairly quiet between us. I think he believes if he gives me some room, I'll come back. I don't know if I'll last an hour alone. Probably I'll pick up the phone and call A and if he's distant move to lower scum in the pond—B. Maybe even a few days after the one year anniversary of the crash, I'll find myself with Beck. Then what will all of this have been about—all this writing about Beck, about A. A in Boston, then Washington, then the South of France, then too busy, then too tired, then quite friendly, then me telling him I'm leaving my husband, then I do it and I call him and he blanks?

Day 365
Last night I took double Valium, climbed into bed, and stared at Neil's back as I've done for several thousand nights. I couldn't sleep. A litany of "Best Book Yet," "We'll See Scan," "Call Me" tightened around my brain as if it were a strap on its shortest notch, creating a headache that wouldn't quit.

≈ ≈ ≈ ≈ ≈

I've bought a gun. It's buried deep among my softest lingerie. Its hardness lays so lovely against the lace. I think a lot about putting it in my mouth—

and then nothing. The reverse of how most scientists believe the universe began. Although, I still think the pill-alcohol route is best—less mess. I can't conceive of John's rope.

Jason tells me, "We're all just passing time until we die." He's gone out and bought a motorcycle with all the necessary equipment to zip around jazzily with the time *he* has left. I spent my money on *that*? I'm always paying for men. Tonight I'm supposed to buy A dinner. Yes, I called him early this morning and he said, "The more upscale the better." Then he laughed. I'm worn out as can be, too tired for sex with him or anyone. All I can think about is that I've lost my publisher.

≈ ≈ ≈ ≈ ≈

God's a kind of publisher—I've never thought about it, but it's true. And two days ago, on Rosh Hashanah, I didn't go to temple because I feel I've lost *Him*, too. Right now, He's busy with His next books: *The Book of Life* and *The Book of Death*. I've helped him along by penciling my name into one of them.

Only Mandy's very present. Wants me to meet her "here" or meet her "there," meet her "Anywhere," but *please just meet her*. I listen to her messages on my answering machine. She *NEEDS* to talk to me. Sy has taken his wife to London and then on to Barcelona and Majorca to appease her. Mandy is frantic—tells me again, "This time I'm *really* done with him. This time it's *really* over."

As I walk into the bathroom, looking for my pills, I think, so is the chronicling of these days. *I need my mother.*

≈ ≈ ≈ ≈ ≈

In my chair, I shakily write this: The phone is ringing. I'm too sleepy. The answering machine takes it. In what seems a far distance, a familiar male voice is leaving a very long, soft-spoken message—it sounds so nicely inviting. Only his last two words are louder—clear and passionate and urgent. He says, "Call Me, *CALL ME* . . ." Neil? A? Beck? . . . JOHN? Then, I think about the asked-for—*prayed-for*—ending of the play, but it doesn't come . . .

Staged Reading
(October 5 Version)
City Theatre Club of Chicago

The Play

Nijinsky's Dog

In Two Acts
by
Jennie Silver

I do not like the fire that destroys lives.
I do not like war.
—Vaslav Nijinsky

CAST OF CHARACTERS
(in order of appearance)

NIJINSKY: A dancer.

LISSA: A poet.

BECK: A critic.

MICHAEL: Lissa's estranged husband.

LETTIE: Lissa's mother.

A: A novelist.

* * * *

The voices of BEN and the TELEPHONE OPERATOR are recorded.

All punching of telephone numbers are heard throughout the theater as are telephone dial tones.

* * * *

NIJINSKY is always in ballet tights. When he is the Faun, he wears a gold cord wig with two little horns woven into it and sometimes carries the nymph's veil.

LISSA'S clothes consist of faded blue jeans, a white T-shirt, a red sweater, black slacks, a black shirt, a black silk T-shirt, a black leather jacket, a worn gray robe. In the scenes with LETTIE she is always in a black pantsuit. Sometimes her long hair is clipped back with two side barrettes, sometimes it's in a ponytail, and when she is disheveled, it is loose.

BECK is always in blue jeans and a black T-shirt.

MICHAEL is always in black pants and a white dress shirt and a tie.

LETTIE'S clothes consist of a hospital gown and a long white robe.

A is always in khaki pants, a white T-shirt, and a tailored designer sport coat.

SET

The center of the stage (or perhaps a little off-center—stage left) is divided by a partition that serves as a wall between Lissa's bedroom and Lettie's hospital room. This is the only wall for both rooms. On either side, farther back, there are three platforms. Two on stage right, one on stage left. The lower platform on stage right is Beck's room with a door to it at a right angle to the stage Over Beck's room is another platform—the rooftop—which serves as the roof of Beck's room and also the place where NIJINSKY dances. The third platform is on stage left at a middle height between Beck's room and the rooftop. This platform is the restaurant/coffee shop, where A always appears, and sometimes MICHAEL.

Lissa's room has an overstuffed chair, a dresser with a large mirror over it and a hand mirror on it, a bed with feminine bedding, a nightstand with an answering machine, a cassette player, and a vase of daisies. There are several small shopping bags on the floor with cassette tapes stuffed into them. Also on the floor is a dictionary and a thesaurus. The partition wall is where LISSA marks the days with a black marker.

Lettie's room has a hospital bed and a mobile hospital tray on a floor stand. On the tray is a telephone and a cassette player. There is a chair for visitors and on the partition wall a medicine cabinet with a mirror for its door. In Lettie's room the light is always brighter—these scenes take place in the past.

Beck's room (first platform, stage right) has a chair with flat wooden arms and a dark leather seat and back. There are hand weights on the floor. A telephone rests on the right arm of the chair. If there's room, a small futon is on the floor with a pillow on it and a dark rumpled wool blanket. There are steps to Beck's room.

The rooftop (second platform, stage right) has nothing on it. These are the steps to the rooftop.

The restaurant/coffee shop (third platform, stage left) has a table with two chairs. When it is the restaurant, it has a crisp white tablecloth on the table and a vase with daisies in the center. When it is the coffee shop the table is bare. There are steps to the restaurant.

TIME: The last decade of the last century.

PLACE: A city with a prestigious university.

MUSIC BEFORE ACT I: As the audience enters, music plays from Debussy's *Prelude to The Afternoon of a Faun,* and Stravinsky's *The Rite of Spring.*

NOTE: Nijinsky choreographed *The Afternoon of a Faun* and danced the Faun role in Paris in 1912. He choreographed *The Rite of Spring* in Paris in 1913.

Nijinsky's Dog
(A play in two acts)

<u>Act I</u>

Scene 1   The rooftop.

Scene 2   Lissa's room. Beck's room. Lettie's room.

Scene 3   Beck's room.

Scene 4   Lissa's room. Beck's room. Edge of stage.

Scene 5   Lettie's room. The rooftop.

Scene 6   Lissa's room. Restaurant.

Scene 7   Lettie's room. Beck's room. The rooftop.

Scene 8   Lissa's room. Beck's room. Edge of stage.

Scene 9   Lissa's room. Restaurant. Beck's room.

Scene 10   Lettie's room. The rooftop. Lissa's room.

Intermission

Act II

Scene 1   Lissa's room. Beck's room. Restaurant. Edge of stage.

Scene 2   The rooftop. Lettie's room.

Scene 3   Lissa's room. The rooftop. Coffee shop. Outside of coffee shop.

Scene 4   Lettie's room.

Scene 5   Lissa's room. Outside of coffee shop.

Scene 6   Lissa's room. Coffee shop.

Scene 7   Lettie's room.

Scene 8   The stage. Beck's door. The rooftop.

Act I

Scene 1

Music from *The Afternoon of a Faun* plays. Lights up on the rooftop. NI-JINSKY, in dance tights and his gold cord faun wig, is warming up with ballet stretches.

BLACKOUT.

END OF SCENE.

Scene 2

> Lights up on Lissa's room. There is
> one tally mark on her wall. LISSA is
> wearing a white T-shirt, faded blue
> jeans, and a red sweater. Her hair is
> loose.
>
> LISSA is hanging up the phone. She
> is shaking.

LISSA
(to audience)
**I used only my first name and asked Brigit Sundquist's secretary to
make a record of my call—that's all.**
(pause)
**I called five months ago, then three months ago—and just now. I asked
the secretary, if I ever did come in to speak with Brigit Sundquist,
would I have to name anyone? In other words, I'm not able to name
Beck.**
(pause)
Not then.
(pause)
Not now.
(pause)
Not yet.

> Lights dim on Lissa's room. She can
> be heard punching in a number on
> the phone atop the small end table.
> Lights up on Beck's room. He is sit-
> ting in his chair, lifting a hand weight

with his right arm. He is wearing
a black T-shirt and blue jeans. His
door is half open. His phone rings.
He puts down the weight and answers it.

BECK
(carefully and slowly)

HELLO?

LISSA

Beck, it's Lis—

BECK slams the phone down.
Lights out on Beck's room. LISSA
sits down in her chair, still holding
the receiver. A dial tone is heard. She
pulls the phone onto her lap. She
hangs up the phone. Then, quickly
picks it up and punches in Beck's
number. Lights up on Beck's room.
Beck's phone rings. He picks it up.

LISSA

Beck—

BECK slams the phone down and
kicks his door shut. Lights out on
Beck's room. LISSA slowly puts the
receiver in its cradle. She goes over to
the wall and adds another tally mark.
She sits down and buries her head in
her arms and rocks back and forth.
With her right hand she begins to

rub the spot on her head where her
part ends. The lights brighten and
focus on the top of her head where
she has a small bald spot. Lights dim.

LISSA
(standing, to audience)

Since yesterday, he won't speak to me.

(pause)

I can't work. I can't think.

(pause)

Finally, late last night I took some pills and slept—locked in a deep,
cold sweat of semi-awareness.

MICHAEL enters Lissa's room, sits
down on the bed, takes off his shoes,
loosens his tie, and lies down on the
edge of the bed.

LISSA

I wonder if after you're dead that's what Hell is like.

(LISSA looks at MICHAEL.)

At four o'clock in the morning I woke Michael. He had come over to
take care of me.

LISSA pulls at Michael's shirt. MI-
CHAEL gets up and sits on the edge
of the bed. LISSA sits in the chair.

MICHAEL
(to audience)

She seems to be having a breakdown.

(pause)

I can't say certain words such as *loss* or *death*.

LISSA

Take them back!

MICHAEL
(sighs)

I-take-back-*loss*. I-take-back-*death*.

> MICHAEL gets up and takes a
> comb from the dresser and starts
> combing Lissa's hair.

MICHAEL

How does this feel?

LISSA

Good. It feels good.

> MICHAEL continues for five more
> strokes.

LISSA

How many hairs do you see?

MICHAEL
(parting her hair, he looks at the top of her head.)

I see three trying to break through. If you could just stop touching it.
If you could just leave it—

LISSA

How big? A quarter? A dime? Valium—five milligrams?

MICHAEL
(sighs)

Somewhere between a quarter and a dime.

LISSA
(handing him a piece of paper and a pen)
Draw it?

MICHAEL
(pushing the paper and pen away)
Lissa, I'm tired. Really tired. I've got to stop for now. Okay?

LISSA
Sure. Okay.

MICHAEL
Try to get some rest.

> MICHAEL lies down on the edge
> of the bed and goes to sleep.

LISSA
(looking at MICHAEL)
How easily he falls into that blank, enviable sleep.
(LISSA touches her bald spot.)
(to audience)
Since yesterday, I mostly sit in my chair touching the stubs roughly.
(laughing a bit)
So far nothing sacred has come from it.
(pause)
The bald spot atop the center of my head, where Orthodox and Conservative male Jews place the yarmulke and where, according to Far Eastern religions, the seventh chakra can be found, is pretty much rubbed clean of the few pathetic hairs that had begun to break through.

> LISSA gets out of the chair and
> sits down on the floor and bangs

her head against the partition wall.
MICHAEL in his sleep turns away
from the noise.

LISSA
(to herself)

Here, mommy. Here, is where it hurts so much.

Lights dim on Lissa's room and go
to a glaring bright on Lettie's room.
LISSA looks toward Lettie's room.
LETTIE is sitting in her hospital
room in a hospital gown with her
back to the audience. She has very
little hair on her head. A white robe
lies across the foot of her bed.

BLACKOUT

Music from the song "Skylark" plays.

END OF SCENE.

<u>Scene 3</u>

> Beck's room. Lights up on LISSA
> banging on Beck's door. She is wear-
> ing her white T-shirt, jeans, and red
> sweater. Her hair is pulled into a
> ponytail. BECK is standing on the
> other side of the door.

LISSA

Beck, please open the door. I know you're there. Beck, PLEASE. I need
to talk with you. Beck, PLEASE. I'm not going to leave.
   (pause)
Beck, if you don't talk to me, I'm going to have a breakdown. Is that
what you want? Is it?
   (pause)
Please, just open the door.

BECK

LEAVE. JUST LEAVE.

LISSA

BECK, PLEASE. PLEASE.
   (pause)
Last week you told me you think about me all the time. Can't get me
out of your mind.
   (pause)
Beck, PLEASE open the door.

BECK

LEAVE. JUST LEAVE.
   (pause)

I have to pick up my kids. I have to leave to pick up my kids. I can't be late. Do you understand that? You DO understand that? Do you not?
(pause)
JUST LEAVE.

LISSA

BECK, PLEASE. Just give me a minute—a minute. Open the door. See me. BECK, PLEASE. I'M A MESS. I'm wearing the same clothes I wear when I go to the cemetery to visit her. GRIEF CLOTHES.
(to herself)
Now, she's in that goddamn hole, dressed in that red suit. What exactly was she celebrating? Leaving this world?
(sadly)
Leaving me?
(She tugs at her red sweater.)
(pleading, to BECK)
Beck, you DANCED with me in the dead weight heat of August in your apartment. You *danced* with me. You made me feel so light. Even after all that's happened—happened between us.
You are *still* the only one who can do that. You are the only one who can make me *feel*—feel *not* dead.
(pause)
Beck, PLEASE open the door. PLEASE. See me.
(more desperately)
SEE ME.

BECK

I have to get my kids. My kids are waiting. Do you understand that? You DO understand that? Do you not?

LISSA

Beck, I'll do anything, just tell me what.
(pause)
Then I'll leave.

BECK

I want a letter.
(pause)
I want you to write a letter.

LISSA

A letter? I don't understand. A letter to whom? To whom should I write
a letter?

BECK

I want you to write a letter.
(pause)
A letter I can show to WHOMEVER I choose.

LISSA

A letter?
(pause)
A letter
(pause)
like a disclaimer?!
(pause)

BECK

Yes. A disclaimer.

LISSA
(astonished)
A disclaimer that you can carry around and show to anyone—anyone
who might have seen the poem? Heard—

BECK

A disclaimer I can show to ANYONE I CHOOSE TO SHOW IT TO.

LISSA

To whom?
(pause)
People at the university?
(to herself)
To Brigit Sundquist's Office of Complaints?

BECK

People at the university. Anyone who has seen *the poem.*
(pause)
SEEN-THE-BOOK. Anyone who has *heard the rumors.* And they *are* rumors, Lissa.

LISSA
(in disbelief)

Something you can pull out of your shirt pocket and show to anyone at a moment's notice?

BECK

Yes! Now leave! I have to get my kids.
(pause)
Call me tomorrow and we'll talk. Call me at twelve o'clock.

LISSA
(surprised)

We'll talk? We'll talk at twelve o'clock? You'll talk to me tomorrow at twelve o'clock?

BECK

Yes. Now *leave.* Talk to you tomorrow at twelve o'clock.

LISSA

Okay.
(pause)

Okay.
    (pause)
Good.
    (pause)
Talk to you tomorrow at twelve o'clock. I'll call you tomorrow at twelve o'clock.

                    LISSA leaves, almost buoyant.

                    BLACKOUT.

                    Music from the song "Skylark" plays.

                    END OF SCENE.

Scene 4

Lights up on Lissa's room. LISSA,
in the same clothes, goes over to the
wall and adds another tally mark.
She smiles at the marks. She sits
down in her chair. Her hair is loose.
The lights dim as she falls asleep.
Slowly the lights brighten on her;
she is awakening. MICHAEL enters
and puts a note on her lap.

MICHAEL
(exhausted, whispering)
Call me if you need me to come back. Here are the numbers where I'll
be this afternoon. Give me a call so I know how you're doing.

MICHAEL exits.

LISSA wakes up, reads the note, and
tosses it on the floor. She looks at her
watch.

LISSA
(to herself)
Eleven fifty.

LISSA jumps up from her chair and
tries to straighten her clothes. She
goes to the large mirror hung behind her dresser and stares at herself.
Then she adeptly climbs onto the

dresser. She picks up a hand mirror with her right hand and parts her hair with her left hand to expose her bald spot. She focuses the hand mirror on it so she can see its reflection in the larger mirror. She stares at it a moment, then puts down the hand mirror and with a comb tries to cover the spot by parting her hair a little more to the left. She looks at her watch again, slowly climbs off the dresser, and goes back to her chair. She places the phone in her lap. She picks up the receiver to check if the phone is working. The dial tone is heard throughout the theater. She gently places the receiver back into its cradle and looks at her watch. Her left hand goes to search out her bald spot, but she stops herself. She waits. She is calm. She sits erect, a slight smile crosses her face. She looks at her watch. She picks up the phone and carefully punches in Beck's number. Lights up on Beck's room. He is sitting in his chair waiting, his door is half open. His phone rings. Beck slowly picks it up.

LISSA

Beck. Hi! This is Lis—

BECK slams down the phone. LISSA sits in her chair, stunned. After

about ten seconds she again punches
in Beck's number. It rings and BECK
slowly picks it up.

                    LISSA
Beck.

BECK slams the phone down with
a crashing sound that is the loudest
of all his hangups. He kicks his door
shut. LISSA sits, immobile. She curls
into her chair, assuming the fetal position.

Lights out.

Pause.

Lights up on Lissa's room. She is adding another tally mark to the wall.
She then drops to the floor.

                    LISSA
                 (to audience)
The last time I saw him
        (pause)
before yesterday—you can't count talking to him with a shut door between us as SEEING HIM—was ten days ago. We walked along the
lake.

Lights up on Beck's room. BECK
slowly opens his door and comes out
of his room. He looks down at LIS-
SA on the floor.

> BECK

I'm having these fantasies. I want to do more.

> LISSA
> (to BECK)

More?

> BECK

Yes. *More.* What do you think of that?

> LISSA
> (to audience)

I listened. After all, we were calmly walking hand in hand along the
calm, still-warm early autumn water. We looked like any other couple
walking calmly together. No bash—bash of waves
　　(a small, bitter laugh)
or waves of bashes—yet.

> BECK
> (quietly)

I want you to get tattoos with my initials on your breasts. *And* I want
to watch.
　　(pause)
What do you think of that?

> LISSA
> (to BECK)

Interesting.
　　(LISSA looks at her left wrist, sadly.)
Go on.

> BECK
> (quietly)

Lissa, do you understand?

(pause)
Lissa, do you understand what I'm asking?

LISSA
(to audience)

His voice was so gentle and quiet—like in the beginning. Only what he was saying was so different.

(pause)

I first met him after he called me seven months ago—March. March 2, to be exact. He asked me to come to his office to discuss my poetry. There, he showed me a review he'd written about my last three books. How he praised them! He gave my work—and me—such focus, such attention. How I loved it. He was so interested in what I had to say. Let me talk about my writing, my feelings in such a seamless fashion. Never interrupting, never contradicting—in the beginning.

(taking a deep breath)

Everything he did in the beginning seemed so caring,

(sadly)

then so—

BECK
(interrupting, quietly)

Lissa, do you understand what I'm *asking*?

LISSA
(returning to the question, to BECK)

Yes.

Lights out on BECK.

LISSA
(to audience)

I thought I could handle it. I'd been handling everything else that had happened—though some would say not very well and I'd have to agree.

(pause)

And they don't even know what's really gone on.

(pause)

Anyway, I also thought

(half-smiling)

what great material. The next day I woke up repulsed, feeling I was going to vomit. Disgusted by both myself and him.

(pause)

The day after, I was once again intrigued. I wanted to *feel* something. I couldn't keep up with my emotions

(pause)

and I was lonesome.

(She tugs at her red sweater.)

(sadly)

She'd been gone less than two weeks.

> The phone rings. LISSA leaps up to get it.

LISSA

Hi! Hello!

> Lights up on edge of stage. MI-CHAEL is sitting there on his cell phone.

MICHAEL

Hi.

LISSA
(deflated)

Oh, Michael.

MICHAEL
(with an edge to his voice)
You were waiting for *another* call?
(pause)
Beck?

LISSA
Why do you say that? What makes you say that?

MICHAEL
(sighs)
Lissa, *just* because he was once *nice* to you doesn't mean—

LISSA
Stop. Please stop.

MICHAEL
If only you'd talk to me about what *exactly* happened.
(pause)
Talk to *anyone*.

LISSA
(irritated)
Michael, why did you call?

MICHAEL
I wanted to know how you were.
(pause)
How are you?

LISSA
I'm fine.
(pause)
I'm okay.

MICHAEL

Have you changed your clothes?

LISSA

No. I haven't changed my clothes. I don't care how I look. Stop asking me questions. PLEASE. I'm going to hang up.

> LISSA hangs up gently. MICHAEL rubs his face in frustration. Lights out on edge of stage. LISSA picks up the phone and bashes the receiver into its cradle. She does this eight times.

LISSA
(pleading, to the phone)
PLEASE. PLEASE RING. MAKE IT BE BECK.

> BLACKOUT.

> Music from the song "Skylark" plays.

> END OF SCENE.

Scene 5

Bright lights up on Lettie's room.
LETTIE is quite sick and is in her
hospital bed in her hospital gown.
She bashes the receiver of her telephone into its cradle, turns on a
small cassette player, and listens
to music from *The Afternoon of a
Faun*. It plays softly. LISSA walks
into the room with a vase filled with
daisies. She sets the flowers on Lettie's tray. LISSA is wearing her black
pantsuit. Her hair is pulled into a
ponytail. Lights up on the rooftop.
NIJINSKY, in ballet tights and the
gold cord faun wig, dances with the
nymph's veil as he sadly looks down
at LISSA and LETTIE. LETTIE
looks up at NIJINSKY. LISSA kisses LETTIE on the cheek. LETTIE
turns off the music. Lights out on
the rooftop.

LISSA
I heard that. Heard it all the way down the hall. Whom did you hang
up on?

LETTIE smiles.

LISSA
Why do you have such a huge smile on your face?

LETTIE

Leah. I hung up on Leah.

LISSA

Good.
(pause)
Finally.

LETTIE

She calls every day. Every day she calls to tell me what she's done—
where she's gone. And at *the end* of each conversation she asks how I
am. Asks what *I am doing.* Today I told her that if she hadn't already
noticed, I was busy. I was very busy.
(pause)
I was very busy
(pause)
dying.
(smiling)
Then I smashed the phone down.

LISSA
(smiling)

I know. I heard.

LETTIE
(still smiling)

I thought you might like that.
(no longer smiling)
Leah's the real survivor and she wants to prove that to me.
(pause)
Well, I guess she has her reasons.
(pause)
Can you imagine? She's still angry, still jealous. Still thinks *I'm* the

blessed one. *The Chosen One.*
(laughs bitterly)
Yes. The Chosen One.
(pause)
The more I've tried to make it up to her, the angrier she's become.
(pause)
It wasn't my fault she couldn't have children. It just wasn't.
(pause)
Was it Lissa? Was it? Maybe if we were both childless, she wouldn't
hate me so much.

LISSA
Mother, please, please don't start that again.
(pause)
I'm here. Aren't you glad *I'm here*?

> LETTIE stares at LISSA. LISSA
> takes Lettie's hand.

LETTIE
Yes. Yes, you *are* here.

> They stare at each other.

LISSA
Mother, would you like me to comb your hair?

> LETTIE nods yes. LISSA takes a
> small comb from the tray and very
> carefully combs Lettie's sparse hair.

LISSA
Does this feel good? Does it help?

LETTIE
(her eyes closed)

Yes. Yes.

(almost dreaming)

When you were a little girl you'd comb my hair. Remember? Once you even kissed the sores. I yelled at you to stop. I *am* sorry for that.

(pause)

Lissa, do you remember? Do you? You were the only one I'd let see the mess, the mess underneath—the mess I made on my head.

(pause)

How I hated picking at myself. I tried to control it. Doing the petit point helped—helped keep my hands busy, busy pulling those thin strands of thread through the almost invisible holes in the canvas.

(pause)

But no little girl should have to see . . .

(LETTIE starts to cry.)

no little girl—

> LISSA kisses the top of Lettie's head—the place where LISSA tears out her own hair.

LISSA

Mother, it's okay.

(pause)

Really, it's okay.

(pause)

Everything is okay.

> LISSA continues to comb Lettie's head. Lights focus on Lettie's globed head, then slowly fade to dark.

BLACKOUT

Music from *Prelude to The Afternoon of a Faun* plays.

END OF SCENE.

<u>Scene 6</u>

> Lights up on Lissa's room. LISSA is
> wearing her worn gray robe and up-
> dating her wall to five. Her hair is
> loose. She sits down on the floor and
> starts fussing with the phone cord, a
> suction cup, the cassette player, and
> the telephone. She places the suction
> cup on the phone's receiver. She is
> preparing to record the call she will
> make. She picks up the phone.

LISSA
(to audience, defensively)
I'm *not* calling Beck. I'm calling A—the novelist A.

> She clicks on the cassette player. She
> punches in a number. Ringing is
> heard. The phone is picked up on
> the third ring. Lights up on A sitting
> in the Restaurant answering his cell
> phone. He is wearing khaki pants,
> a white T-shirt and a tailored sport
> coat.

A
Hello?

LISSA
Hi.
(pause)
A. It's LISSA.

A

Hey, Lis. How are you? God, I'm tired. I just finished working out at
the gym. Just sitting here having a cappuccino.

(pause)

Lis, you should see my body. It's beautiful. Hard. *Really hard.*

LISSA

(giggling)

It's good you're working out. It's healthy.

A

Hey, Lis. I'll be back at the university this winter. Going to teach another course. They're paying me big money.

LISSA

That's great! What will you teach? Can I sit in?

A

Anything I want. I can write my own ticket. I think I'll do Tolstoy, or
maybe Hemingway—or Proust. Who knows? Someone large.

(pause)

Very large, someone very large and very brilliant.

LISSA

Like you.

A

Yes.

LISSA

Can I sit in?

A

Yep.
 (pause)
But that department. Who are those people?

LISSA

I only know one.
 (pause)
Know one well.

A

Who?

LISSA
(hesitating)

Beck.

A

Beck? Beck!
 (laughing)
He looks like an animal long dead. Road kill. Yep. Road kill.

LISSA
(laughing)

Road kill?!

A

Hey, Lis. Got to go. People waiting for me.

LISSA

Maybe we can have dinner when you come to town? When do you think—

A

Absolutely. Got to go. Bye.

> A snaps his phone shut. Lights out
> on restaurant. A dial tone is heard
> on Lissa's phone.

LISSA
(puzzled, she speaks to the dial tone)

Bye.

> LISSA hangs up the phone, clicks off
> the cassette player, gets up from floor.

LISSA
(somewhat hyper, to herself)

A is better than Beck. A could cancel out B. B doesn't equal A. A's much more impressive.
The secret to holding his interest will be to be somewhat distant and ambiguous about myself. About who I am.
(sadly)
Who am I?
(pause)
(confidently, to audience)
I will no longer be Anna about to throw herself under the train. I will be Odette—the mysterious Odette whom no man could resist.

> LISSA sits down in her chair. Lights
> dim.

LISSA
(deflated, to audience)

I hardly go anywhere. Mostly, I stay home waiting for the phone to ring and playing A's tape. Playing Beck's tapes.

(She reaches into a bag and pulls out Beck's tapes.)
"Beck on Pleasure," "Beck on His Wives,"
(pause)
"Beck on His Dog."

> LISSA holds this tape up and then
> places it in the cassette player and
> pushes "play."

BECK
(on tape)

I was *good* to her, Lissa. I *loved* her. I really *loved* her. *How could you
write that I didn't?*
It's bad enough that you've published the poem with some online literary rag, but I'M WARNING YOU NOW—DON'T-PUT-IT IN-
YOUR-BOOK. JUST DON'T.

> LISSA snaps off the cassette player.
> She bows her head, puts her face in
> her hands, then looks up.

LISSA

I like it when A talks about Beck—calls him road kill.
(pause)
He really did smell as bad as road kill
(pause)
sometimes.

> LISSA takes out the tape and places
> another tape in the cassette player.
> She pushes the "play" button.

LISSA

I've talked to you before about PLEASURE—about giving you PLEA-

SURE, about wanting you to give me PLEASURE and about wanting the times we're together to be PLEASURABLE and I do think it should have been possible to give each other much more PLEASURE than we've successfully done.

> LISSA snaps off the cassette player.

LISSA
(shaking her head, to herself)

Pleasure.

> Lights up on Beck's room. BECK comes out of his door and looks down at LISSA, who is still focused on the cassette player.

BECK

I can't stop thinking about you. How beautiful you are. Your face. Your hair.
(sighs)
Your breasts.
(pause)
How you became so wet.
(pause)
It's called *passion*, Lissa. It's called *sex*.

> BECK goes back into his room and slams his door shut.

LISSA
(startled, looking up at him)

BECK? BECK? BECK!!

BLACKOUT.

Music from the song "Skylark" plays.

END OF SCENE.

Scene 7

> Bright lights up on Lettie's room.
> LISSA is combing Lettie's few thin
> strands of hair. LISSA is wearing her
> black pantsuit. Her hair is in a pony-
> tail.

LETTIE

He's a real rascal, that one.

LISSA

Well, that's a generous way of putting it. But there's more to it than
that. Beck—

LETTIE

I had a few rascals in my day. Viktor—

LISSA

Mother, Viktor was a Na—

LETTIE
(interrupting)

Was a what?

LISSA

Never mind, mother. Never mind.

> LISSA looks up to Beck's darkened
> room.

BECK
(from his room)
It's called *passion*, Lissa. It's called *sex*.

LISSA quickly turns back to LET-
TIE.

LISSA
Mother, tell me the Morris story—tell me about Morris again.

LETTIE
Morris? Oh yes, Morris. When I was seventeen, I had this boyfriend
Morris.

LISSA
Yes. Morris.

LETTIE
Well, he adored me.
(pause)
At least he did until he saw my knees.

LISSA
Ah yes, your knees!

LETTIE
Yes, my knees. I was on stage doing Juliet's speech from her balcony,
but it was a rehearsal and I had just come from gym class and had on
these awful bloomers. Morris came to the rehearsal to surprise me.
Well, I guess he was the one who got the surprise.
(pause)
He saw my knees. When we were finished, I hurried off stage to greet
him. I'd done Juliet perfectly and was excited that he had seen me. All
he said was I DIDN'T REALIZE YOU HAD SUCH FAT KNEES.

(sighs)
He never came around again. I waited and waited. But he never did.
Now, THAT'S a rascal, wouldn't you say?

LISSA
(laughing a bit)

Yes, I'd say *that's* a rascal.
(pause)
What happened to him?

LETTIE

Who?
(pause)
Morris? Romeo?
(laughing a bit)
They're both dead.
(pause)
Yes. Morris,
(pause)
Romeo, both dead. Very dead.

LISSA

Beck calls every day to ask how you are. He stays on the phone and
listens and listens to the hard time you're having—how hard it's been—

Lights up on Beck's room.

BECK
(from his room, standing, looking down at them, lifting a weight with his
right arm)

How is she today, Lissa? Tell me. How is she? How are you? I want to
know. Tell me.

Lights out on Beck's room.

LETTIE

That's nice.

LISSA

Well, it's much more complicated—

LETTIE

Michael calls *me* everyday.
    (LETTIE pats Lissa's hand.)
You two should get back together. I can still picture the two of you as
you walked down the aisle. Such a handsome couple. Such a nice boy.

LISSA

Yes, a nice boy.

LETTIE

So what's wrong with a *nice* boy? There's no need to go looking for trouble. Trouble has a way of finding us, without our help. There's no reason to seek it out.
    (pause)
How long has it been, Lissa?

LISSA

Three and a half months, Mother.
    (sighs)
He needed a break. I guess I exhausted him with my extremes—the
extremes of my emotions and then there was the whole Beck issue.
    (pause)
He does visit.
    (pause)
Michael's a middle-ground man.
    (pause)
Feet firmly planted on the ground. Emotions steady and deeply rooted

in the ground.
(pause)
He's very grounded.

LETTIE

Stop it!

LISSA

What?

LETTIE

The words—the playing with words. This is *your* life!

LISSA

Mother, words *are* my life.

LETTIE
(tired)

He still cares about you, Lissa.

LETTIE turns from LISSA, lifts her
hands to feel her head.

LISSA
(sadly, to herself)

Yes, Mother. Maybe it's your daughter who can't care about someone who really cares about her. Your daughter who keeps holding out hope for a man who now won't stop insulting her body, her mind with what he calls acts of affection.

LETTIE
(her hands still touching her head)

Lissa, would you feel my head? It feels spongy to me. I think IT'S spreading. Spreading to my head.

> LISSA gently touches Lettie's scalp
> with both her hands. Her hands fill
> with dead hair follicles. She stares at
> what's in her hands.

LETTIE

Yes, I know. No more hair will ever grow there.
(pause)
They feel like grains of sand, don't they? You can roll them around on
the tips of your fingers.
(pause)
Lissa, remember when you were a little girl and we'd go to the shore for
the summer? How you loved to run into the lake and then roll around
in the sand. Cover your body as if it were in a crust. Then you'd jump
up as if you were about to take to the air—burst forth like a butterfly.

> LISSA gently hugs Lettie's head and
> kisses the top of it.

LISSA

Yes, like a butterfly about to break free of its shell.

> Lights out on Lettie's room. Lights
> up on the rooftop. NIJINSKY, wear-
> ing his gold cord faun wig, dances to
> music from *The Afternoon of a Faun*.
> Lights up in Lettie's room. She's
> alone, watching NIJINSKY dance.
> NIJINSKY pauses and looks down
> at LETTIE.

BLACKOUT.

END OF SCENE.

Scene 8

> Lights up on Lissa's room. She is adding five more tally marks to the wall. Then she sits in her chair. She is in her worn gray robe. Her hair is loose.

LISSA
(to audience)
Someone slams the phone down on you and what they're really doing is slamming you out of their life.
(LISSA looks up at Beck's room)
Forever.
(pause)
She never spoke to her sister again. Had a few weeks free of her before she left. We'd let the phone ring and ring and when we couldn't stand it anymore, we'd turn the ringer off.
(sighs)
How Leah hates the sight of me.
(pause)
She doesn't feel that way about my father—he just shuts her up with money.
(pause)
Here Leah, have a check.

> LISSA gets up from her chair and gets into her bed. She curls into the fetal position on her left side and with her right hand goes straight for the bald spot on her head. She is hypnotizing herself by touching the spot.

The lights dim.

Pause.

Lissa's phone rings six times before she jumps out of the bed to answer it. When she picks it up all that is heard is a click and then a dial tone. She doesn't put the phone down and yells into the receiver over the sound of the dial tone.

LISSA

Hello? Hello?! Beck? Beck?! Is it you? Beck?
(pause)
A? A?
(pause)
Michael? Michael, are you there?

Lights up on edge of stage. MICHAEL, looking frustrated, is sitting there with his cell phone turned off. Lights out on edge of stage.

OPERATOR
(recording on LISSA'S phone)

If you'd like to make a call, please hang up and try again. If you need help, hang up and then dial your operator.

Three beeps are heard and then the recording plays again.

OPERATOR

If you'd like to make a call, please hang up and try again. If you need help, hang up and then dial your operator.

LISSA hangs up.

LISSA
(mimicking the OPERATOR)
If you need help, if you need help—I need help. I need help.
(pause)
MOTHER, I NEED HELP.
(pause)
Mother, you're so lucky you're out of all of this. You're safe.
(pause)
At least I hope you're safe.

> Lights out. Lights up. LISSA, still
> in her robe, is updating her wall to
> fifteen marks. She then climbs onto
> her dresser, stares at her face in the
> mirror and traces her mouth with
> her right hand which she holds like a
> paw. Her back is arched like a fright-
> ened cat and is toward the audience.
> The audience sees her face as reflect-
> ed in the mirror.

LISSA
(to mirror)
He rarely made me laugh. Could never laugh at himself. He had a terrible fear of gossip—gossip about him.
(pause)
People said he only married his third wife because he believed she'd be
"a good breeder."
(pause)
Yes, a good breeder.

Lights up on Beck's room.

BECK slowly opens his door and steps out.

BECK

GOSSIP. MORE GOSSIP.
(pause)
HAVE I NOT BEEN YOUR FRIEND? HAVE I NOT BEEN A GOOD FRIEND TO YOU?

LISSA looks up at BECK, then turns toward mirror.

LISSA
(to mirror)
The captive is intensely grateful for small kindnesses shown to her by the captor. The captive denies the captor's violence against her when the violence or threats of violence are actually occurring. The captive denies her own anger at the captor, to others
(pause)
and to herself.
(to audience)
Some call this result of imprisonment Stockholm Syndrome. I call it The Avigdor Element Effect. Beck learned such behavior from his mentor at the university and his mentor learned it directly from the then most celebrated living author in this country, the cad Avigdor Element.
(sighing, to BECK)
Yes. Yes, Beck. You've been a good friend to me.

BECK

Right. That's right.
(pause)
Lissa, I really don't want to *quarrel* with you.

LISSA
(to audience)
It was the *quarrel* word that would stop me dead.
(pause)
The more of an emotional mess I'd become, the more he'd elevate his language, and when I was finally able to compose myself and become somewhat coherent—

BECK
I can't *address* this right now.

LISSA
It was the *address* word that was so off-putting.
(pause)
So high-minded. If I tried to continue, tried to make a rational point—

BECK
YOU ARE FILLED WITH REPROACH. YOUR STATEMENTS ARE PURE REPROACH.
(pause)
I can't *address* this right now.
(pause)
LISSA, I really don't want to *quarrel* with you.

LISSA
Can we talk about it another time?

BECK
Yes. But I've got to go. I've got a lecture to give. My students are waiting. Do you understand that? You DO understand that? Do you not?

LISSA turns toward the mirror.

LISSA
(to mirror)
The captive is hypervigilant to the captor's needs and seeks to keep the captor happy. The captive finds it psychologically difficult to leave the captor, even after her physical release has been won.
(to BECK)
Yes. Yes, Beck. I understand.

BECK

Good!

BECK re-enters his room and slams his door. Lights out in Beck's room and Lissa's room.

Lights up on edge of stage. MICHAEL is still sitting there.

MICHAEL
(to audience)
Sometimes, I go over there when she can't sleep and just lie next to her, reading to her from the biographies of the Russian poets—Akhmatova, Mandelstam, Tsvetaeva, Pasternak—and as she's about to fall asleep she'll often sigh and quietly say, "How could they stand such oppression and still be so brilliant, Michael? Do you think they were made more so because their words were the only things they had to hold on to—like others do their jewels?"
(pause)
I like it when she says my name.
(pause)
I know she believes she wouldn't be able to deal with what they had to endure—the censorship, their unending exiles. That she wouldn't have their courage to rebel against such subjugation with only the power of words.

(pause)

I can't decide. I've seen Lissa jump over many hurdles. Seen her hold her own, but then again, I've seen her tumble down into a pit, filled with demons.

(He looks over to Beck's room.)

(sighs)

She'll say, "Mandelstam jumped out of a window in exile and survived. But Tsvetaeva hanged herself." Then, she'll repeat it in a tone that teeters between sadness and envy. She doesn't seem interested in what the American poets did to themselves—Plath, Sexton, Berryman, Lowell. It's a large outward force, an outward tyranny—history's dictators trying to suffocate words—that absorbs her attention.

(pause)

And yes, to some extent, I do understand why.

BLACKOUT.

Music from the song "Skylark" plays.

END OF SCENE.

Scene 9

> Lights up on Lissa's room. LISSA is
> updating her wall to twenty marks.
> She is in her gray robe. Her hair is
> loose and very snarled. Her phone
> rings. She picks it up quickly.

LISSA
(frantically)

Hello? Hello? Who is this?

> Lights up on restaurant.

A
(on his cell phone, from restaurant)

Hey, Lis. It's A!

LISSA
(nervously)

Oh. Oh, A. Hi!

A

What's wrong? Were you sleeping?

LISSA

No. Well, yes. But I was about to get up. Go out.
     (trying to gain some composure)
A! How are you? I'm so glad to hear your voice. What's up?

A

Well, Lis. I need to rent a place for the winter semester. Something fantastic. A loft. Yes, a loft. A place where I can throw great parties.

LISSA

Will you invite me?
(more urgently)
Can I come?

A fingers the petals of the flowers in
the vase on the table.

A

Absolutely. But, you can't wear pants.

LISSA

What?!

A

No underwear. I won't wear any either. When we see each other, both
our asses will be bare.

LISSA
(ignoring what A just said)
Do you want me to find you a real estate agent? I know a few.

A

That'd be great.

LISSA

Can I give them your number?

A

Absolutely.
(pause)
Are any single?

LISSA

Single? A, I thought you were married.

A

We've decided to separate. We're still friends. She's the best and still crazy for me. It's just that—well, you know—hell, we've been married for *twelve* years. Anyway, I really don't care if they're single, married, divorced, widowed. Women—god—they're all over the place. All over me. Especially ones in their early thirties.
(pause)
Lis, I do a hundred sit-ups every morning. A hundred. My abs are so hard.
(laughs)

LISSA

I'll see what I can do.

A

Thanks, Lis. A loft would be great. Money's no problem. Something with a view. Maybe overlooking the river. Bye.

LISSA

Bye.

Two clicks of phones are heard. Lights out on restaurant.

LISSA
(to audience)

He's fifty-nine. Still beautiful, BUT, FIFTY-NINE.
(pause)
He talks so damn much about his body.
(pause)
Was I supposed to ask to see it? Was that my introductory chance? Was

that my only chance?

(pause)

Then, I've messed up.

(pause)

And, that "no pants" thing. What was that about? Was that supposed
to arouse me? Well, it didn't.

(pause)

Beck's forty-eight.

(pause)

And now he's talking to me about getting tattoos

(pause)

on my breasts.

> Lights up on Beck's room. BECK
> stands in his room.

BECK

HOW DO YOU FEEL ABOUT THAT?

LISSA

I think—

BECK
(interrupting LISSA)

AND, I WANT TO WATCH.

LISSA

Yes, you've told me that.

> Lights out in Beck's room.

LISSA
(to audience)

Can you see his semi-saggy, still handsome face sweating with excitement? I can.

(sadly)
Whatever beauty he saw in me, eventually he seemed to need to contain,
    (pause)
mark,
    (pause)
wound,
    (pause)
ruin.
Tattooed.
    (She looks at her left wrist, sighs.)
The area could become infected, take months for it to calm down.
    (pause)
Forever marked.

> Pause.

> LISSA takes her marker for her wall and marks her left wrist, looks at it, kisses it, then touches her bald spot with her right hand.

LISSA

Rubbing it erases thought.

> She bows her head to show the audience. Lights brighten and focus on the spot.

LISSA

Sometimes, I go outside and spread my hair to the sun and it feels like its light is shining right into my soul.

> She raises her head. Lights soften. She sits down on her bed and smooths the sheets.

LISSA

Waking up can last hours. I barely move. I feel both myself and the world are of no worth and that I am, in fact, a stillbirth.

(pause)

A stillbirth.

(slight laugh)

Leah would have liked that.

BLACKOUT.

Music from the song "Skylark" plays, sounding scratchy, as if the needle is stuck.

END OF SCENE.

Scene 10

> Bright lights on Lettie's room. LET-
> TIE is sleeping. The cassette player
> is playing music from *The Afternoon
> of a Faun*. Lights up on the rooftop.
> NIJINSKY is dancing to the music,
> wearing his gold cord faun wig. LIS-
> SA enters, wearing her black pant-
> suit. Her hair is in a ponytail.

LISSA
(looking at LETTIE)

She's pruned to almost bonsai dimensions—no excess, just the shape
of pure grace.
(sadly)
The doctors say she has between two weeks and a couple of months left.
Then, they say *not* to hold them to this.
(a bit sarcastically)
Just like most people, they don't want to be *pinned* down. Pinned down
to their words.
(pause)
Unlike a poet.

LETTIE
(awakening)

Ben?

> LETTIE turns the music off. Lights
> out on the rooftop.

LISSA

No, not father. It's me, Lissa.

LETTIE

Of course. Of course.

LISSA

Mother, aren't you glad to see me?

LETTIE stares at LISSA.

LETTIE
(looking at the rooftop)

I was having a dream.
(to LISSA)
There was music and dancing and Nijinsky was there.

LISSA
(sighs)

Ah, yes, Nijinsky.

LETTIE

Yes, sometimes when I hear music play, if I look up, I can see him—see
him dancing. *Even* when I'm not asleep.
(pause)
Lissa, do you ever see him?

LISSA
(laughing)

No Mother, I have yet to see Nijinsky.

LETTIE
(serious)

I never told you, because I *thought* you'd laugh.
(pause)
Well, if you ever *do*, Lissa, *it will be a gift.*

LISSA
(more curious, more serious)
So Nijinsky just shows up?

LETTIE
(quietly)
Yes.
(pause)
He appears when I'm the most frightened.
(sadly)
He has since I was twelve.
(pause)
Anyway, in the dream, suddenly, I needed eyeshadow. Can you imagine, *eyeshadow*?

LISSA
When you're better, we'll get you some. We'll have lunch and then we'll shop. We'll shop for eyeshadow.

LETTIE
(humoring LISSA)
And new clothes? I'm probably a size two by now. Well, I always wanted to be a size two.

LISSA
(to herself)
Beckett had a nervous breakdown after his mother's death. So did Marianne Moore.

LETTIE
Lissa, I don't think I'll be able to finish the pillows, my eyes—

LISSA

Mother, you have to, and while you're doing that, I'll write more books so there will be more titles that you can petit point onto pillows.

> LETTIE reaches down near the foot of the bed and hands LISSA an unfinished canvas of petit point, with a threaded needle still stuck in the canvas.

LISSA

No, Mother. No.

LETTIE

Please. Take it. My eyes are so tired. So tired.

> LISSA reluctantly takes it and puts in her purse.

LISSA

I'll bring it back when you're stronger.
(pause)
I even have a new series—I call them "The Petit Point Poems."

LETTIE

In the new book?

LISSA

No. But the "Dog Poem" is. I asked my publisher if they could add it at the last minute. It fits so well with the rest of the manuscript—no one could ever guess from the poem she was *his* dog.
(pause)
Then it was published by an online journal and he saw it.
(sighs)
He must be tracking me on the Internet.

LETTIE
(confused, tired)

What?

LISSA hits Lettie's tray with her fist.
LETTIE flinches and turns slightly
away from LISSA.

LISSA

He says if he sees the poem in my book, he'll ruin me. I don't know what's
going to happen if I don't comply, comply with his every demand. And,
the most horrible part is that I can't seem to stay away from him.
(pause)
It feels almost okay for him to interfere with *me*, intrude on *me*, *but my
writing is—*

LETTIE
(turning toward LISSA, patting Lissa's hand)

Lissa, you should have been a dancer, not a poet. I should have made
you practice more. Mama always wanted her children to be dancers.
Leah was to be named Pavlova—
(laughing)
and I—well I—was to be Isadora—yes, Isadora, the free one, the
free-spirited one. Though no one really thought of Isadora as a *great*
talent.
(to audience, sadly)
It was our little brother, Jascha, who had *all* the promise of becoming
a great dancer.

LISSA

Mother, I was telling you—

LETTIE
(absorbed in her own story)
Papa wouldn't stand for it—calling his daughters Pavlova and Isadora.
(pause)
But when Mama saw Nijinsky dance, she knew she *had* to have children who would be dancers.
(pause)
Yes, Lissa—*my* Mama saw the great Nijinsky dance.

LISSA
(to audience)
Diaghilev forced Nijinsky into sex acts with him and when Nijinsky finally pulled away and married, he threw him out of the Ballet Russes.
(to LETTIE)
I know, Mother. Your mother saw the great Nijinsky dance.
(pause)
He treated movement as a poet does the word. No extra—

LETTIE
(ignoring LISSA)
Her mama took her to Paris when she was twelve. Imagine that! Mama saw Nijinsky dance in Paris in 1912 when she was twelve.

LISSA
(patting Lettie's hand)
Yes, Mother.
(pause)
Remember, I read you my poem. Do you? My poem Nijinsky's—

LETTIE
The poem?

LISSA
The "Dog Poem." The poem *"Nijinsky's Dog."*

LETTIE

What about *his dog*?
(pause)
Nijinsky *had* a dog?

LISSA
(frustrated)

No, Mother. She was really *Beck's* dog. But I thought of her more as
Nijinsky's dog. She was so sad. So scared. So aware. So—

LETTIE

Oh yes, Beck's dog. The one you thought you looked like. Really now,
Lissa! Really!

LISSA
(sadly, to herself)

All that soul-broken grace.

LETTIE
(taking Lissa's hand)

Lissa, sometimes I really worry about you.
(pause)
You need to see the *real* Nijinsky
(a little laugh)
not some poor sad dog.
(patting Lissa's hand)
That—yes, *that*—will be my gift to you.
(pause)
I will leave you the *real* Nijinsky.

LISSA
(a little laugh)

Mother, sometimes I really worry about you.

LETTIE
(again, absorbed in her story)
The Afternoon of a Faun. No one had seen anything like it. Nijinsky as the faun. On that stage, they say he truly became half-animal, half-human.
(to audience)
I've looked at *all* the books with the pictures of him dancing. I've listened to *all* the music.
When I see him dancing, it does make me forget, at least for a bit, the world's ugliness. The awful things people do to each other.
(to LISSA)
You know Lissa, he went mad. Such a shame.

LISSA
(sadly)
The last dance—*his* last dance, "World War I"—he choreographed it so as to try to capture all the cruelties of war.
(pause)
Then, he had an irreparable break—

LETTIE
(interrupting with a bitter laugh)
Art choreograph a war, *capture* a war—a *real* war with *all its cruelties*?!
(softly)
You'd think all that talent could have saved him.

LISSA
Dr. Sam Guttmacher might agree.

LETTIE
Who?

LISSA

Dr. Sam Guttmacher. The chief psychiatrist at the university believes
talent can *possibly* save you. But I'm not so sure.
(laughs a bit)
Talent can be to the artist what alcohol is to the alcoholic. What sex is
to the nymphomaniac.

LETTIE

Lissa, such talk!
(waving her hand)
So dramatic. Too dramatic.

LISSA

No, Mother, I mean it. While you're in the talent—*in it*, hypnotized by
it—you're saved, but as soon as you awake from it, you return as naked,
as exposed as ever, to everyday truths. Maybe more so—the heat of the
high-pitched fever over, and what's left is just the fall to the cold, real
world
(sighs)
with the possibility of landing among some of the terrible people who
inhabit it.
(more thoughtfully)
But if art can't always save the artist, maybe it can save someone else.
Someone who is terribly upset, but upon hearing the music, reading
the poem or
(moving closer to LETTIE)
seeing the dancer—

LETTIE
(mesmerized by what she remembers)
Mama said the difference between his flesh and costume was indecipherable. He wore coffee-colored tights with brown spots; they were
painted on his arms and hands, too.
(She raises her hands to her head.)

A tight gold cord wig with two small flat curled horns cupped his head.
  (pause)
Mama talked and talked about it always.

  (pause)
Leah and Jascha and I took lessons every day
  (pause)
until the train—

> LISSA takes a book out of her book
> bag. She opens it to a place she has
> flagged.

                          LISSA
            (interrupting, trying to distract LETTIE)
Speaking of talent, Mother, listen to this—
"Divinity must live within herself:
Passions of rain, or moods in falling snow; . . .
All pleasures and all pains, remembering
The bough of summer and the winter branch
These are the measures destined for her soul."
What do you think? Wallace Stevens.

                          LETTIE
                        (smiling)

Nice. Very nice.

                          LISSA

See mother, poetry—

                          LETTIE

I can't decide if I want to come back as a tree or a bird—maybe a skylark. That's as close to being a dancer—a dancer in the afterlife—as you
can get.
  (laughing a bit)

A skylark. Yes. What music it makes as it spirals higher and higher into
the sky, farther and farther away from the ground—this earth.
(angrily)
This dirt!
(pause)

Tell me, Lissa. HOW MANY TIMES IN A LIFE DOES ONE PER-
SON HAVE TO BECOME SO BALD IN THIS WORLD?
(softer)
Tell me? How many?

> LISSA bows her head.

LETTIE
(to audience)

They shaved our heads, they said, "to prevent lice."
(sarcastically)
They said it was good for us. *Everything* they did, they said was *good
for us.*
(pause)
They shaved *all* our hair off our bodies.
(pause)
I looked almost brand new. The truly old people looked like withered
children.
(LETTIE looks at her own body.)
Yes, like a withered child.

> LETTIE turns away from LISSA
> and falls back to sleep.

LISSA
(to audience)

The cancer was busy eating her body, but it never reached her brain.
The sicker she got the more and more she talked about Nijinsky, about

how she wished she could have become the dancer her mother had hoped for her.
(pause)
How she'd performed Juliet at the Goodman Theatre.

> LETTIE awakens.

LETTIE
(sarcastically)
The hemline *way* below my knees.

LISSA
Mother, you're tired. I'll see you tomorrow.

LETTIE
(weakly)
Yes, tired. Really tired.
(pause)
Exhausted.

> LISSA kisses the top of Lettie's head.
> LETTIE raises her left arm and gracefully waves goodbye to LISSA.
> LISSA leaves the room but quickly returns. The stage dims.

LISSA
Mother. Tomorrow. I *will* see you.

> LETTIE again gives LISSA the same delicate wave. The stage goes dark.

LISSA
(offstage)
The wave. *That* wave. *Her* wave had the same arc and flutter and grace
as a bird's wing. The same arc, flutter, and grace.

> The lights brighten in Lettie's room.
> NIJINSKY, wearing his gold cord
> faun wig and carrying the nymph's
> veil, enters Lettie's room, lifts LET-
> TIE out of her bed, into his arms,
> wraps the veil around her, and
> dances to the music—no lyrics—of
> "Skylark." LETTIE awakens and em-
> braces him as if he were a lost love.
> He then carries her offstage.
>
> Lights out.
>
> Lights up.
>
> Lissa's room. LISSA is in her chair
> in the same clothes she wore to the
> hospital. The wall is out of sight be-
> cause it is covered by a blank white
> sheet and this is taking place in the
> past. Her hair is loose. She has fall-
> en asleep, pen in hand and a pad of
> yellow paper in her lap. She wakes
> up suddenly. Startled, she presses the
> "play" button of her answering ma-
> chine on the nightstand. Her mes-
> sages begin.

BECK
(recorded)
Lissa, it's Beck. How are you? How's your mother? I want to know.
Give me a call. Maybe we can get together tonight. LATE. It has to be
late. I have my kids tonight. You could come over after they're asleep.
(pause)
I know the book is due out in a couple of weeks. I've checked.
(pause)
I am assuming you *did not* put the poem in the book. I am assuming
right—*am I not*?

One beep.

BEN
(recorded)
LISSA, IT'S YOUR FATHER. IT'S ALL OVER. LISSA, ARE YOU
THERE? I SAID, IT'S ALL OVER.

Beep.

Stunned, LISSA rewinds her father's
message and plays it again and then
again.

BEN
(recorded)
LISSA, IT'S YOUR FATHER. IT'S ALL OVER. LISSA, ARE YOU
THERE? I SAID, IT'S ALL OVER.
(rewind)
LISSA, IT'S YOUR FATHER. IT'S ALL OVER. LISSA, ARE YOU
THERE? I SAID, IT'S ALL OVER.

LISSA turns off her answering machine. The phone starts ringing, then

stops. Then the ringing starts again and goes on for twenty seconds. She takes the phone off the hook, puts the receiver on the arm of her chair, and curls into her chair.

The lights dim.

LISSA goes to her nightstand drawer and gets Lettie's unfinished petit point canvas from it. She sits down in her chair and starts pushing the attached needle and thread into the holes in the canvas in an imprecise, agitated way.

LISSA
(to herself, in a broken voice)
When the days and nights were of equal length
and the autumn equinox warned
the birds to migrate toward the equator
to escape the falling temperatures,
we watched—landlocked—
the leaves in their last dance
of color. How flushed and fevered
they were in their final daze—
a petit point of terror, their panic
sewn into the strict canvas
of nature, the extreme stage
in the fear sequence before us.
The plummet toward Earth's crust
where all becomes organic litter—
the dream over—was days away.
Reel and keel. Past topsoil

and humus, the interlock
with silt and sand and fragments
called parent material,
came so fast, the zero
down to unweathered bedrock—
a place where you are now woven
into an indecipherable, invisible pattern.

> LISSA sits down on the floor and
> bangs her head against the parti-
> tion between her room and Lettie's.
> NIJINSKY enters Lissa's room, sits
> down next to her. He starts bang-
> ing his head against the partition in
> unison with LISSA. LISSA, startled,
> stops and stares at him. NIJINSKY
> stops and looks at her. NIJINSKY
> takes her hand and kisses it.
>
> BLACKOUT.
>
> END OF SCENE.

INTERMISSION

Act II

Scene 1

> Lights up on Lissa's room. The wall
> has thirty-two tally marks on it.
> LISSA is dressed in freshly pressed
> black slacks, a black silk T-shirt, and
> a black lightweight leather jacket.
> Her hair is combed. She is standing.
> Her hair is neatly clipped with two
> barrettes.

LISSA
(to audience)
Saw "La Boheme" with Michael—it seemed tame. Even when Mimi
dies, I wasn't that moved. Too much that happens, happens offstage.
It's hard to care these days unless everything unfolds before me—all
passion, high-pitched, and slapped in my face.
(pause)
And it's hard to call Brigit Sundquist's office to file a complaint against
Beck when all I really want is for him to call. I pick up the phone a lot
to call her, but always stop before the last digit.
(LISSA sits down in her chair.)
I'm doing research for a long poem. Purses—womblike, vaginal, sexual
containers we women carry around with all our little junk inside. Stuff
to make ourselves look better. Make ourselves look good enough for a
Beck to come on to us. Come BECK to us.
(laughs slightly)
For an A. For an A and a B. A plus B equals C.
(smiling)
You figure out the empty "C" container word.

> LISSA goes over to the wall and adds
> the thirty-third mark to it.

LISSA
(half-smiling, looks at the wall)
Thirty-three. Christ was crucified when he was thirty-three.

She picks up the phone and punches in a number. Lights up on Beck's
room. He is in his chair reading. His phone rings. He picks it up.

BECK
HELLO?

LISSA
Hello.

BECK
Hello.

LISSA
Will-you-talk-to-me?

BECK
No.

LISSA
Will you talk to me sometime?

BECK
I don't foresee it now.

> Pause.

                          LISSA
                         (weakly)
Okay goodbye.

                          BECK
Bye.

They both hang up. The two clicks of the receivers are heard. BECK
gets up from his chair, opens his door, and looks down at LISSA. Then,
he quietly shuts the door. Lights out on Beck's room.

                          LISSA
                    (excited, to audience)
He talked to me! He didn't hang up. He actually seemed glad to hear
my voice. Didn't he?
      (pause)
He doesn't "FORESEE" it now.

                              LISSA grabs for both her dictionary
                              and thesaurus, which are on the floor.
                              She sits down on the floor. With
                              both books in her lap, she opens the
                              dictionary.

                          LISSA
FORESEE: to see as a development beforehand. Apprehend. Antici-
pate. Foreknow.
      (pause)
Good. Good. THAT'S NOT SO BAD.
      (She opens the thesaurus.)
FORESEE: Foretell. Predict. Expect. Envision. Envisage.
      (pause)
I don't like Expect, Envision, Envisage. Just don't. But, FOREKNOW,
ANTICIPATE, PREDICT—there's an opening here. Better than
thirty-three days ago.

(pause)
Yes, it's progress.

> LISSA gets up and climbs onto her
> dresser. Almost dazed, she speaks to
> the mirror.

LISSA

Small kindnesses by the abuser create hope. The captive is intensely grateful.

> LISSA picks up the hand mirror on
> the dresser. She unclips her barrettes
> and exposes the bald spot. She uses
> the two mirrors so she can see it.

LISSA

I have to stop picking at it. It can't become more visible. It just isn't attractive.
(She puts down the hand mirror.)
(to audience)
There's nothing appealing about a woman with a bald spot atop her head. On a monk, okay, but not on a woman who wants to be wanted.
(pause)
"I don't foresee it now." It's the crack in the once solidly slammed shut door. It's the crack in the vault that her coffin is locked inside of—it's the crack in the coffin that can give her some air.
(looking down)
Oh, mother, how do you exist down there? Don't you need some *air*?

> Lissa's phone rings. She jumps off the
> dresser and speaks to the theater as
> if she's searching the entire space for
> someone.

LISSA

HELLO? HELLO?

>She then remembers to pick up the
>phone. Lights up on restaurant. A is
>on his cell phone in the restaurant.

A

Hey, Lis.

LISSA

A? Oh, A! How are you?

A

Great. I'm just great. Hey Lis, did you get me a realtor's name? I'll be in
town on the nineteenth.

LISSA

Yes. Yes. I did.
   (pause)
Can we have coffee?
   (pause)
Or maybe dinner?

A

When?

LISSA

When you're in town.

A

Well, sure, maybe. What's her name?

> A fingers the petals of the flowers in
> the vase on the table, then breaks the
> stem of one and puts it in the upper
> pocket of his sport coat so that just
> the head of the flower shows.

                    LISSA
Who?

                     A
Lis. *The realtor*? Her name. What's her name?

                    LISSA
Alison Abeles. Alison Abeles, 773-668-3357.

                     A
          (writing the name and number down)
773-668-3357. Ali Abeles. Okay. I'll give old Ali a call. Hey, she does
know lofts, doesn't she, Lis?
    (laughing)
She *is* "Able?"
    (pause)
Hey, Lis, is she avail-able?
    (laughing more at his cleverness)

                    LISSA
                    (sighs)
Yes. Yes A. She knows lofts.
    (pause)
And no, she's married, but—

                     A
                   (laughs)
No problem. Thanks, Lis. See you.

A turns off his cell phone.

Lights out on restaurant.

LISSA looks at the receiver of her
phone, hangs it up.

LISSA
(to herself)

"See you?" "See you?"
(pause)
SEE ME.
But, she's not pretty enough, you'll be disappointed—
(to audience)
that's what I wanted to tell him.
(pause)
It's just a stub of a possibility he'll *see me*, even if he is disappointed
with Alison. There's nothing really there to hold on to—like those
miniscule hairs pushing through the center of my scalp.
(pause)
I KNOW he's an egomaniac, but he's less cruel than Beck.
(pause)
A's a different kind of poison. It's just for now, that I'm labeling him
"The Beck Cure."
(pause)
"Sorry, I'd really like to see you, but I'm *tired*. That's what he'll say.
That's what he *did* say last year. We *had* a plan. I had come down to his
class, dressed really nice. He arrived in worn jeans and a T-shirt and I
knew at that moment there'd be no dinner.

A
(offstage)
Really *tired*. Just flew in from Paris to teach this class. Had to come

back, the university is paying me big bucks for just this two-hour class
once a week. PRETTY GOOD. Huh, Lis?

> LISSA
> (to audience)

I then called Michael and asked him if he'd like to meet me for dinner.
He said yes. When he arrived he looked especially dressed up as if he
knew A would cancel.

> LISSA sits down in her chair.

> MICHAEL enters Lissa's room. His
> clothes are somewhat rumpled. He
> sits on the edge of Lissa's bed and
> rubs his face with his hands.

> LISSA
> (to MICHAEL)

In two days it will be six weeks since she died.
> (pause)

Is it too late for a complete breakdown? Or does it come slowly—pieces broken off that huge terrain the mind inhabits until eventually all
thought, all intellect, all emotion, becomes chipped, cracked, frag-
mented, and scattered?
> (LISSA parts her hair.)

It is better than when it slipped into an ice-white baldness, slick and
moist, from my constant touch. Isn't it?

> MICHAEL stands up and looks at
> the spot.

> MICHAEL

Yes.

LISSA

How many?

MICHAEL counts the hairs.

MICHAEL

Nine.

LISSA

Just nine?

MICHAEL
(looks again, sighs)
Yes, nine. With about four about to break through.

LISSA

Well, that's better. There's hope. Isn't there?

MICHAEL
(despairingly)

Hope?

MICHAEL picks up the comb from
the dresser and combs her hair.

LISSA
(to audience)
From the box where we were sitting at the opera, what fascinated me
most were the tops of the women's heads. Their crowns. So many of
them had too—wide parts—their scalps showed through. Some had
quite obviously tried to cover over where their hair had naturally begun to thin—or had they been picking at *their* heads in *their* rooms
in *their* chairs? The men's bald spots didn't bother me as much, but I

thought a lot about how much of the audience was slowly beginning to disappear, starting with their hair.

(to MICHAEL)

My mother's head had become so granulated at the end. I could roll her hardened dead hair follicles around on my fingertips.

> MICHAEL sighs, then kisses the bald spot.

LISSA

Your cool lips feel so good against its hot irritation.

> MICHAEL puts down the comb, pauses, stares at LISSA, and exits. LISSA watches him leave.

LISSA
(to audience)

What he did felt almost sacred.

> The lights brighten. LISSA climbs onto her dresser. She picks up her hand mirror and twists to look at her lower back. She then turns around.

LISSA

Every time a spot darkens on my body, I blame Beck. Beck has this thick strip of warts above his butt. They looked like something I could, or for that matter, anyone could catch. After I saw them, my lower back itched for months. Sometimes, it still does.

(pause)

I'd ask Michael if he saw any warts on me. He'd say no.

> She twists around to see if she has missed an area.

> MICHAEL
> (offstage, totally fed up)

Good God, Lissa! Enough!

(slyly)

I don't mean to get *this* stuck in your mind, but *he* is the spitting image of John Wayne Gacy.

> LISSA

Take it *back*!

> MICHAEL
> (offstage)

Okay. Okay. I take it back, he's the spitting image of John Wayne Gacy.

> LISSA
> (to audience)

Unfortunately, I can almost see it—the bulky head. The goat-white hair. Though in BECK'S defense he does have beautiful eyes that he would focus so directly into mine.

(pause)

He's very practiced with the look of kindness.

> Lights up on Beck's room. BECK
> gets up from his chair, slowly opens
> his door, and walks through it.

> BECK

THEY'RE MOLES. I'VE ALWAYS HAD THEM. I AM NOT DIS-EASED. WHY DO YOU OVERSTATE EVERYTHING? THAT'S WHAT GOT YOU IN TROUBLE IN THE FIRST PLACE.

(pause)

LISSA, DOES THE WORLD REALLY NEED ANOTHER CRAZY LADY?

> LISSA, shocked to hear Beck's voice,
> turns and looks up at him from her
> dresser.

                         LISSA
BECK?!

                         BECK
JUST ANSWER THE QUESTION.

                         LISSA
Yes. Yes.
   (pause)
A Blanche.
   (to audience)
Romanticism and sadomasochism—its conjoined twin—battled within her.

                         BECK
A Blanche?
   (pause)
A what?!

> LISSA turns away from BECK and
> toward the mirror.

                         LISSA
A Blanche. An "I've always depended on the kindness of strangers"
Blanche. But one who *will report* what's happened and NOT be hauled
off to an asylum—her tongue silenced behind steel doors, slammed
shut.
   (to audience)
The captive never shows her rage directly to the captor. Sometimes she
attempts to speak in metaphors or uses literary allusions.

> She smiles.
>
> Lights up on restaurant. A is sitting
> there.

A
(to himself)
My body is clean and hard and beautiful.

LISSA
(looking at A, then to audience)
HE arrives in two weeks.
(pause)
It's important that my desperation doesn't show. Though, sometimes I think it might, especially if he's listening carefully. Then again, I doubt if he ever is—his ego too involved in a dervish dance with "He, Himself."

> A beeping noise is heard from the
> restaurant.

A
Sorry, Lis. My beeper just went off. What did you say? Did you say something about ME?

> Lights out on restaurant. Lights up
> on edge of stage. MICHAEL is sit-
> ting there. His clothes are freshly
> pressed.

MICHAEL
(to audience)
I've started dating. Women are easier to find than I imagined. In fact,

after our separation was made known, some found me first. I take each to a nice restaurant, but never one I'd gone to with Lissa.

(pause)

The most surprising thing I find happening on these dates is how many of these women tell me they are, or aspire to be,

(sighs)

a poet.

(pause)

Most of them arrive dressed in black—Lissa's outfit. Some try to look like young, hip students, others like borderline goths. Most, however, just go with an expensive, dramatic look. Yet, no matter how they present themselves, all of them at some point in the conversation tell me how much they *love* Lissa's poetry. Then, follow it with a "but," which means *they*, of course, are different. Different in style, in content—*whatever*. Forever the implication being if they were just discovered, they could come to be regarded as good, if not better, than she. At this point, I usually start to tune out, especially when they attach how *healthy* they are—implying that *possibly* Lissa is not.

(pause)

Some tell me how much they exercise. A couple even have asked—still at dinner—would I like to feel their biceps? Their triceps? I, of course, accommodate them, however odd it might look in a public place.

(half-smiling)

Anyway, I'm used to "odd."

(pause)

I've also come to learn that any kind of physical reference to their bodies is always a prelude to what they inevitably will offer later in the evening.

(He raises his hands to his face, looks down, then looks out to the audience.)

I miss her.

BLACKOUT.

Music from the song "Skylark" plays.

END OF SCENE.

Scene 2

Lights up on the rooftop. NIJINSKY
is dancing "The Sacrifice" part in *The
Rite of Spring*. The music is coming
from Lettie's cassette player. Lights
up on Lettie's room. LETTIE is sitting up in the bed—it is earlier in her
hospital stay. She looks healthier and
has more energy. She also has a little
more hair. There are fresh daisies in a
vase on her tray. LISSA and LETTIE
are listening to the music. LETTIE
has her glasses on and is trying, with
difficulty, to work on the petit point
canvas. LISSA is dressed in her pantsuit and her hair is in a ponytail.

LETTIE
You used to like to hide from me when I took you shopping.

LISSA
You were always in my full view. I liked to see the upset on your face—
it's true. I liked to see how you looked at the very moment you thought
you'd lost me. It showed me that you loved me.

LETTIE turns off the cassette player. NIJINSKY sadly looks down at
LETTIE and LISSA. Lights out on
the rooftop. LETTIE, frustrated,
continues with the petit point.

LETTIE
Well, I didn't like it. Didn't like it at all.

LISSA
Then I'd pop out from in back of a mannequin and you'd smile. It was a game. I wanted to show you I could disappear and then come back. It was a game.
(pause)
I guess it made me feel I was in control of what was happening.

LETTIE
By scaring a mother into thinking she had lost a daughter?!
(pause)
I don't understand such games. I never got used to the disappearing, even for a second. It wasn't a game. Don't you understand THAT? Why would you do a thing like that? You knew—

LISSA
(interrupting)
I'm sorry. I just wanted to show you I would always come back.
(pause)
Mother, we're both still here. Look at me. SEE.

> LETTIE tries to continue with the petit point, then gives up, puts it down on the bed, and takes off her glasses.

LETTIE
(to audience)
After my parents and brother disappeared, I started having this dream that they'd come back.
(mesmerized)
They'd take my hands—Mama the right, Papa the left, with Jascha next

to Papa—and we'd walk away together.
      (pause)
In the dream the air is always clean and warm and clear
      (pause)
and it is always summer.
      (pause)
And for years, whenever I'd walk into a room—any room—here in
America, I would look for Jascha, and sometimes I'd think I'd see him.
But the closer I got, it was never him.
      (sighs)
      (to LISSA)
Lissa, I think *this* time, I'm *not* going to get out of here.

                          LISSA
Mother, of course you're going to get out of here.

                          LETTIE
I mean
      (pause)
alive.

                          LISSA
                          (upset)
Mother, how about putting on some lipstick. It will brighten your face.

                          LISSA goes to the medicine cabinet
                          and gets Lettie's lipstick. LETTIE
                          lets LISSA put it on her. LISSA
                          takes a small mirror from her purse
                          and hands it to LETTIE. LETTIE
                          stares at herself.

LETTIE

A GHOST IN LIPSTICK.
(small laugh)
That's what I'll be for Halloween.
Yes, I will be a ghost in lipstick by Halloween.
(pause)
What a *strange* holiday.

> LETTIE puts down the mirror and closes her eyes.
>
> Lights out on Lettie's room. The click of turning on the cassette player is heard and music from *The Rite of Spring* plays. Lights up on the rooftop where NIJINSKY dances "The Sacrifice" part. Lights up on Lettie's room. She is alone, watching NIJINSKY.
>
> BLACKOUT.
>
> END OF SCENE.

Scene 3

> LISSA is updating her wall to for-
> ty-seven tally marks. She is dressed
> in a nice black shirt and black pants.
> She looks completely put together.
> Her hair is clipped with the two
> barrettes.

LISSA
(to audience)

A'S HERE! Since losing Beck, I've been waiting for tomorrow. For A.
The cure. THE CURE IS HERE. At least somewhere in this city to-
night.
(She bows her head.)
YOU CAN'T SEE IT? CAN YOU?
(pause)
I DIDN'T THINK SO. What do you think of this outfit? Rather put
together, I think. This is what I'll wear.

> LISSA sits down in her chair and
> waits.

> Pause.

> She looks at her watch. Smiles. She
> gets up and turns on her cassette
> player. Lights up on the rooftop. Mu-
> sic from the *The Rite of Spring* plays.
> NIJINSKY dances "The Sacrifice"
> part. LISSA looks up at NIJINSKY
> and dances it, too. Finally, exhaust-

ed, she turns the music off. Lights
out on the rooftop. Lights dim on
Lissa's room. LISSA falls into her
chair and sleeps.

Pause.

Her phone rings. Awakened, she
awkwardly grabs for the phone.

LISSA

Hello? HELLO?
(pause)
NO. You have the wrong number. There's no one here by that name.

She bashes the phone down, gets up
from her chair, and starts pacing.
She looks at her watch. She tries to
smooth out her clothes, then picks
up the phone, punches in a number.
Lights up on coffee shop. A is sip-
ping coffee and has his feet propped
up on the table. A's cell phone rings.
He answers it.

A

Hello?

LISSA
(talking too rapidly)

A? I hope I didn't wake you. Someone woke me and then I realized
it wasn't all that early and that you were probably up and even if you
weren't I wouldn't wake you because your phone would be turned off
and I could just leave you a voice message.

(She takes a breath.)
So you're here! How are you?

A

Got a cold, Lis.
(He coughs, then coughs again.)
I'm just waiting to meet Ali. She sounds great. Really great.

LISSA

Great.
(pause)
How about coffee late this afternoon?
(pause)
or maybe
(pause)
dinner?

A

Sorry, Lis. I'm meeting some students from last year for drinks. Then I'm having dinner with a friend.

LISSA

A friend? Oh.

A

And this cold.
(He coughs again.)

LISSA

Tomorrow?

A

Well, sure, maybe, tomorrow. What's your number?
(pause)

But, by tomorrow the cold could be worse.

                         LISSA
It's 773-742-0902.

                          A
GREAT.

                         LISSA
Tomorrow's pretty free. I could meet you just about any time.

                          A
Got it. But if not this trip, I'll be back after Thanksgiving. I'll be in
Austria—Innsbruck, you know—skiing. Talk with you soon. Bye, Lis.

                         LISSA
Happy Thanksgiving.
     (pause)
Bye.
                              A turns off his phone. LISSA hangs
                              up.

                         LISSA
                       (to herself)
He *has* my number. Didn't he *even* bring it with him?

                              LISSA picks up the phone and
                              punches in a number. Lights up on
                              MICHAEL outside the coffee shop.
                              His cell phone rings. He answers it.

                         LISSA
Michael, could you meet me for lunch?

MICHAEL
Lissa, I can't. I wish I could, but I can't. I have a date.

LISSA
(sadly)
A date?

MICHAEL
(uncomfortably)
Well, not really a date.
(pause)
An appointment.

LISSA
(softly)
I understand.

MICHAEL
I'll call you tomorrow. Are you Okay?

LISSA
(softly)
Sure. I'm Okay. Bye.

MICHAEL
Bye.
(MICHAEL hangs up.)
Damn it.

Lights out on MICHAEL.

LISSA
(hanging up phone)
DAMN IT. DAMN IT. GOD DAMN IT.

(pause)
GOD DAMN IT
(pause)
BECK.

> Lights up on the rooftop. Music from
> *The Afternoon of a Faun* is playing.
> NIJINSKY is dancing. He is wear-
> ing his gold cord faun wig. LISSA
> looks up. NIJINSKY stops dancing
> and looks at LISSA. He smiles. LIS-
> SA gives him a tentative smile. Lights
> dim on Lissa's room. She curls up in
> her chair and goes to sleep. NIJIN-
> SKY starts dancing again. Lights out
> on the rooftop. Lights up on Lissa's
> room. LISSA wakes up. She checks
> her answering machine for messages.
> There are none.

LISSA
(to audience)

He hasn't called. He won't. Not this trip. I had my hair trimmed, my
nails done.

> LISSA looks at her nails, then goes
> over to the wall and updates it to
> forty-eight tally marks. She switches
> off the lights to her room. The stage
> goes dark. The punching in of num-
> bers on a telephone is heard.
>
> Pause.

> Lights up on Lissa's room.

LISSA
(ashamed, to audience)

I called Beck. I didn't want you to see.

(pause)

I guess the gods of small minds and even smaller acts were looking out for me—his line was busy. If I could just talk with him, I'd be better.

(pause)

One drink. Just one. That's how an alcoholic must feel.

(pause)

That's how *this* alcoholic is.

> Lights up on Beck's room. He slowly opens his door and steps out.

BECK
Have I not been a good friend to you? I *have been* a good friend to you.

LISSA
(tired, looking up at BECK)

Yes, Beck, yes. You have been a good friend to me, except—

BECK
EXCEPT WHAT? ACCEPT YOUR RESPONSIBILITY IN WHAT HAPPENED. ACCEPT YOUR PARTICIPATION. ACCEPT THAT YOU *DID* PARTICIPATE.
ACCEPT THAT YOU *STAYED* IN THE RELATIONSHIP.

(pause)

ACCEPT THAT YOU *PUT* THE POEM IN THE BOOK.

(pause)

I NEVER *HURT* YOU, LISSA.

(pause)

I NEVER HURT *HER.* I LOVED *HER.* AND NOW YOU'VE

WRITTEN ABOUT
HER. WRITTEN THAT I *HURT* HER.

> BECK steps back into his room and
> slams his door.

> Lights out on Beck's room.

LISSA
(angry and upset, to audience)
I may not be able to call Brigit Sundquist's Office of Complaints, but
on the other hand, I just *couldn't* pull the poem from the book.
(pause)
He *did control* her.
(sighs)
He *did hurt* her.
(pause)
I just couldn't do it. There was a limit to what he could *take* from me.
And the limit was *he couldn't take the poem*.
(pause)
And now—and now, *I can't handle any of it. I just can't.*

> LISSA grabs at her hair with both
> hands as if she's going to pull it all
> out. NIJINSKY enters Lissa's room.
> He is holding a straitjacket. He of-
> fers it to LISSA.

LISSA
No. No. Not that.

> NIJINSKY starts to leave, but LIS-
> SA pulls him back.

LISSA

Please?

> Music from "Skylark" plays softly.

LISSA

Come with me?

> NIJINSKY nods. LISSA takes his
> hand. He drops the straitjacket.
> They leave Lissa's room and go up the
> steps to Beck's room. Lights dim on
> Beck's room. She opens Beck's door
> slowly. BECK is not there.

LISSA

I know. So dark. So dirty. After he left his last wife, he moved here—
moved here with his dog. Her coat so unkempt, so gnarled, so uncared
for. I wondered why she stayed—why she didn't just run away?

> NIJINSKY stares at LISSA for five
> seconds, then tries to pull her from
> the room. She resists.

LISSA
(speaking quickly)
The dog was sitting quietly next to me when it happened.

> LISSA points to different places
> in the room where the action took
> place.

LISSA
She was as startled as I was, when he bounded from his chair in the

middle of dinner and yanked me from mine. His hands were already on my breasts. Then, I felt the dog's paws at my waist. I could feel her quiver.

> As LISSA is talking NIJINSKY begins to tremble.

LISSA

Was she trying to protect me or was she wanting me to protect her? *She* seemed half-human, half-animal. *I* seemed half-animal, half-human. Were we one and the same being?
(pause)
He yelled at her, kicked her, and she ran under the table—hid there. I saw her silhouette as he pulled me to the futon. One of his children had napped there earlier—I could smell the urine.

> NIJINSKY backs away and bends into himself.

LISSA
(to herself)
The more I cried for him to stop, the more he ripped at my clothes. My hair went flying all over my face, my now bare skin and the dog—
(LISSA bends down as if she sees the dog.)
she stayed huddled, frozen, frozen in her own mountain of fur, except for the chewing, *that* unrelenting chewing, *her* unrelenting chewing on herself, her eyes crazy from the chaos.

> NIJINSKY slowly straightens, pulls LISSA up, spins her around and out of Beck's room, down his stairs and back to her room. Music from "Skylark" plays softly.

                                LISSA
                         (to NIJINSKY)
Now she's dead. She jumped—

                                     BECK opens his door and steps out.

                                BECK
                     (sadly, to audience)
I was good to my dog. I loved her.

                                     Startled, LISSA and NIJINSKY
                                     look up at BECK.

                                LISSA
                         (to NIJINSKY)
Suicide. She committed suicide.

                                BECK
DOGS—DON'T—COMMIT SUICIDE.
   (to LISSA)
SHE FELL. DAMN IT, YOU BITCH.

                                     NIJINSKY stares at BECK, then
                                     wraps the straitjacket around both
                                     LISSA and himself.

                                     BLACKOUT.

                                     END OF SCENE.

Scene 4

> In Lettie's room, it is nearer to the
> beginning of her hospital stay. She
> is out of bed wearing her white
> robe. She is weak, but she is walking
> around. She stops and stares at her-
> self in the mirror on the medicine
> cabinet. She tries to fix her hair.

LETTIE
(horrified, to mirror)

Like then. Yes. Like then. The hair, just stubs or tuffs or fragile strands, trying to grow back.

> LETTIE goes over to the vase of dai-
> sies on her tray and proceeds to care-
> fully pull out each petal of one flow-
> er. LISSA enters wearing her black
> pantsuit. Her hair is in a ponytail.
> She is carrying a large sack filled with
> books. She watches LETTIE. When
> LETTIE is finished and there are no
> more petals on the flower, LETTIE
> stares at the bald flower and then at
> LISSA. LETTIE sits down on the
> edge of the bed.

LISSA

Mother, I brought the books you asked for, but I'm not sure they're what you should be reading.

LISSA sits down on chair. LETTIE
is still staring at her.

LISSA

No, I didn't tell Father. Anyway, I doubt if he'd notice even if I walked
past him with them. He just hides behind the newspaper. Just reads the
business section, over and over.
(pause)
But the books—

LETTIE
(quietly)
They're familiar. They make me feel safe.
(assertively)
My eyes are still strong.

LISSA

Safe?! How can *these* books and *that* place make you feel safe?

LETTIE
(agitatedly)
Because I had no choice. This was the life that was given me and EV-
ERYONE kept telling us we were in a safe place.
(pause)
And I was twelve. And the red brick building with the small windows
that were brightened by white frilled curtains and the picket fence
around it LOOKED SAFE. And eventually everything became so
familiar—the uniforms, all of them, and the bodies that inhabited
them, the strong healthy ones, the bird-thin sick ones, all the smells
that were created when they commingled—this place where life and
death collided and the earth opened herself like the whore that she
was and swallowed everyone into her putrid womb. This womb became my home.
(strained)

I'm *still* looking for them: for my mother and father—and Jascha.
(pause)
And because my journey is almost over—and thank God for that—I
need to keep looking for them among the ruins so I can go on to whatever's next.
(pleading)
Lissa, do you understand? *Do you?*

LISSA

Yes.
(pause)
I want to go, too.

LISSA reaches to take Lettie's hand,
but LETTIE pulls it away.

LETTIE

It is *not your journey.*
(softly)
It has never been, and for this you should be grateful.

LISSA

Mother, because it's yours, in part, it's mine, too.

LETTIE

OH, NO. NO. YOU WEREN'T THERE.
(softly)
You have your *own* journey to travel.

LISSA
(softly)

Yes, yes Mother, I know.
(sighs)

LETTIE

Do you, Lissa? Do you really know that? I sometimes wonder. Do you really?

> LISSA, not responding, reaches into the sack and pulls out a pint of chocolate ice cream and two spoons wrapped in paper napkins.

LISSA

I brought two spoons. We can eat it right out of the carton. We can eat the richest chocolate ice cream in the world and no one can stop us. No one.

(pause)

Mother, remember the story I wrote when I was six about the little girl who tricks the monster by telling him she likes vanilla so he'll give her the chocolate? Mother, do you remember?

> LETTIE just stares at LISSA. LISSA, ignoring the stare, hands LETTIE a spoon and takes the lid off the pint of ice cream. LISSA dips her spoon in the carton and then puts the spoonful of ice cream in her mouth. She watches as LETTIE does the same. They both swallow.

BLACKOUT.

END OF SCENE.

Scene 5

> Lights up on Lissa's room. LISSA is
> not there. There are sixty-five tally
> marks on the wall. Loud noises are
> heard offstage—crashing sounds of
> things being overturned. Then, from
> offstage LISSA starts chanting hys-
> terically.

LISSA
(offstage)
"The art of losing isn't hard to master;
so many things seem filled with the intent
to be lost that their loss is no disaster."
(pause)
"Lose something every day. Accept the fluster
of lost door keys"—
(pause)
I CAN'T FIND THEM. I JUST CAN'T FIND THEM.

> More crashing sounds are heard—
> things being overturned and draw-
> ers being opened and shut.

LISSA
(offstage)
OH, MOTHER. PLEASE HELP ME. PLEASE. HELP ME.
(pause)
EVEN THOUGH YOU'RE GONE, CAN YOU SEE ME? SEE ME?

> LISSA rushes into her room wear-
> ing her jeans, white T-shirt, and red
> sweater, and throws herself onto her
> chair. Her hair is loose and she is
> completely disheveled.

LISSA
(to audience, more calmly)
Lota Soares, Elizabeth Bishop's lover, had a breakdown and then killed
herself after Bishop left her.
(pause)
Did Bishop have a breakdown, too? Or did she put all emotion into
finishing her poem "One Art"? All grief locked into a poem about a
person lost to her forever?
(sighs)
A person who never comes back.
(pause)
And hanging on to the "foresee" word with the tip of your fever-sick,
wet tongue or the tip of your split fingernail dug deep into a stub of
hair as if it were a thick rope that will save
you is setting yourself up to slip straight into some kind oblivion—be
it death or madness.

> LISSA spots something under her
> dresser near the right leg. She jumps
> up and runs over to it. She bends
> down and grabs it—it's her keys. She
> kisses them and she looks up.

LISSA
Thank you, Mother. Thank you.
(She sits down in her chair, clutching her keys in her right hand.)
(to herself, sadly)
The art of losing is *impossible* to master.

LISSA'S phone rings. She picks it up
quickly and stands up.

LISSA

Hello?

Lights up outside of coffee shop. MI-
CHAEL is standing there with his
cellphone.

MICHAEL

Hi!

LISSA
(softly)

Hi.

MICHAEL

You sound strange.

LISSA
(half-laughing)

And this surprises you? It's nothing.

MICHAEL

It's *not* nothing.

LISSA

I just couldn't find my keys. But I did just find them.

MICHAEL
(half-laughing)

And were you running around reciting the Bishop poem?

                          LISSA
Yes. Yes, I was. Aren't you glad you're out of all this? That you don't
have to *waste anymore of your time*—

                          MICHAEL
                       (interrupting)
No. Not particularly. How about dinner—dinner tomorrow night. I'll
come over at six o'clock. Then we can decide where to go.

                          LISSA
Dinner?
    (pause)
Maybe, okay.
    (pause)
I don't know.

                          MICHAEL
Let's just leave it at "okay." See you tomorrow evening, Lissa. Bye.

                              LISSA hangs up. MICHAEL shuts
                              his cell phone. Lights out on MI-
                              CHAEL. LISSA sits down, immo-
                              bile, clutching her keys. The lights go
                              slowly to dark.

                          LISSA
                       (to herself)
"Lose something every day. Accept the fluster . . .
the hour badly spent.
The art of losing isn't hard to master."

                              LISSA gets up and disappears into
                              the darkness. She is adding one more
                              tally mark to her wall.

LISSA

The art of losing is *impossible* to master.
(pause)
The hour badly spent.
(pause)
All the hours, the days, the months, *badly spent.*
(more determined)
ALL THE MINUTES, THE HOURS, THE DAYS, THE WEEKS,
THE MONTHS.

> Lights up. There are sixty-six tally
> marks on the wall. She writes the
> number 66 on the wall.

LISSA
(to audience)

Sixty-six.
(She adds one more 6 to the wall.)
Six, six, six—the devil's number. I don't know why. I heard it once and
then again and again and I guess if you hear something often enough,
you begin to believe it.
(to herself)
Yes, you begin to believe it.
(pause)
The *devil's* number.

> LISSA picks up the phone and dials
> a number.

LISSA

Brigit Sundquist, please.
(pause)
Well, *when* will she be back?

(pause)
Is this her secretary?
(pause)
Well, when will *she* be back?
(pause)
I'll call again.
(sighs)
Just say Lissa called. I've called before.
(pause)
My number?
(scared)
My number is
(sighs)
773-742-0902.
(pause)
Thank you.

> LISSA takes the vase of daisies off her end table and collapses on her floor. She puts the vase in front of her. Her legs encircle the vase. She starts pulling the petals off the flowers, one by one.

LISSA
(agitatedly, to the petals)

The man who loves me hates me.
(pause)
The man who loves me hates me.
(pause)
The man who loves me hates me.
(pause)
The man who loves me hates me.
(pause)
The man who loves me hates me.

LISSA raises both hands to her head
and starts to pull at the long strands
of hair adjacent to the spot, then
stops.

LISSA
(to herself)

Stop it. *Stop it. Just stop it.*

She gets up and runs out of her room.

BLACKOUT.

END OF SCENE.

Scene 6

Lights up on both Lissa's room and
coffee shop. Lissa's room is empty. A
is in the coffee shop. He's making
a call on his cell phone. The phone
rings in Lissa's room.

LISSA'S ANSWERING MACHINE
Hi, this is Lissa. PLEASE leave a message. Thanks for calling!

A
Hey, Lis. It's A. I'm in town for a couple of days to get things settled for
next semester. And Lis, you've got to do me a favor.
(pause)
Lis, are you there?
(pause)
Anyway, you've got to get that Ali person off my back. I mean it—literally and figuratively.
(laughs)
She won't stop calling. You've got to tell her to calm down—to cool it.
I'm going to give you my new number—I *had* to change it. *That woman*
just won't quit.
(laughs)
It was great—to a point. *Great* that she's found me a place and all *that*—
that she's *so friendly*—but enough is enough. Talk to her, Lis. Please.
(a small laugh)
I really need some help here.
(pause)
And hey Lis, I've been hearing some *intriguing* stuff about *you*. You
know, just talk. But it did remind me of Proust's descriptions of the
rumors surrounding the enigmatic Odette.

(laughs)

Yes, you may have guessed, *I'm* going to teach Proust—*Swann's Way.*
The class will love it—love me!

(pause)

Anyway, Lis, you and I should get together—have *that* dinner. Get to
know each other better. Okay? Maybe tonight? I know it's sort of short
notice, but *I am* available, just not to Ali Abeles.

(laughs)

Now, don't tell a soul. It's 773-664-7709. So give me a call, Lis. Lookin'
forward!

> A turns off his cell phone.
>
> Lights out on coffee shop.
>
> MICHAEL enters Lissa's room.

MICHAEL

Lissa? Lissa? Where are you?

> He looks around, then disappears
> offstage.

MICHAEL
(offstage)

LISSA.

> He returns to Lissa's room.

MICHAEL
(desperately)

Lissa, where did you go?

> MICHAEL exits. Lights dim on
> Lissa's room. Lights up on Lissa's

room. NIJINSKY enters, picks up different items of Lissa's, and dances with them—e.g., a cassette tape, the dictionary, the hand mirror. No music plays.

BLACKOUT.

END OF SCENE.

Scene 7

> Lights up on Lettie's room. She is
> at the very beginning of her hos-
> pital stay. She is wearing her white
> robe and is pacing around her room.
> She pauses at the medicine cabinet
> mirror where she looks at herself in
> horror. She takes out a comb from
> her pocket and runs it through her
> thin hair. There is a box of mints on
> her tray with a blue ribbon around it.
> She takes the ribbon off the box and
> holds it.

LETTIE
(to audience)

So here I am *again*,
(pause)
another treatment.
(pause)
An experimental one.
(softly)
An experiment—
(She looks at the ribbon in her hand.)
When we got off the train they shouted
(pause)
WOMEN TO THE LEFT. MEN TO THE RIGHT. WOMEN TO
THE LEFT. MEN TO THE RIGHT.
(pause)
They called out for doctors and twins. DOCTORS AND TWINS.
Mama gently pushed Leah and me out of the line. I guess she thought

this was good. That we might be given special attention because we were twins.

(smirks)

Viktor saw us—saw me—he ignored Leah.

> LETTIE moves closer to the audience.

LETTIE

(sadly)

He came toward me, came very close, and he touched my hair. He CHOSE me.

(pause)

Leah was sent elsewhere.

> LETTIE moves back to the mirror.

LETTIE

(to mirror)

When they grabbed my satchel away from me, I was left holding just the string that had helped to keep it shut. I tied it around my head and made a small bow of it.

> LETTIE takes the ribbon and ties it around her head. She looks at herself in the mirror.

LETTIE

He laughed when he looked at it.

(to audience)

He asked my name and called me his pretty little maiden.

(to mirror, dazed)

My name is Lettie. Lettie.

(pause)

And I'm not that pretty.
    (to audience)
He asked how old.
    (to mirror, dazed)
I'm twelve. I'm Lettie.
    (to audience)
I'm twelve.

> LETTIE, exhausted, sits on the bed.

LETTIE

Their hands were quick and rough when they shaved me.
    (sadly)
I had red curls.
    (pause)
When Viktor came back, he seemed to like it.
    (sarcastically)
My brand-new child look. He touched my scalp. He took my hand
    (LETTIE looks at her hand.)
and we walked a path that led to his door.

> LETTIE takes off her robe and lays it on the bed. She is left wearing her hospital gown. She exits. Lights dim on Lettie's room. Lights up on Lettie's room. NIJINSKY enters, picks up different items of Lettie's, and dances with them—e.g., the comb, the petit point canvas, a book about him. No music plays.
>
> BLACKOUT.
>
> END OF SCENE.

<u>Scene 8</u>

> LISSA is running toward the rooftop. She is wearing the blue jeans, white T-shirt, and red sweater. She is disheveled and her hair is loose.

LISSA
(angrily, to herself)
JUST-STOP-IT. STOP-IT. STOP-IT-*ALL*.

> LISSA runs up the stairs to the rooftop. NIJINSKY enters, wearing his gold cord faun wig and carrying the nymph's veil. He sees LISSA and pauses.

LISSA
(on the rooftop, assertively to audience, trying to catch her breath)
Nijinsky danced his last dance, "World War I," in 1919. He then suffered an irreparable breakdown.
(pause)
Nijinsky's dog, if he had one, died last July.

> LISSA puts both hands to her chest, still trying to catch her breath. LETTIE enters and walks toward Beck's door. She is wearing her hospital gown. The blue ribbon is in her hair.

LETTIE
(dazed)
My name is Lettie.

(pause)
I'm twelve. I had red curls.

LETTIE reaches Beck's door, pauses, and looks up. Lights brighten on
the rooftop. Lights dim on LETTIE.
LISSA moves slowly around the
edge of the rooftop while reciting
the poem "Nijinsky's Dog." LET-
TIE listens.

LISSA

She was a beautiful animal
with all that was rational
beaten out of her strong,
cleanly chiseled head.
We'd circle each other,
lonely, in the heat
of the late summer nights,
both of us waiting for you—
for some crumb of attention.
When I didn't finish the dinner
you'd sometimes offer,
you'd slip it into her bowl
and she'd spring toward you,
more starved for love than food.
I'd watch her from my chair,
passing the time until you'd turn yourself
toward me—remember, O please,
I was there. Out on the ledge
she'd sit, elegant and damaged—
her scars buried in her dense, gnarled
fur. Since I've come up here I twist
my hair so hard it snaps

NIJINSKY crosses stage and
starts up the stairs to the rooftop.

and now I have a bald spot
that my barrettes can barely cover. You   NIJINSKY arrives on the
almost seemed to cry   rooftop and kisses the top
when you told me that she died.   of Lissa's head, then
But as I came closer I saw   smoothes her hair. She's
your eyes completely   too distracted by what
dry. You left her   she's saying to notice.
on that hot July roof—   NIJINSKY jumps small
the tar blistering   jumps on the rooftop.
her dog feet. She couldn't stand
to touch the surface
so she sat and sat
on that asphalt edge,
her mind on fire with memory
of how you once took care
with her, gave her a yard
to play in, rolled with her
in cool green grass.
She'd dream of that
and want it back—before
the war that destroyed her world: NIJINSKY cringes.
your wife's shrieks: *take the goddamn
dog if you leave
me*. And the dog
in her dog mind thought and thought
it was all her fault.
I wish I'd been there
when she took her leap
into the too-blue parched
air, over the anchored   NIJINSKY agitatedly looks
oak tree and the naive lilies   out to what lies
reaching toward the idle sky,   beyond the roof, toward
to see her resolve—the pause,   the audience, the ground.
then the quick   Lights go brighter on the

amazing move–the elevation, the gift
of rising, her thick mane ablaze
against the dazed noonday sun.
How she broke
free in that *grand jeté*,
sailing in holy
madness past her dog life,
her soul bounding out
of her sad dog eyes
while her ragged body hit
a barren patch of earth.

rooftop.
NIJINSKY dances with
quick moves. LISSA
sees NIJINSKY dancing
and dances next to him as
she continues reciting the
poem. MICHAEL enters,
sees LISSA, and quickly
crosses the stage toward
the rooftop.

NIJINSKY raises the veil and puts
it loosely around Lissa's shoulders.
LISSA touches it. Spotlight shines
on LETTIE who is looking up, staring at NIJINSKY. LETTIE opens
Beck's door. Lights out on the rooftop. LISSA continues poem.

MICHAEL
(frightened)

LISSA?!

LETTIE walks through Beck's door
into darkness. Spotlight shines on
shut door.

Pause.

Lights out on entire stage.

A howl—half-animal, half-human—
is heard from LISSA.

Lights up on the rooftop. LISSA is standing there alone with a look of exhausted relief on her face. MI-CHAEL reaches the top of the stairs and holds tightly to Lissa's arms. Lights up on NIJINSKY who is at the bottom of the stairs. Music from *The Afternoon of a Faun* plays. NIJINSKY dances across the stage. LISSA turns to watch NIJINSKY. NIJINSKY looks up at LISSA and gracefully waves to her with the veil. Lights fade to dark on the rooftop. Spotlight shines on NIJINSKY as he does a leap and exits.

BLACKOUT.

END OF PLAY.

The Novella

Specula Karma

by
Jennie Silver

You are for pleasure's sake, my greatest.
—Avigdor Element

I

The Woman Who Loved Halloween

She's given up the huge
festivals—the bonfires on
the hilltops, the days when the devil's
help was evoked
for health and luck—the twisted
world a tumble down
the tenured land. She's given

up the trick or treat—
the carved-out grin of the night watchman.
O how she misses him:
his long bones, his skeleton
heart that she tried to glue
flesh on, his hand
movements—*flexion, extension,*
abduction, adduction; ADDICTION
to the pelvis girdle—
that deep cavity, the flared-
up ilium, the drop
to the pubis that she worshipped on

an autumn evening not unlike this one.
All Hallows' Eve. Eve of the dried-out
garden, *what is there left to tend?*
Eve, who walks the earth with her jack-
o'-lantern—neither in hell nor in heaven.

Idy Cometh

II

When Ida Cometh, better known to most as "Idy C" or simply just plain Idy—although there was nothing plain or simple about her—met Randolph van Straaten, better known as "Dolph-the-Strap" because he wasn't just any old poetry critic, for his reviews could lacerate life-lasting wounds into souls of poets, each had met their match in hell.

Their first encounter, fifteen years ago, was a little strange, but pleasant enough—at least that's what Idy thought. She remembered a man with a mop of gray hair, a youngish, bulky face, in the mid-phase of middle age, with a too-pronounced chin. A chin that she considered at the time would help his face photograph well, but in reality did look a bit "Dudley Do-Right" or "über-Supermanish." Yes, she thought to herself, the kind that almost mandated him to become a leading man—or thug—even if it were just in the world of poetry, which she would eventually learn had its own matériel of weapons—both metaphoric and real.

Immediately, Idy found Dolph both appealing—and not. For the impression she had of the chin and how it almost jutted into her own as he moved his head up and down and sideways with a forceful enthusiasm upon greeting her, invaded the small space between them, making her feel both flattered and crowded. And that the chin at the moment of their introduction felt and looked like something more—a calcification that had the ability to invade her, hurt her. Then, she dismissed such a thought, attributing it to her overactive imagination.

Unfortunately, she was right. The chin *would* become a dangerous conceit for their future—the years of intrusions and damage each would cause the other. Yet, neither could have known this at the ever-so-cordial, heightened instant of their introduction.

≈ ≈ ≈ ≈ ≈

Idy shook his thick, spongy, hot, massive palm, noticing, too, the complex-
ity of his hand, with its long, slender, graceful, cold fingers. Then, there
were the large, too-thick black frames of his glasses and her thought that
rimless ones on such a large face would work better, giving the mass of his
head a less weighty look.

After what felt like too-prolonged a moment of his excessive leaning
into her, she did—with a pleasant smile—back out of the office where
their first encounter had happened. The office also included four male
poets, each vying for Dolph's attention, each of them hanging on to his
knife-sharp words, laughing too loudly at his cutting comments about
the poetry world in general and specific poets who were absent from the
room. They chose to ignore what they knew to be true, that there were—
and always would be—other groups with Dolph in full command, groups
laughing with equal delight and vigor *at them*. However, for a short time,
they were feeling too special, too included in Dolph's circle, to think
about any of this. In a year or two or five they would, if they were "lucky,"
find out what Dolph really thought of them and their work. Even then,
they would consider his insults better than having their writing completely ignored by him—or so they'd try to convince themselves. For the slice
of his "sentences" could cut deep, past flesh right into the quick of their
writing souls, making them doubt what they had produced—more than
they already did.

Then again, artists, and especially poets, were used to such injury, either self-inflicted or caused by others. That romanticism and sadomasochism—its conjoined twin—battled within them. However, the majority
would be appalled by such a blatant assessment and argue deep into the
night about its untruth, both to others and, when alone, to themselves.
Mostly, they would stick such psychological analyses onto dead poets—
something about which they could safely bob their heads in agreement—
allowing the hardening frost of their own insecurities to temporarily melt.

III

Going back to her own cubicle at the literary magazine where she had just been promoted from an editorial assistant to poetry editor, Idy's equilibrium completely returned. In the seconds after her meeting "Dolph-the-Strap," Idy Cometh couldn't have imagined that in the months that followed, her first book of poetry would be accepted, published within a year, and land on Randolph van Straaten's desk for his possible review. Had she known this, she would have replayed their encounter over and over in her head and convinced herself that everything had gone wrong—that her face had flushed too much and she had said too few words.

She also didn't know—how could she?—that at the moment of that handshake, Randolph van Straaten felt for her not the usual attraction he felt for most women—his tastes being rather eclectic and Jello-like—but the beginnings of what would mushroom into a strident, unbridled, complicated lust and that because of these burgeoning feelings, he would burst. Meaning, he would come to rape her. Something he, too, would have found appalling, because however much he took pride in seducing people, his best handiwork came from raping them not with his proud, thick penis, but rather with what thinly snaked out from his highly prized Mont Blanc pen—his typist left to decipher his handwriting and to transpose it on to what he ironically called "that inhumane machine," better known as the computer.

In many ways Dolph remained an old-fashioned guy, too, when it came to women, living in more genteel, upper-class, past societies' manners—that no matter ladies' talents, when "taken by men," they became objects to be taken, but taken more artfully than outright rape. He was the perfect inheritor of the legacy left at the university by the much-celebrated novelist Avigdor Element and Dolph's own mentor, the critic Ivan Durmand—who had been a direct disciple of Element.

≈ ≈ ≈ ≈ ≈

Yes, Randolph van Straaten had been more than merely "bitten" by the charms of Idy Cometh. So much of his fantasy life from the moment he touched her slender, warm hand with its delicate fingers tapering to the "virginal" color on her nails, which he remembered as a soft pink with a hint of light peach, now involved her and an escalating obsession to completely devour her. He imagined all the ways he could turn her entirely naked being well past that color. He knew he could ignite her. Flame her.

Obviously, he didn't like the growing power his obsessions and fantasies about Idy were having over him. He was used to being totally in charge of both his inner and outer atmospheres, and consequently he realized the only way to get command over what had been set in motion within himself was to get closer to her and take control.

Needless to say, her first book of poetry received a superb review from him. People were perplexed—actually astonished—by the way he cooed about it, using many empty adjectives such as "amazing," "stunning," "gorgeous," and "pure" to describe it.

IV

Dolph was living in the voraciously hungry id of his inner life with his thoughts of Idy. His analyst, whom Dolph quit four months after he met Idy, would have smiled a droll smile and then have been horribly aggrieved, believing that the abrupt, crass way Dolph terminated his therapy would ultimately lead him to act primitively.

Years later, when the whole mess of the story about Dolph and Idy publicly aired, the analyst did take some liberties and publish a book about a patient such as Dolph—his identity barely veiled in his minor alterations of some specific facts about the real Randolph van Straaten.

The book used a character he renamed "Adolph," giving the Jewish analyst some amount of pleasure in its easy connection to Hitler as the supreme example of how the "wounded child" can become the adult narcissist, then one of history's most heinous sociopaths. And he did, rather brazenly, leave in a few of the exact details of Dolph's life—his mother being a former Rockette, then a model for brassieres, then a known alcoholic with a suggestion of a possible descent into prostitution, and his father, a frustrated, mediocre jazz pianist, who did rub shoulders with some of the New York greats and womanized with the best of them. Of course, with such facts, no one in the claustrophobic circles of the literary world—no matter how high or low—could miss whom the book was about.

The analyst would use as the centerpiece of his book, entitled *The Oedipus Complex, Even More Complex*, that "Idy," now renamed "Abby,"—whom he would not give any accurate details about—looked a great deal like Dolph's deceased mother before she bloated into her alcoholic despair. Dolph had detailed their physical similarities to the therapist. Such information would be reveled in by any psychoanalyst—and perhaps the unabashed, visible relish he did take in this *was* at least part of the cause of Dolph's sudden, cruel tirade and exit.

≈ ≈ ≈ ≈ ≈

Clearly, the therapist had his own unfinished business with Dolph (and his own self), and one day Dolph stormed out of his office—Dolph, in his rant taking down the entire psychiatric profession and targeting the therapist specifically with his bulldozing, yet ever-so-articulate tongue in full motion as he exited, slamming the door so hard that much of the paint from its frame snapped from the wood as if it, too, were frightened by the heft of such a man.

Something Dolph had said to the therapist knifed into his own ego. It was guessed this had to do with the therapist's seemingly secluded ways and that Dolph had intruded by so aggressively interrogating him as to *why he had no family, no wife, no woman, and that by living like a hermit—a "troll"—how could he possibly give any advice to anyone about having a life.*

Few people would ever be Randolph van Straaten's equal in retaliation, but with his book, the therapist proved to be of them—no matter that it was a slow one.

However, even if Idy had been handed such a book about the dangers of a man like Dolph, it wouldn't have stopped the unrolling of the red carpet to hell that she was on with him. Idy had her own history, her own issues, that too neatly locked into the jigsaw pieces of Dolph's own puzzle. For this man, whom she would come to hate, would also be the man she would fall in love with and want to fix, want to believe in again—no matter the strength, the independence of her outward behavior and the originality of her poetry. The force of him would encapsulate her and hold her.

≈ ≈ ≈ ≈ ≈

"A captive of the Marquis de Sade," some would come to say, especially years later when both scholars and students of poetry would read and dissect Section VII of Idy's long poem "The Pornography of Pity":

Sorry Sade I say. I do
not feel sad for you
nor would you care me
to, which is even
sadder than the saddest
path that self-pity
ever rode on bare-
backed, bare, back on
abstract concepts—

poetic trots of no responsibility.
But this is not your ordinary cross-
word puzzle, cross in
the road, cross mad-
woman, crossing herself, genu-
flecting to the timid wind.
This is the real thump and crash
and bruise and bash over
the stone-strewn road
that no hooves will not crack over.
This is the nature that convulses

Over. Over
is what Sade said in bed.
Over. Over. Please Turn
Over. A new leaf(?)
one that does not grow
on the erotic tree
with its flash and ram-
ifications? Forget It.

Turn. Turn. Turn
and do not look back.
(This is worse, I thought, than turning
to salt with its awful pillar taste,
this lull in the lull-
a-by as I lie stunned, still.)
Goodbye, Sade said, *GOODBYE,*
he shouted bare-
backed, bareback
when so easily he galloped off.

≈ ≈ ≈ ≈ ≈

Yes, Idy and Dolph would clearly and keenly leave more than metaphoric
welts on each other. Ones that would never quite fade away on Idy's pale
skin or within her fragile self, as Idy would leave markings—initially less
visible—on Dolph. Ones that in the end he would not be able to rub out.

V

Fifteen years after that first casual encounter at the literary magazine office and thirteen years after he raped her, Idy Cometh left Randolph van Straaten's house, again broken.

Again, she was on that long ride home into what seemed like a clearer, cleaner air (which she really did know held as many pollutants as any other). Exhaling too much, her breathing becoming almost a pant—her whole being rising up to the verge of complete panic, her eyes barely able to focus on the road—the only sharp image coming to the fore was the face of Cecilia.

Although she didn't want to, Idy couldn't stop thinking about the poet Cecilia Slaughter—years gone—who, after her death, had become an icon in the poetry world, her reputation almost equal to that of Sylvia Plath's. Cecilia had grown up in a suburb just five miles north of the one where Idy lived. No, Idy didn't want to think about her—to make a parallel of their lives—but she couldn't help it, especially after what happened between Idy and Dolph thirteen years before. Idy truly didn't envy Cecilia Slaughter's after-death fame, as some others did, nor did she want for herself Cecilia's ending. Sure, she would privately think, that kind of universal acknowledgement for her own work would be great, but in life. After Dolph had raped her, Idy fought every day not to make Cecilia Slaughter's fate her own.

How she hated that Cecilia had lived in the next town. Its proximity to where she lived sometimes made her think that her backyard hung directly over Cecilia's grave.

VI

Cecilia Slaughter had killed herself approximately twenty minutes after she killed the critic Ivan Durmand. The newspapers had reported the murder/suicide with as much specificity as they could, seeking out any morbid, lurid, sad fact of their relationship. Several even excerpted Cecilia's novel right after it was posthumously published, in their magazine sections, which did detail at length Ivan Durmand's attack on her.

No, Idy Cometh hadn't any interest in such belated attentions or such a public revenge. She didn't even like the comparisons people made between her poetry and Cecilia's—not because she didn't believe Cecilia had been a great talent, but because it made her too anxious. She feared that people knew what had happened between her and "Dolph-the-Strap" and she wanted to deal with the rape in her own way—certainly far more discretely, much more indirectly, than what Cecilia had done.

Anyway, Idy believed her poetry was more submerged in metaphor when she wrote about Dolph than Cecilia's had been when writing about Ivan Durmand. That she was better at this because of the assistance she had from David. That their acts against Dolph helped sustain her and lead her work to a place where she could write about such abuse in a surreal or abstract way, yet any human being who had been hurt by another—and who hadn't?—could be touched by it, if only in their preconscious minds. At least that's what Idy hoped for in her hubris.

And she did do this so well at first that even Dolph didn't get it—or so she thought—for he continued only to praise her three books that followed the first. Which confused Idy a bit and eventually she did begin to question—both to herself and to David—"Why doesn't he get it? At least some of it, if he's such a great critic? Why doesn't he see that I'm referring to him? Why can't 'The Great Critic' see through the similes, the meta-phors? Why can't he see that this is about what had happened between us—*what he had done?*" As time passed, she ruminated over these ques-tions even more, while David listened, fairly quietly—taking all of it in, not letting anything out, yet.

It wasn't that she wanted him to get it, for she didn't. That frightened her too much. But she just couldn't help writing about the rape—its vio-lence—forever returning to it. Then, she'd wonder if Dolph took it all as a form of flattery. "Was he that twisted? Or was it that he just didn't care?"

Or maybe, Randolph van Straaten just wasn't finished with Idy Com-eth. Sadly, the latter thought never entered her awareness . . .

VII

"No," she cried, her face now completely masked by tears—it felt like spit secreted by a large insect now covered all of her skin—as she remembered Dolph's sweat of this night and how soaked she was in it. "I don't want to be the next generation's Cecilia Slaughter."

She *had* different plans and she had been somewhat successful with them, yoking in her rage both through her writing and, of course, with what she and David had done. Her "different sort of revenge" from the abuse she had suffered years before from Randolph van Straaten was always in motion, the clock of punishments for him set ticking with his initial, primal penetration.

Although now, a new thought had started to nag at her, one that would continue for the rest of her life—that Cecilia Slaughter would never have given Ivan Durmand a second chance. With this, the seed of her own stupidity grew as large as a diseased tree—its trunk and branches overhanging a swamp, its leaves wet, polluted, and sick. On this ride home the toxic tree was now covering her brain, soaking her mind—overwhelming any sane thoughts.

In her judgement she was becoming not a woman who lived in the Midwest, where she could be as resilient and changeable as the seasons, but rather a Southern one, who lived near predators in murky waters and was driven into madness by her own obsessive inclinations and profound misjudgments in getting too close to the creatures who lived nearby. She was becoming as hallucinatory as Susanna in *Raintree County*, as delusional as Blanche in *A Streetcar Named Desire*.

No, she was not romanticizing herself here; it was that Idy lived in far too literary a way and also believed too literally that such things as "poetic justice" did exist—a karma, of sorts. And her biggest mistake of all—that such a fairness could be exacted—that all insults, all debts, all bad deeds could be paid for, and with that, all scales of justice could be balanced.

VIII

As she entered the quiet of suburbia miles away from the intellectual, reptilian pit Dolph inhabited, her thoughts of Cecilia Slaughter grew larger—which made perfect sense, since it was at the same university that Ivan Durmand had attacked Cecilia. Something you just couldn't make up, its fabrication—the redundancy of such events, the similarity of them—would never have been believed. Idy reflected on this as she also considered Avigdor Element. For it was there that this much-decorated novelist, decades before, would line up a few of his most attractive female graduate students—topless—so he could choose one to take on his annual spring vacation trip to Bermuda—*wasn't it!?* She questioned this with both outrage and bewilderment. The stories of this happening in the late 1960s through the 1970s were still talked about. And it was said that one rather buxom blonde student of Element's—Christiane Juul—had actually won a Genius award. For what? Idy smirked. Then she said out loud to no one, wishing everyone could hear, as she hit her right hand on the steering wheel too hard, almost swerving the car into the curb, "No. Nothing's changed."

She also thought, as she did often, that at least Cecilia had a witness to Durmand's attack on her, even though the witness was just a dog. A year before the Durmand/Slaughter murder-suicide, which did spin a tornado into the murky puddle in which the poetry world existed, Durmand's dog had jumped off his roof. No one except Cecilia could report on the dog's life with such specificity—nor would dare to: how Durmand would kick the animal and leash her to the flat arm of his Toms-Price chair when she got in the way of any of his dark intentions. Cecilia had witnessed this and had written about it directly and expansively in her poetry and then in her posthumously published novel and had also made reference to it in the notes the police found in her apartment afterward. All of which are now meticulously archived at the very same university that had employed Ivan Durmand and now, Randolph van Straaten, and years earlier, the great Avigdor Element.

IX

Only once, when asked by the *New Yorker* for a statement upon Element's death in his hundredth year, did Christiane Juul open up a bit. "E"—as she was allowed to call him, along with a few others—had shared almost nothing about himself with the public, so what she said was devoured with great hunger and left everyone wanting more.

"Born in Hungary, he was captured by the Russians while serving as an Austrian officer on the Russian front and imprisoned in Siberia until 1917. After the Russian Revolution he rather quickly immigrated to Palestine and then to America and eventually to the university. He hated the way the Jews were treated. He hated their underdog status—their need to always be searching for a patch of land on which to live. He wanted so much more—more than a patch of everything, where he could spread the full force of his being onto this earth.

"My first assignment as his research assistant was to find his brother, which I could not. Most of his life and much of mine we searched. It was the one thing he felt he had failed at and he suffered it as an enormous insufficiency within himself. Few knew he had a lost brother and that he searched for him everywhere he went, whether in the records of governments or in the faces on the streets or in restaurants—the brother he had left in Hungary so long ago, the young Shemuel standing there with his huge, dark eyes tearing, waving to him as he, Avigdor, left: first for the Russian front, then returning to Hungary temporarily after the revolution—and after his imprisonment—then to Palestine and finally to America.

"He left the young Shemuel with the promise of his return, his protection. It was years later that he realized how much he needed to find him. Shemuel's face becoming more and more debossed into his dreams, haunting him more directly in his days—his look of innocence and trust that his older brother would come back for him and save him.

"In every book he wrote there was always a boy left and lost, whether in the center of the narrative or on the periphery—either way 'the boy' was always a force in E's emotional and creative universe.

"All of this—and all his history—I believe, was the basis of his need to dominate, embrace, take over, control everything in his life, and with this attitude he set a bad example for some of his finest male PhD candidates to follow—with those he was fondest of taking on the role of 'younger brother' whom he would instruct in the uses of power."

It was this last sentence that proved so controversial—everyone's curiosity building. And it was then that Christiane Juul disconnected her phone and became a complete recluse. To this day there are still rumors: "She's down there, somewhere near the university, perhaps writing—writing something, maybe the full, untold story."

≈ ≈ ≈ ≈ ≈

It should be added that parallel to Christiane's statement, the *New Yorker* reprinted one of the few poems Avigdor Element had written and published—published with them many years before—which reinforced a part of her statement and incited further arguments about this forever incendiary topic:

Pity Jerusalem
    by Avigdor Element

City of too many Sabbaths
that sleeps with one eye shut,
the other open, checking
if the gate is locked. Too many

donkeys and push-
carts roll down the narrow streets,
hauling the dead
to their respective gods.
Site of Supper and Sacrifice—
ascensions to heaven from
a cross or a stone—
a bullet, a message jammed
into the crevice of the body-broken
wall—*always the craving to reach*

God in this desert of deserted
space, where prayer rises
and falls like a cloud
come to fog. How many
amulets can be sold,
stuffed into pockets, hung on
necks thrust forward, looking
apish! How many clawed feet

can dig into an inch of land
until it gives itself up and caves in?

X

In Cecilia Slaughter's unpublished novel, a roman á clef if there ever was one—which, of course, got published rather quickly after her death to rave reviews—Idy had read that Cecilia believed the dog had reached her own breaking point with Ivan Durmand and Cecilia had concluded she committed suicide to get away from Durmand. The result of this being a continuing debate among dog experts, poetry critics, and literary biographers if it really could be characterized as such. "Could a dog *choose* to commit suicide, if so abused?" became the heightened question of the day.

Even two decades later, new opinions continue to be written, read, and presented sporadically at academic sessions of conventions such as the Modern Language Association and the Associated Writing Programs. It is still a sure thing to be accepted on to such a panel if one has a fresh angle on, or analysis of, this topic. The latest was last year at the MLA convention, entitled "Critics Critical of Their Poets/Pets." The auditorium was fully packed and many had to be turned away.

Thinking about this did bring a grin to Idy's face, even with all the physical and psychological pain she was now experiencing, and did help in evening her breathing and making the image of Cecilia's face and the gossip about Christiane fade—some.

Then, as the calming of her body improved, she returned to upping the ante of doing damage to Dolph's life. Even though at this point doing more made her sad for she truly believed this past year she and Dolph had been travelling a redemptive path . . .

≈ ≈ ≈ ≈ ≈

Driving through the sweet, moist, warm, early May air with her car's windows rolled down, she saw, with the help of the many streetlights and lit-up houses, the bursts of nature's renewal and the outside world's predictable, steady blooms, which stimulated her. Pushing through the wild, amorphous overgrowth of this evening's grief, she was temporarily able to turn her energy outward into the night with its promise of even more dazzling eruptions.

Then her mind uncontrollably revisited the darkness of Dolph's house. A little less hysterically—was it shock?—she went over how at the end, when he was through with her, he lay on his back and said, "I'm tired. Perhaps it's time for you to go. Go home to your husband or brother or *whoever* he is. Anyway, I think I'm getting a cold sore." Following this, he laughed, and with a self-satisfied sigh and a smile from his too-thin lips, he folded his arms behind his head, making of them a pillow, and uttered to himself, "I'm good." It was then Idy Cometh silently dressed and silently left. It was only in her car, after she started the ignition, that the trembling began . . .

As it did again full force when she reached within a mile of where she lived. And her poem "Directions to Where I Live" raced around in her brain and she screamed it into the dewy night air:

> "Pass the fragile hepatica and wild
> geraniums that trim the tollway,
> exit at Willow and travel east
> against the sun on its excitable
> noonday rise, ride with caution
> five miles to the street cordoned off
> the day they couldn't stop
> the crazy girl from shooting
> six children in school.
> Where the road ends, turn west
> for about a block, then north to Oak.
> It's second on the left,
> facing south, with the heart-

shaped blossoms dangling
on delicate arched stems
tangled below the windows—
a sheltered locale. Enter my house
as if it were my body,
with gentle eyes, trustworthy smile."

"He had praised that poem in his review of my first book," she shouted to her car's interior. "Didn't he know me? Didn't he care? Didn't he? DIDN'T HE?" she yelled, her voice then going to pathetic whisper, "Didn't he?" as she recalled in detail his attack of her thirteen years earlier, just four months after his public applause of her first book in the *New York Times*.

XI

She felt the chill deep inside her body against the warm, sultry spring air, as the surface of her inner thighs and upper arms began to swell, overheat, and ache from the recent, full weight of Dolph's body on hers.

Yet, sadly, after being in the car over an hour, all Idy Cometh could think of was, he didn't call me once on my cell phone to see if I'm okay— and, now, if I'd made it home safely. Then, after a few seconds she did laugh at the absolute idiocy of such thoughts and her continued expectation of any gesture of true concern from Dolph. That something she could/would do could actually reinvent (rewrite?) their miserable history—even though a large "I love you" had so easily slipped from the slit of his mouth, past his now yellowed teeth as prelude this evening, during their final coffee shop encounter in his efforts to re-engage her. Also, his mention of the "cold sore" now began to haunt her . . .

She would soon spend many hours on the computer looking at images of them as she did whenever she or David would develop a rash and then worry about all diseases of the skin. After all, that's how it had started with her mother so many long years before. "Idy," Naomi Cometh asked her small daughter three decades ago, "can you see this small bump on my neck? Can you feel it? Doesn't its color look peculiar?"

Now, in the months to come, on her decreasing entries into the outside world, she would stare at the lips of people who faced her, always looking for an incipient lesion or one in full blossom.

≈ ≈ ≈ ≈ ≈

In her bathroom was a large magnifying mirror attached to the wall and an equally large hand one on the radiator cover. Idy was always ready to see if she could figure out what was going on—what impending, or fully bloomed, occurrence she could capture and control, be it physical or psychological. She was always looking for the lost or buried cities in the fissures of the brain and in the body, as if the answers to existence and human behavior lay there—although she did leave some room for the metaphysical and the theological.

XII

It was better than thirteen years ago—wasn't it? Idy repeatedly tried to convince herself in the days after—still wondering about his emergent cold sore and wanting to question him more about where he had gotten it and if it were the sexually transmitted kind.

"Maybe he *had* missed me, did love me in a narcissistic, sadistic, kind of way? Maybe that was all he was capable of," she'd whisper as she tried to straighten her and David's house, or run small errands to the drugstore or the market or wait too impatiently for a friend for tea, while answering herself with reproachful sneers or quick, bitter laughs.

She Googled "Herpes" innumerable times and kept touching her lips as she imagined them beginning to tingle. Repeatedly looking in the mirror at her mouth, she saw nothing irregular and thought there's nothing here . . . nothing. Then she'd grin a wicked grin at her own image and the double meaning of her words, wondering if Dolph *were* far more clever than she—that perhaps she was completely out of her league in retaliation—that she and David were no match for The Devil From Hell.

≈ ≈ ≈ ≈ ≈

The grief of what had happened between them thirteen years earlier had left her hysterical for months—until, with David's help, they devised their plans. Yes, Cecilia Slaughter's rage after Ivan Durmand's assault and her final acts of aggression were obviously more direct, but Idy, in her arrogance, thought herself more clever.

However, more and more now, she silently would envy Cecilia for her "cleaner cut," if you could call it that, and eventually she, like too many others, would make of Cecilia the perfect, vengeful goddess—a mythic, archetypal creature.

Yet, her early plans for retaliation against Dolph had felt more true to who she was, who she had become, which also made her sad, for who she had become was not who she had set out to be. *Something that could also be said about so many.*

In the very beginning all she wanted to do was to write poems—small, incisive, diamond-like poems surrounded by clean, white silky space— that space being equally as precious. True, after the first attack her poetry did become less direct—more elusive, more obscure, and, in some ways with their hidden meanings, sharper—more universal, more of the universe. Quite the opposite of a "Willy O'Dell" kind of poem. Willy sold more books than any living poet and thought himself to be quite "wonderful"—believing himself incredibly envied. The more talented poets did find him, at best, quite jolly and, at worst, impossibly silly. The frivolity of his verse fading away as quickly as a sugary snack. He came to be known in not-so-closed circles as "Silly Willy." It was Dolph who first penned this moniker.

XIII

For a dozen years (only in this last one—the thirteenth—did she let up, to see if, in fact, Dolph had been "reborn") her writing had been focused on "an eye for an eye." Or, "an I for an I," as she would tell David, and they'd smile—contorted smiles as warped as their thoughts. As their deeds.

She'd also ponder whether Christiane Juul held any rage toward Avigdor Element, and if she did, where had she put it? Where did it go? As she would also wonder where Christiane was—where did she go? Except for her statement several years ago in the *New Yorker* it seemed as if she'd ceased to exist. "Had *she* recently quietly killed herself—or maybe she had just faded away and died?" Or if she survivies, how is she? *Could Christiane help her?*

≈ ≈ ≈ ≈ ≈

For now, as upset as she was and as much as she had come to idealize Cecilia, Idy Cometh still wanted to live and to continue to write poems, however odd they were increasingly becoming—as was Idy.

She tried to find a balm to balance herself, but then she returned to the lotion she had bought thirteen years earlier, called "Lethal," and once again covered her body with it each night before sleep and even wrote a poem called "Lethal." It was the name that had first drawn her to this scented lotion, because of how much she did want to die after Dolph's first attack—something to which she could not directly admit, although it was hard to fight off, hard to resist. And ten years ago, when Idy read that the lotion was going to be discontinued because it had coated the skin of too many young women after their suicide notes had been found, Idy bought enough of it to last for years, even though she was better and had promised herself never to use it again.

Its perfumed odor was actually quite lovely, a sachet of crushed wild-flowers. In its aroma lay the temptation to breathe it again and again and to smother her body with it—as were the temptations of Dolph's cumulative attentions and her own thoughts of him, of his possible reformation, and how she finally gave in and revisited his skin, his sweat.

XIV

After the first attack, during the flat, fallow rot of their relationship, Idy spent so much time focusing on Dolph, making the afterimages of his assault ever more horrific, more obscene, and yet she couldn't stop thinking about wanting "a correction" for what had happened.

She would, however, question herself over and over: "Just what kind of redemption, cure, CORRECTION, am I looking for?" There was no love song (Billie Holiday's rendition of "Mean to Me," Sarah Vaughan's "Smoke Gets in Your Eyes") or poem (Yeats's "Never Give All the Heart," Dryden's "Farewell Ungrateful Traitor") that Idy could ever latch on to that explained what was going on inside her, no self-help book (*Women Who Love Too Much; Get Rid of Him*) she could find that could stop her from thinking about Dolph both in the positive and in the brutally remembered negative. Also, his repeatedly positive reviews of her books didn't help. His plans for retaliation for what Idy had been writing paralleling her burgeoning creations . . .

When they would unavoidably be at the same poetry events, she would intentionally stay as far away from him in the room as she could. However, increasingly, as time passed, Dolph would carefully capture her attention—if just with a smile or a "so good to see you"—and a too-large, too-happy hope would well up in Idy, which she couldn't understand, so she just labeled it "sick." Yet, even with Dolph's decisive plan to "reconnect" with her, however pleasant he was in the years following the attack and however excited she silently was about this, Idy knew at some level that the matrix of the track she was on, starting with hers and David's subversive actions, made no good sense—that it was a maze with no positive, karmic way out.

The more deeply she traveled into the underground of her feelings about Dolph and her acts against him—all the while looking for guideposts and answers—the foggier the atmosphere became and the more the path mutated into a thickening, out-of-control bramble bush, its thorns fully prepared to tear into her as if they were a further punishment for her own bad form behavior. Although, she did consider Dolph's slow, but increasing, reappearances possible opportunities to get more clarity—the "why" of it, the "why" of any of it, the "why" of ALL of it.

XV

Idy was always looking for more clarity as to the "why of anything," and thought herself rather good in her investigations to understand things. Added to this, she couldn't let go of the hope that answers in all cases could lead to corrections. She romanticized that with more knowledge she could possibly reverse things, always carrying with her the sad belief that had she been older than six-and-a-half when Naomi Cometh had died, she could have learned something that would have protected her mother from death, be it a potion or a chant. She also believed that had her mother been alive all those lost years, Naomi Cometh could have helped her—saved her. And it was true that sometimes what Idy did, did temporarily help her, protect her, calm her. Yet, nothing had prepared her for Randolph van Straaten's entry and then reentry into her life.

$$\approx \; \approx \; \approx \; \approx \; \approx$$

Inspections, psychological, physical, and metaphysical, captivated her—books on medicine, philosophy, and religion sat on the table next to her writing chair. That's why many called her "Idy C"—the "C" of course a play on the word "see" and how in sync it was of her last name. Everyone who knew her well knew she was always looking to get inside of things. One of her favorite writing professors in college compared her mind to that of a Russian nesting doll where there could be found another smaller doll "living" inside the larger one. Idy liked this comparison—that inside the body of the large doll there existed a smaller one with more clarity. Her goal being someday to find the one that contained the most dolls—up to several dozen—with the smallest, innermost doll a baby lathed from a single piece of wood. For Idy, that would be the one that held "The Answer" as to why things were the way they were. That in the shape of its simplicity would lie "The Truth." The thought of this excited her spiritually and aroused her physically.

≈ ≈ ≈ ≈ ≈

Her grandmother, Ida—her namesake—was Russian. And although it was against Jewish tradition to name a child after a living person, Ida Brodsky Pinsky secretly very much liked it when her daughter, Naomi, insisted that she was going to name her baby daughter after her.

Ida had lost her grandparents to the camps. As an adult, Ida would only say, "Yes, sent to Dachau—once an artists' colony, once a place of beauty. The playground of kings and tsars—wasn't it?" Then, she'd laugh, an angry—almost demonic—laugh, in part because she had intentionally misdirected her audience to the wrong camp, which was perplexing and disturbing to those who knew her and also to herself. *As if she could change history*. Yet, the sarcasm of her tone could never hold back her voice from cracking a bit, however strong the stitch she made to tie down any show of heartbreak.

The camps had not only killed Ida's grandparents, they eventually killed her parents—their grief and survivor's guilt too deep, as they stood in their new land of "milk and honey"—it might as well have been quicksand.

Ida had escaped the Holocaust as a child, coming to this country when she was three and her parents in their mid-twenties. The small Ida Brodsky with her small family arrived in this country with a large hope and three huge, worn trunks, held together with six frayed straps.

Idy hadn't known her grandmother's history at all well—no one did, not even Ida's daughter, Naomi—except that when Ida's parents died within two months of each other from the flu, twelve years after their arrival and one year after World War II, the sixteen-year-old Ida went to live with distant cousins who had a son named Levi, whom Ida would marry.

Idy's grandfather Levi died young, too, years before Idy was born. His friends would lower their voices and nod their heads in unison, agreeing,

"That marriage to that sad, abrupt, aggressive woman didn't help—Levi had been a pawn." For it was well-known that Ida arrived into Levi Pinsky's house with some amount of wealth. Ida's grandmother had sewn the considerable family jewels into the lining of Ida's mother's fur coat and Froma Brodsky wore the coat across the ocean and it lay across the foot of her deathbed when she bequeathed it and its secrets to her daughter, Ida. It was then that Ida Brodsky took the coat, put it on, and wore it straight into Levi Pinsky's house.

Ida had kept so much of her own family's story to herself, even deliberately slurring the name of the shtetl where her family was so suddenly forced and where she was born and from which she and her parents had fled, so no one could find it on any map. More than once Idy had asked her grandmother to spell it, but each time Ida did, she said the letters too quickly for her small granddaughter to write them down and when Idy persisted, Ida Brodsky Pinsky would pull hard on her granddaughter's right ear to stop all such questioning. She was not a woman to be pushed around without consequences, which Idy in some ways enormously admired, and through the years of her own life Idy would have the impulse to yank at someone's ear when she wanted them to say more or to shut up; when she couldn't understand exactly what they were talking about or were asking *her* why she did the things she did—but she never acted on this urge, at least not directly.

≈ ≈ ≈ ≈ ≈

Idy viewed her mother's mother as an escape artist. Hadn't she escaped death, unlike the rest of her family? Hadn't she, however horrible it was, lived longer than her own daughter by forty years? Yes, to Idy Cometh, her grandmother had become the supreme escape artist who knew many tricks—knew many corrections, many secrets to living a strong, independent life—and Idy, too, hoped she could do that. It was what she aspired to—and unfortunately this became even more pronounced an obsession after Dolph's first assault—her plan being to escape what had happened to her as "artfully" as possible. The pitfalls in all this she refused to notice.

XVI

Precocious as a child, Idy craved as direct a vision as possible into every ex-
ploration. She was fascinated by speculation, investigation, precision, and
specula, believing that by looking "under rocks" or directly into cavities
she could see exactly what was going on—what was wrong—and thereby
create what she ultimately came to call "a correction." This feeling—this
hope, this fantasy, this fallacy—made her feel safe, or safer, for Idy Cometh never felt completely safe in this world and she was in continued disbelief that anyone really could—or did.

She'd say to David such things as, "Maybe the people who played golf
all year, following the consistent perfect weather around the country, had
the answer." Then she'd feel embarrassed for envying them, yet still craving their naïveté, nonchalance, stupidity, wisdom(?) or whatever it was,
and with her hands raised in bewilderment or despair—or both—continue: "Their game plan, to focus only on the putt, putt, putt of that small,
white ball into that little, empty hole, as if it were the filler, the plug, the
opium suppository, 'The Answer.'"

Being interested in all holes, she believed, would lead her to the larger
whole. All openings and the devices used to look into them intrigued
her—the tubes or blades of instruments that allowed for direct vision:
the nasal speculum with its two flat blades that, when the handles were
squeezed, spread the inside of the nose laterally; the aural speculum,
which looked like a funnel and came in a variety of sizes, for examining
the labyrinth of the ear; the rectal one, which resembled a tube that had
a removable bullet-shaped insert; the vaginal one, with its duckbill—the
two blades hinged and closed when inserted to facilitate entry, and how,
when opened, it could be arrested by a screw mechanism so that "the op-

erator" was freed from keeping the blades apart and thereby more able to get the fullest view. In this instance, starting thirteen years ago, the operator in her mind was always Dolph and she wondered what she might have looked like to him and, of course, what he felt when he saw her so completely, so totally exposed. Whatever it was, it was the furthest thing from love—actually a deep hate, perhaps for all women, starting with his mother: her long legs, her large breasts, her mouth the perfect funnel for a vodka bottle.

Of course, she was more than a little worried that she could never really correct what had occurred years before by this time consenting to being spread so physically and emotionally wide for him, even though he primed her with grand praise about her brilliance as a poet ("Haven't I shown *this* to you in all my reviews of your books?" he'd say) and huge apologies of what he called his "runaway passion" for her—for what had happened, what he had done. She had read many psychology textbooks on men like Dolph and that for such men there was rarely a cure. And yet, and yet again, she secretly couldn't give up the splinter of hope that he could be fixed—that if she found the right "tweezers," the one with the perfectly angled tip, she could pull out all his rage and correct him.

XVII

"A second chance for me—for us," he'd plead in various coffee houses around the city, leaning forward, his new rimless spectacles on, his face cleanly shaven, a breath mint recently popped onto his tongue. And with this Idy did begin to feel hopeful, saying to herself in a café's ladies' room, "Yes, this would wash away the ugliness of what had happened. A cleansing. 'The Cleansing.'"

She began to believe she was the beneficent heroine in some romance novel. Although she had never read even one, she had seen enough junk television—the soap operas of rape, revenge, and redemption relaxed her. "In General Hospital hadn't Luke raped Laura, but then they fell in love and got married? Yes. Of course, everything after that was downhill," as Idy recalled Laura's spiral into madness. Idy couldn't remember if Laura's mother had warned her. But, then again, Idy didn't have a mother to warn her—Naomi was long gone.

≈ ≈ ≈ ≈ ≈

Now, with this present end result of Dolph's pursuit, Idy felt she had become part of a hardcore pornographic script—a very badly written one at that, although weren't they all? she'd question. She had only seen one such movie, *The Devil and Miss Jones*, and had walked out in the middle—when the snake was about to enter Miss Jones's vagina. *Dolph.*

XVIII

It became clear to Idy, after Dolph's reentry into her life—and his second concrete inner space journey into her—that he was as cruel as ever, but this time the damage, the filth of it—"The Cold Sore Of It," as she now called it—was proving even worse for her psychologically. "Maybe because I'd never gotten fully clean of it the first time? Maybe because I'd given him a second chance without examining it more thoroughly? Maybe because I'm the stupidest woman on the planet Earth?"

She became all reproach for herself as she began to pull out her hair. Then, upon remembering Cecilia Slaughter's hair-twirling and head-picking, which Cecilia had made reference to in so much of her poetry and her novel, Idy would quickly put her hand down. Yet, she couldn't stop tearing into the psychology of herself, the reexamining and deconstructing of her own behavior and flagellating herself for who she was—who she had become. Sometimes she would slap her face so hard that the end result on several occasions would be a bruised cheek or a blackened eye.

Finally realizing that perhaps she couldn't do the best job of helping herself—that maybe she needed professional help—after much research she found a female therapist whom she hoped she could be honest with, because, "After all, how could a man understand?" Although she did consider Dr. Sam Guttmacher, the esteemed psychiatrist who lived so near the university and knew so much of its history, its many stories. But he was far into his nineties and, anyway, she had just learned he had recently retired. Still, she wished he were available. He would have been a good choice. He had a great love for artists, especially poets. It was said he had known Wilfred Owen well—that Owen had saved him in the trenches during World War I. And that he had Owen's poem "Arms and the Boy" framed and signed to him in his office.

≈ ≈ ≈ ≈ ≈

Returning to her self-recriminations: "I did return—return to the 'sick scene of the sad crime.' 'The sick crime of the sad scene.'" She now, in the days after the not-quite-assault, rather "his horrid, planned insult," flipped and flopped her language even more. Her self becoming a fish out of water flailing on the hostile ground, her mind a foreign country called "subtext" where the inhabitants sometimes spoke in puns, a place where everything had double meanings and every sentence contradicted the previous one— where everyone had double intentions. She even began to make David take things back twice if he said anything that disturbed her further or had what she considered two messages, as if the two times Dolph had entered her had become a double entendre for just about anything she said, or was said to her.

She knew she needed help . . .

XIX

When Idy entered the upscale house—even for this upscale North Shore suburb—and went into the enormous living room to wait, as she was told to do, there were many pillows—all needlepointed—carefully positioned on the three large couches, two overstuffed chairs, and two elaborately sculpted wooden ones with plush upholstered seats. Many of the pillows had the face from different angles of a striking woman with blond hair.

There was also a huge—ceiling to floor—regal portrait of a woman with blond hair from the eighteenth century on the far wall. The obvious implication being that she was royalty. As Idy was studying the painting's overdone courtliness and the elegant mishmash of furniture from different eras, Dr. Ariella Greenberger announced herself in full glory. Her bleached hair had several shades of blonde in it and was carefully dyed red at the tips. Idy quickly thought it looked as if a lampshade trimmed with fringe had been dropped onto Dr. Ariella's head. She wore an orange feathered boa wrapped twice around her neck, a chartreuse tunic, and black pantaloon pants, topping all this off—or rather bottoming it all out—with designer cowboy boots that had brightly colored flowers painted on them. Idy stood up and smiled—not from any great pleasure of meeting her, but from the expensive hodgepodge both on Dr. Ariella and in the room. She thought it almost funny and questioned how anyone who lived and dressed such a mess—however high priced—could bring any clarity to my own mind.

Idy became double-sure of this after sitting down in her large office—cushioned with yet more pillows of a much-too-positive facsimile of Dr. Ariella's face. That nothing of value could be talked about with this woman, however sweet her surgically lifted smile, which revealed too-thick, too-white, capped teeth. She reminded Idy of her stepmother, Mitzi, all made up in celebration of herself, except Dr. Ariella had several degrees attached to her name, which were ornately framed on her expensive, off-white, grass cloth walls, whereas Mitzi Cometh had none, unless you counted her line of last names from deceased husbands as accomplishments—which, money-wise, they were.

Added to all this was "Gerda," a German shepherd, laying on the floor, her cubic zirconia–studded leash looped into the arm of the chair where Dr. Ariella sat. Whatever statement was intended by the dog's presence was lost on Idy, for all she could think of was Cecilia's reportage of Ivan Durmand's German shepherd and her leap off his roof and with this Idy wondered if Gerda, too, wanted to commit suicide because she was tethered to the unending, high-pitched gush of Dr. Ariella's voice.

The rest of the furnishings—aside from the large, dark-haired dog—were a calm off white and the only thing that intentionally popped inside the room were the pillows, the hand-carved gilt frames, and Dr. Ariella herself, where she collected large amounts of money from anguished women, allowing her to pile on more necklaces and bracelets, which Idy also noticed with each additional visit, distracting her further. "From the Southwest, Greece, Africa, Singapore!" Dr. Ariella spurted. The places she had travelled, which she was quick to bring up whenever Idy mentioned anything geographical, however local.

After eight sessions of asking Idy the same questions at least twice (it was clear to Idy the woman was having memory problems) and Dr. Ariella saying—with what seemed a rote, faux empathy—to just about anything Idy told her, "We are ALL just wounded healers," Idy quit. It was obvious to Idy that she was liked by this woman, for she called her six times, asking, "When will you be back?" Finally, she stopped making excuses for her cancellations and let her answering machine deal with Dr. Ariella's chirps, which Idy would then quickly erase. How easily I can leave her—dismiss her—Idy thought, and wished she could do at least a quarter as well with Dolph.

XX

With the failure of her visits to Dr. Ariella, Idy's cleansings of herself escalated, giving even more attention given to her mouth and, of course, to her other openings. Her mind, too, increasingly became an incubator of viral thoughts she could not wash out. She now saw herself as completely diseased, as David watched, helpless . . .

She could not deny that she had been given enough cues and clues that Dolph hadn't changed, as he so relentlessly had proclaimed: "Idy, I'm so much better with reining in my powerful emotions." With his calls to her rather erratic this past year, she'd now wonder if the gaps between them had meant he was having a full-fledged outbreak of the herpes virus or just "reconnecting" with other women. Silence, then a barrage of calls with his sudden longings for her presence, giving her little time "to be there." His reasons for his long pauses sometimes too vague or nonsensical.

She'd listen intently to his excuses and then would often mark her calendar with the word ENOUGH and not pick up the phone the next time. But there were many calls and her resolve always weakened, no matter how many ENOUGHS were threaded through the weeks and days and hours of the past year. And she met him, again and then again.

Part of her attraction to him was that his reviews were as acerbic as ever—except for the superb ones he gave her and a few others who she believed actually deserved them. In their world, which reeked of hyperbole and cronyism, most of what he wrote was refreshing and to her mind fairly accurate. However, with his inconstant behavior, she did begin to look under what he was saying to her. She would come home from their encounters and write down his words—sometimes even taking notes right afterward in her car. She did study their subtext. She wanted to be careful, but, then again, she also wanted that correction. She'd ask herself, "This is good, isn't it?"—that question mark always following her like the stepped-on, broken tail of a small animal.

≈ ≈ ≈ ≈ ≈

Idy Cometh knew that night, after Randolph van Straaten had plumbed the depths of her that second time, that in the not-so-deep recesses of his being, pure evil festered and that this time she had ALLOWED herself to be touched by it. But as a panhandler sweats in his stamina to find gold, Idy sweated in her stamina to find her correction, ultimately just finding herself filled with devil's milk. No Freud. No Jung. No Ariella Greenberger could have saved her. Not even the renowned Dr. Sam Guttmacher, if he had been available—of this she was sure.

XXI

When she got within a few blocks of her house, she parked the car so as to calm herself further, for she worried that David would be waiting in full alert and he would see both her inner and outer dishevelment when she entered the house. David, with whom she had shared this place for over three decades. David, who was always there for her—David, her "half-brother," her "half-husband," although they weren't related by blood or certificate.

Her father had brought Mitzi and David Adler into their house a little over thirty years ago. Mitzi became Sidney Cometh's second wife and his worst nightmare. Idy's mother had passed away the year before. Mitzi had already buried three husbands: suicide, heart attack, stroke. David was the result of his mother's third marriage. Upon learning Mitzi's history, Idy quite understandably worried that Mitzi would bury her father, too. Especially after the then-nine-year-old David filled her in on details of his mother's life. "Yes," they agreed with nervous giggles, as they shook their child heads mopped with curls—still innocent haloes over them—"Mitzi Adler was a husband killer." After this, Idy worried every day for her father's life.

When first introduced to Mitzi, Idy couldn't help but think of how her last name was the same as that of a snake—but she was mistaken, for she heard "Adder" instead of "Adler." Still, the more experience Idy had with Mitzi, combined with what she'd learned in second grade about the snake—it being responsible for more fatalities than any snake in Africa—led her association of Mitzi with the puff adder to stick. With Mitzi's arrival, the entire atmosphere in her house changed so much that it made Idy feel that she was in fact living in a foreign country, one she knew little about—one with a large and poisonous creature who could kill.

After Naomi Cometh died, during their year of being alone together, Sidney Cometh had covered all the snake pictures in Idy's second-grade book with the cardboard backings that came with his shirts when they were returned from the cleaners. Idy had a terrible fear of them ever since she was three and a neighbor boy of ten had cut one in two and dropped the still-wiggling tail part down the back of her clean white pinafore. Even now, coming across one in a book or seeing one in a movie will make her scream, and with her father's introduction of Mitzi "Adder" Adler into her life, Idy felt a similar terror begin to crawl down her back.

≈ ≈ ≈ ≈ ≈

Predictably, Mitzi's demands, which had begun with husband number one, were carried into Idy's and her father's home. Her need for more—more shoes and jewelry and furs—did make her "more," as in attractive and noticeable. With her curvaceous form and platinum blond–dyed hair, she did, when gussied-up, make heads turn with her hysteria of perfume, hair spray, and expensive cloth and color.

Idy was the opposite of all of this, with long black hair parted to one side and casually swept into a ponytail, the whole effect being that of a thoroughbred—be it person or horse. "What long legs! A thoroughbred!" Idy's mother Naomi would exclaim to her husband about this daughter they had produced. Then, the gentle, self-deprecating Naomi would say, mostly to herself, "How did I give birth to a thoroughbred?"—even though Naomi Cometh was herself quite beautiful in the most unadorned and natural of ways, before disease turned such fairness to bruise and rot. With her untouched auburn hair, soft brown eyes, and wide smile that exposed perfect, naturally white, even teeth, Naomi Cometh was memorably lovely.

≈ ≈ ≈ ≈ ≈

Idy's long black lashes that would never need mascara and her naturally pink lips—inherited from Naomi—that would never need any extra embellishment, made Mitzi hate her stepdaughter at first sight. Mitzi, being so trained in the illusion of perfection, could see that Idy, even at seven-and-a-half, would need no help in trying to achieve it, for it had already arrived. Idy would never need a dressing table cluttered with mascara, eyeliners, powders, creams, concealers, or any other concoctions to fuss with to present herself as perfect in public. It was a scary fairy tale scenario—father, daughter, stepmother, and doom to follow.

So it was inevitable that with the arrival of Mitzi Adler, Sidney Cometh in his temerity stopped complimenting his daughter, for he, too, could feel Mitzi's fury toward Idy. Idy noticed her father's growing distance from her quickly, although he had never been a particularly warm man, except for that year—that "awful time" as they came to call it—when Naomi left. Then, Sidney Cometh did hug his daughter a lot, even hold on to her as they silently sat together and watched too much television. Idy liked this, almost to the point of feeling guilty that it was the result of her mother's death, and she missed it so much after the "Adder's" arrival into their house. And she would look for it more and more as she grew older in the coldest of men. Men who were capable of creating the illusion of warmth where there was none. Randolph van Straaten being the master magician of this trick.

XXII

David knew his mother to be "a witch" and he and Idy would pretend they were the children in a Grimm's fairy tale—in particular for Idy, "Snow White," for she hated doing anything domestic and anyway the Seven Dwarfs were so efficient with the household tasks.

Sometimes she and David would lie naked behind the dense yew bushes in the backyard, their hair laced by Idy with picked flowers, which Idy also inserted into each of their openings—ears, mouth, buttocks . . .

She would even make up little plays for David and her to perform—their only audience being the trees and carefully planted flowers—always insisting that David play the evil mother, for, "After all," she'd say, "you brought 'the witch' into *my* house." David went along with this for he had learned under Mitzi's fist to be agreeable and cooperative, and he also enjoyed these permissions to be mean, demanding, irrational, and experimental—something Mitzi never allowed. Plus, he had quite quickly fallen in love with his new, unconventional stepsister, whom he would always love and protect as much as he could in his earnest yet seemingly impotent ways.

As the years passed and Idy realized she couldn't change her father's awful mistake of marrying Mitzi Adler, no matter how much she wished it every night, when she came to think of David as the correction for this, it did help. Just as David tried to help her correct the fact of Dolph's existence after the rape. For David eventually came to believe in corrections, too—perhaps even more so than Idy.

XXIII

Ultimately, Idy's worst fear was realized when she was sixteen. Sidney Cometh died suddenly—a blood clot in the brain. An explosion of blood. Idy imagines to this day that's where all pressures placed on him by *that woman*—as she came to call her—coagulated, and the silent rage he felt toward Mitzi had imploded there. That the inside of her poor father's head became one large encapsulated blood blister from all the years of *that woman's* pus. The pressure he was under from her grew so obvious to Idy when, within the year of Mitzi's entrance, he became short of breath. From then on his face took on an almost constant unhealthy flush, which disgusted Mitzi so much she'd flee the house even more frequently to shop and God-knows-what. Mitzi liked men too much—compliments that too obviously invited supple complements to slide into her. The shrewd ones gave her both, then left in a rush.

≈ ≈ ≈ ≈ ≈

Mitzi's collective inheritance from all four husbands made her a wealthy woman, and two months after she buried Sidney Cometh, she moved away to Miami, leaving David and Idy alone in the house, which had been included in Idy's inheritance. Of course, this infuriated Mitzi, however irrational it was, and she told everyone with great disgust, "*She got the house.*" In Miami, Mitzi lived quite close to Idy's grandmother. But Ida would have nothing to do with any of them—Idy included. She would never forgive Idy for allowing Mitzi into her deceased daughter's home. It was the most bitter, irrational, cruel act of Ida Brodsky Pinsky's life. And try as she could,

Idy could never figure out her grandmother's behavior—the "why" of it—which only made her try harder with people who were just as difficult.

≈ ≈ ≈ ≈ ≈

David and Idy went to the same university, David becoming an architect and Idy a poet. Both liked creating things, their goals similar—to produce a perfect, pared-down-to-essence structure, be it a building or a poem. Both craved a correction for their childhoods of garish accumulation, excessive demands, and caked-on vanities. In loss—or less—both could see a plus.

XXIV

Idy now believes the rumors—however quiet—were true. That all the student/ professor troubles at the university started with the arrival of Avigdor Element. It was said: He could be all oxygen or all arsenic or all helium—having only a boiling point, never melting. At least not in the conventional ways we think of people as being capable of becoming softer. And sometimes he could be all nitrogen—that smothering substance. His words were considered all gold for they won him many awards, large sums of money, and the highest "word" praise—the Nobel Prize. Yes, he was still talked about as a pure substance that refused to decompose into a simpler one. And with Christiane Juul he did suck away her breath—only to be reborn when she'd hear his deep, commanding voice.

Yet, like a star in the universe-worn sky as it grows older, it does decay and come to an end, blow itself apart like a bomb, remaining in space until it's drawn into the core of other stars, other astronomical bodies—Ivan Durmand, Randolph van Straaten . . . Ivan being Avigdor's graduate student, then colleague, with Dolph taking the same route with Ivan, both were allowed to directly call him 'E," as were Christiane and a few others—especially those Avigdor or Ivan had mentored.

The air on that campus polluted three scholarly and creative generations and almost sixty years of female students and visitors—most especially the "prettiest" ones.

Of course, everyone knew "Element" was not really his last name. (No one, it seemed, knew his real one.) Although Idy had never met him, the legend of him, now more hushed, was still long-winded and Idy did listen. Even after he moved to Palm Springs in his late years, it seemed as if one could still find him in his large paneled office on campus, left as it was—as a monument.

Avigdor Element kept to himself his real last name as he did many other things—the unending permissions he gifted himself as if he had been anointed by some royal court. He knew the name "Element" would always be associated with what was essential, what no one could live without. The "Avigdor" he was born with and he kept. And he liked giving permission to those closest to him to call him "E," as if he were the 119th addition to the periodic table—although many called him this, just not directly to his face, pretending to others that they, too, were so included, so special.

≈ ≈ ≈ ≈ ≈

Avigdor Element became Christiane's mentor and lover—her first, last, and only muse. So it was inevitable that ultimately he also became her silencer, when he'd tear up what she had written because he thought himself too exposed—that he was *too* present. Her initial express lane to success came easily as he hacked a path for her with his tongue sharp as a scythe. One call from him and she had a publisher, then a "Genius award" with a large amount of cash. Then, he became her only reader, for after she began to make her own name in literature, he destroyed her work.

This became most acute and final after marrying his third wife and honeymooning with her on a photographic African safari. It was then that Christiane experienced a huge despondency and turned from writing fiction to poetry. Upon "E's" return, he saw a poem of hers that had recently been published in the *American Poetry Review,* entitled "Goose Pity," and raged at her almost uncontrollably. He read to her a section and screamed, "How can people *not* know *this* is about me?" Then he made the bewildered, shaken Christiane read it out loud to him:

> "It was the stiff flight feathers,
>   the down underneath,
>   that I can't forget.
> How he swam into me, all

grace—the white-blur flutter.
Some days I remember him
as huckster, trickster, monster;
others as the god transformed, zeroing
in on me—the waiting, blazing center.
How mythic. How cliché.
Either way. Better than OK.
Woo. Wound. Woe, Whoa.
I'd scream too loud
How Strange, so he found
another—quieter—and now
I find him only
for certain filling up my page."

After this, she stopped seeing him, wouldn't take his calls, went into therapy. But every day he persisted with grand, desperate pleas that he couldn't
live without her, which she almost believed, and that she was not *just* hurt-
ing him by cutting him off, but more importantly, his writing, which they
both knew was even larger than himself. So she returned to him for "literature's sake" and, also, for what she knew to be true—for herself. Whatever enormous nourishment it was, she re-entered their symbiotic—and
some would say, "sick"—relationship. It seemed a necessary act for both
of their existences.

≈ ≈ ≈ ≈ ≈

Starting out as his student, then his researcher, then his "singular, most
precious mistress" from the age of twenty-one until his death at 100,
Christiane was always that. Never to be one of his four wives. "That small
honor," he would joke to her, "was bestowed upon women with dull hair
who were good typists."

"Yes," he would say as he'd sit naked behind her nakedness, both of
them rubbing her nipples, his head buried in her thick, long blond curls
that swirled well past her shoulders to the middle of her back, "You are for

pleasure's sake, my greatest. For marriage I need someone less lustrous; you are too large!" He even took great pleasure in her name and played with it, repeatedly calling her, "My Christian Jew-el. My exquisitely cut, perfectly set, pure as sunlight, fiery diamond," while Christiane wondered with great worry what her devout Lutheran parents would make of his talk—and their acts. Then he'd laugh a grand laugh and heave her a command to spin around, lie down, and spread her legs in order to bring her center up toward his impatient eyes and mouth. He loved her reluctance, and her acquiescence. He loved her continued, authentic shyness and he loved looking inside her and saying, "Yes, very healthy." His eyes and tongue his specula, with Christiane's karma a quick fame and then a slow shredding of it because of Avigdor's power and paranoia.

XXV

In the time left to her, Mitzi continued to live in the hot Florida sun, blazing into and through the lives of even more men. None dared to marry her, but that didn't matter, for all of them sequentially dropped into those rectangular holes of the Jewish cemetery adjacent to the golf course that bordered her large condo—its insides upholstered with well-cushioned furniture and decorated in calm hues of blues and yellows. Idy, on her infrequent visits, was quick to take notice of this décor and the burgeoning of large, cushiony pillows Mitzi had placed there, giving the deceptive appearance that she had grown softer, while David just became increasingly unfocused and inattentive to all things "mother."

On her final visit Idy recognized—how could she not?—Mitzi's attempt to morph further back into youth—into Idy! With her black aerobic tights, which couldn't contain or smooth her now thick, lumpy thighs, and her pink leather ballet flats, with the fat of Mitzi's feet bulging over their soft edges, Idy was shocked. But more appalling, more frightening, to Idy was that Mitzi had let her hair grow long and had dyed it shoe-polish black, parting it to one side and sweeping the tired, thinned, broken strands into a sickly wisp of a ponytail. With this, Idy cut her stay short, leaving just twenty-four hours after she arrived, David hurrying after her.

≈ ≈ ≈ ≈ ≈

When Mitzi died from the anesthesia of a third face-lift, and a further attempt to chisel her nose, neither David nor Idy buried her. This was left to some semi-retired rabbi who did these kinds of services at least twice a week. By then her son and stepdaughter had carved their own paths for preservation—ones that so easily intersected with each other.

When not working, they went everywhere together. The one exception being this past year, when Idy would leave to see Dolph. David would wait at home like a worried, but all-too-permissive mother: saying to her, "Please don't go; he's not good for you," and then forgiving her when she went. He didn't want to force the issue for fear she'd tell him to leave; it fed into a panic that occasionally would rise up in him that he'd be lost without her. That he'd choke—that there would be no air. He needed her to be near. Plus, he did like helping her with her acts and plans to ruin Dolph, although no matter what they did—the letters, the calls, all their anonymous warnings to others—they believed it only added a mild confusion to Dolph's life, as if someone sporadically sprinkled pepper on his favorite dish, ruining it.

Publicly, he seemed to hold his place—his high position. However, they did feel it was the best they could do short of "buying a gun." Idy would constantly say no to David's suggestion of this, with David forever saying, "I know a man who knows a man," which Idy never really believed was true. "Just talk."

Yes, Idy was adamant that she would not become Cecilia Slaughter and refused to consider there be any gun, any murder. Although David truly and adamantly liked repeating, "I know a man who knows a man," especially in the early months after the rape thirteen years ago.

≈ ≈ ≈ ≈ ≈

The fact was, David *did* know a man who knew a man who would kill a man.

XXVI

Finally, Idy drove into the driveway and saw the front door lights were on, as were the ones in the garage. "Yes, he's still up," she sighed, and then stopped the car, moving the rearview mirror to focus on her face. It was aflame with an uncontained fury and looked swollen.

Then she looked at the two crabapple trees that bordered the door's entry. The apples were at the tiny balloon stage—red-purple buds reminding her of her bruises from Dolph thirteen years before. In the next weeks the trees would flower to bride white and the thought of this made Idy cry.

As she entered the kitchen through the garage door, David approached her from the library and immediately saw her wild disorganization—both physical and psychological. He had been trying to wait patiently by reading some convoluted spy thriller—where the male character was both heroic and not-so-borderline sociopathic—but in the last half hour the book could no longer hold him and he just kept rereading the same page, which he found to be ironic, for wasn't that what he'd been doing with his life anyway—especially with Idy, with not barring her from her returns to Dolph? He was familiar with mocking himself, calling himself a "dunce" and "moronic." Mitzi had set the stage for this name-calling, provided the script, the props. All he had to do was show up for the walk-through.

Since he didn't know how to stop Idy from spending any more time with Dolph—no matter how much he tried to reason with her—and he was incapable of raging at her with threats that he'd leave if she saw him one more time, his anger was left to drain into a large trough, sick with worry, jealousy, and a not-so-submerged wrath.

≈ ≈ ≈ ≈ ≈

His worst fears on this particular evening were confirmed, for no matter Idy's efforts to fix her hair, straighten her clothes, and apply fresh lipstick in the garage, she was not successful. Her whole self was a tinderbox ready to explode—her major distress emanating from her eyes, a burning chaos pushing out from them. A Gordian knot of upset had redoubled itself inside her body from which she would never be able to free herself. It was way too late. David saw this and a fire ignited within him and he, too, felt that he might detonate.

However, controlled and quietly as he could, he asked, "Do you want to do something *more?*" Idy nodded weakly and then said, "David, I'm sorry." At first, he thought she meant "sorry" that they would have to "do something more," but he then realized it was for what had gone on with her this particular evening, for she continued, "I need to shower. I really need to shower"—and ran upstairs and slammed the bathroom door. Immediately he heard the sound of running water, which seemed to last forever.

After staying in the shower, scrubbing herself for over a half hour, Idy emerged, dried herself, and brushed her teeth too hard, as if she were trying to remove all filth that might still be lodged inside her mouth. Her gums bled. She felt like one of those rare, tropical birds who were victims of the deadly oil spill of last year. No one could get them clean enough, their elegant shape—their beauty—of no help to them now that they were soaked in so many toxins—no hand able to save them, human or metaphysical other. She took a hairbrush to her long, wet hair, trying to untangle it, then started beating her head with it, trying to knock something out of it or hurt herself—or both—as if the troubling aches of her body weren't enough. She bit her left wrist and was only satisfied when she could see her teeth marks in it and the small markings of blood. She tugged at her right ear the way her grandmother had done to her when she was little and had asked too many questions, was too curious.

It was late—almost three—when she lay her naked, clean self between the sheets that felt like silk compared to the stiff, sperm-soaked ones on Dolph's bed. She recalled how he complimented her nakedness: her pale skin, the shape of her breasts—their firmness and most especially, her nipples. "Ah," he sighed, "the color and shape of two huge, ripe raspberries. Yes, how I remember. I'd never seen any like these before—or since." How he voraciously feasted on each, which at first aroused her and then made her yell from pain, exciting Dolph further as he bit into them harder.

Hearing David's soft, well-paced breathing next to her (thanks to his taking twenty milligrams of Valium) she felt temporarily safe and fell into a sleep devoid of Dolph or anything else—a gift. It was only in the mid-morning that she awoke in full fright, remembering what had happened the night before.

She tried to distract herself by thinking about how much Dolph had aged—his body hair all gray, his nipples now surrounded by fat, making his own breasts the same size as some women's. He was aware of this, but like everything that was his and everything he did, he knew how to put a positive spin on it, by asking, "Would you like to suck *my* breasts?" so as to give her encounter with his aging chest an erotic twist.

Then, the railing against herself began—self-recriminations that now would never stop. "How could I have believed anything I could do would change him? Who in their right mind would ever understand this need for a correction!?" She looked over to where David slept, except he had left for work with his concrete plans for other people's dreams—the beautiful homes they would come to live in, hope to be safe in. She looked at her body—the numerous bloody cuts on her nipples and the red bruises on her breasts, upper arms, and inner thighs that were beginning to form, and she wondered if David had seen them.

≈ ≈ ≈ ≈ ≈

Dolph didn't call the next day or the day after, as Idy waited by the phone hour after hour, calling herself names like "idiot" and "whore." All those coffee shop talks where Dolph leaned forward, whispering and repeating, "For fifteen years—ever since we first met—I've never stopped thinking about you. Give us a second chance Idy, we both deserve it." And Idy Cometh, in what she now was calling her "primal stupidity," thought this could be the greatest correction of all. That she, "I. Cometh," like some kind of Christ in his second coming, could fix a Judas, an Adolph. Such hubris, she thought, as she tore out a healthy, long strand of hair from her head.

XXVII

In this last year, every time they met, Dolph would compliment Idy on some miscellaneous and rather dull item she was wearing: a pair of well-used boots she had worn before with him, her drugstore sunglasses, an old wool winter coat that—it was true—she liked a lot, but only for its detective look. These compliments seemed so random and without taste (did he have none?)—off base—and she'd wonder if he owned an outdated textbook on seduction that recommended a man compliment a woman on "any old thing," leaving her waiting and wanting—so hungry for him to land on the right thing, meaning her whole being. She'd remember how much she had longed for this from her father and the "sweet year"—as she secretly came to call it—they had together after her mother's death, which continued to make her feel both guilty and happy. But she also knew Naomi Cometh would have understood this need in her daughter, for Naomi, too, had yearned for such attentions from her husband, which she received while he was courting her and quickly evaporated after their marriage. In truth, Sidney Cometh had begun to dry up long before Naomi's sickness and death. With Mitzi, initially, he thought he saw an oasis—a flash of flesh and color, however garish—and felt an unexpected welling up of the juice of life.

≈ ≈ ≈ ≈ ≈

When Dolph was giving Idy his unfocused compliments, Idy would sometimes try hard to see them from a different angle. Wasn't there a sweet awkwardness in how he presented her with these strange flatteries; wasn't it sort of endearing? She'd both ask herself and doubt any validity to this thought at the same time.

She would sit across from him, his large face and too-blue eyes looking so earnest, her well-combed, loosened hair blanketing her shoulders, her body smooth and unmarked—completely healed from his long ago attack, unlike her forever-strained mind, and listen to him talk. "I used to think you were the one who wrote the letters," he said to her more than once. It was at these moments that Idy would try to steady herself further—not fidget even an inch—as he'd continue, "You know, those letters, those calls, almost killed my career," nervously adding another, "you know." Idy liked this, for Randolph van Straaten rarely, if ever, used extra words, and what this meant was that he was unsettled, nervous. And she had made him that. She was learning that what she and David—and maybe others—had done really *did* have more of an effect on him than they'd imagined, and this couldn't help but please her.

Listening to him, Idy envisioned all the women and their husbands and his own two ex-wives whom he had hurt, and she felt they would be pleased that there had been such articulate rants against him, whether or not she had participated in them. She thought, maybe many people spoke out against him, sometimes almost believing that she had nothing to do with any of it. Or even if she had, that she was a member of some good faith religion and an evildoer with an oily tongue had taken it over and now the steadfast, the faithful were trying to overthrow their satanic leader.

Yet, sometimes when she'd calmly sit across from him at these coffee shop encounters, Idy couldn't help picturing him from thirteen years before, pushing her against the wall of his bedroom, pulling her onto his messed bed, tearing off her clothes with no concern that he was permanently ruining them, and spreading her legs with the full force of his powerful, sculpted knees—the legs he inherited from his Rockette mother. How afterward he had offered her some old, used makeup—lipstick, foundation—left there by some other woman, and said with absolutely no affect, "to fix your face"—cover the scratch marks from *that chin*. How his presentation of these items, right after everything else he had just done to her, made her run into his bathroom and double up with seizures of vomit.

Then, she'd shove these memories into the overflowing dust bin in her mind that she created long ago and she'd listen to him further, thinking, I can't correct the world's miseries, but perhaps he's paid enough. The karmic actions of what's been done to him have been sufficient, perhaps even have healed him. At least that's what she hoped. If nothing else, Idy Cometh's hubris remained stubbornly intact and magnified itself with thoughts that she was better than Cecilia Slaughter. That she—Idy Cometh—had been more clever, was stronger, and, most importantly, forgiving.

So when Dolph ended what he was saying to her at their thirteenth encounter (a baker's dozen)—the one that would burn through the full thickness, all the layers of her mind and body—with the statement she had waited and waited for, an "I love you," loud enough for anyone to hear, she thought, "Yes." A new beginning, an erasure, a correction, and she allowed herself to give in to what she wanted to believe was the reborn Randolph van Straaten and that she had been both witness and midwife to his repentance.

XXVIII

She left the cruel world around her—all the pain shooting out from the nightly news on TV and the world happenings online, the awful announcements she awoke to each morning when she turned on her computer, their drip out and over the slick surface of its screen. She left her mother's diseased body—all the horrid visions she still had of the sickness that ate its way into her mother. She left the bitter misery of her grandmother's story. She left the memory and awful ache of her grand-mother's abrupt, final dismissal of her after *that woman's* arrival into their lives because she, Idy, couldn't stop the tornado that was Mitzi. She left her father's bloated red face after he made *that woman* his wife and his growing, suffocating silence, out of his fear of Mitzi's fury—which only made her crave his attention more on all matters "Idy."

She felt drugged by the possibilities of love and redemption, thinking, Randolph van Straaten loves me and maybe the rape *was* just an uncontained passion, ignoring what is so clearly stated in the Dhammapada: "Neither in the sky nor in mid-ocean, nor on entering into mountain clefts, nowhere in the world is there a place where one can escape from the results of evil deeds." Yes, she even pushed aside her own bad actions of revenge against this man and all the years of trying to destroy him.

She believed there was such peace unifying them as she and Dolph left the shop—that an aura of purity encapsulated them against all the evils in this world. A cleansing. Yes. "The Cleansing" she had waited for all these years and she said these words out loud. To which Dolph replied, "What?" Gone from her were all the insults to her body, all the inconsistencies of his behavior—and hers—all the small hints, all the large atmospheric warnings, of a bad ending.

XXIX

Three months later, with still no call from Dolph, David—who by now can't bring himself to go to work, to leave Idy for fear of what she'll do to herself—circles her, repeatedly asking, "Isn't there something we can do? Something *more*?" But Idy Cometh mostly stares blankly into the air as if no one's there and now has completely convinced herself that Cecilia Slaughter had the right idea in killing Ivan Durmand and then herself. Although Idy hasn't enough energy left to even leave her house, yet alone consider how to murder Dolph.

She thinks about Dolph all the time, and that he calmly told her, after their "reconnection"—which she now silently calls by various names: "The Failed Resurrection," "The Ultimate Incorrect Correction," "The Nazi Shower Trick"—"*never to write of me again.*" And with this, the parallels between herself and Cecilia solidify like steel bars locking her into the air Cecilia breathed—the prison where Idy now exists.

≈ ≈ ≈ ≈ ≈

After David leaves to go out for groceries—"You have to eat. I'll get you a treat, something you'll like," he says at the door with a false enthusiasm—Idy takes out a pen and writes a poem:

> Lady Trick
>   For Cecilia Slaughter
>
> Queen of Knives, Talking Skull, The Bodiless,
> always the illusion of something other.
> There, then not. Lover

of mirrors and traps, the romance
of levitation, making the audience
rise to all occasions. Lady

in the wooden box who vanishes
and comes back from seen
nothingness. Magician's assistant, victim,

necessary vision for the trick,
surgeon's patient, payment,
his creation without whom he
could not exist.
Bird in a cage
whose song entertains,
then is silenced. Dictator's

mistress who signed the contract
not to rival or reveal
any secret.

Working on this helps until the writing of it is over. Then she stops. Just
stops. Idy Cometh has now arrived at a place past all questions, all answers,
all corrections, and she completely silences. Maybe this, too, is karma in
action—she meditates on this in her silence, in her stillness.

XXX

Idy still sits, waiting for Dolph. She can't help it. That gnarled seed decomposing inside her—that waiting for a correction, all the while thinking of herself as Miss Havisham from the novel *Great Expectations* and smiling an inward smile at that title. Although she's not wearing a decayed wedding dress, but an old robe gone from bright white to dull gray from David's constant re-washings of it—his unending, unbounded determinations to make it clean with products that promise to correct the color, return it to when it was once new.

Until, suddenly, the stillness cracks open by what sounds to her like short, small shrieks of a weakened animal slowly being tortured. She then realizes it is just the ringing of the phone. Idy stares at it, powerless, as if it is a dying pet all curled up that she can't help. The ringing stops, then starts again. Slowly, she approaches it, picks up the receiver, and hears the rage of someone. She can't tell if it's a man or woman. The unsullied fury of the voice is too amorphous—a non-gendered, too-guttural howl. The fragility of her split-open self seems to be shared by this someone else. She listens to the oozing screams, the wounds in the raw tones, and questions if anyone is really there or if it's just her inner self let loose.

David has begun to search for a place where she can rest—as if such a place does exist—and she can get the best of help—as if such help also exists.

≈ ≈ ≈ ≈ ≈

Soon he will call the man who knows a man who *will* kill a man . . .

XXXI

Avigdor Element had silenced Christiane Juul for the rest of his long life. She was seventy and he ninety-five the last time they saw each other. Even then, he smothered her and dissolved her. "E" was still unbreakable to her and she obeyed what he demanded of her. Except for the manuscripts she was writing—a play, poetry, novels, and the one about their relationship. She had locked them away in a post office box upon each of his scheduled returns to her. After his death, she continues writing them, not particularly out of vengeance or rebellion, rather out of obsession to again feel his presence—and her own. Her talent is still very much alive and maybe ever more so because she's not suppressed it—just hidden it. Gossip, however softer and sporadic, continues about her: "She's down there, maybe in a basement apartment near Avigdor Element's now enshrined office, maybe even writing, writing something. I think I saw her . . ."

XXXII

Dr. Sam Guttmacher watches as Christiane leaves her apartment. He remembers his brother's leaving—his wave goodbye, his promise to return. Which he did, however briefly, after his release from the Siberian camp. It was then Avigdor learned that his mother had died from influenza and too deep a melancholia that both her husband and oldest son had been imprisoned.

Shemuel had cut two curls from his mother's thick hair—one for Avigdor and one for himself—before the rabbi and other old men from the shtetl had lowered her box into the earth.

In the camp, their father had been shot to death. Avigdor had to tell him this. Shemuel wept and wept as he had done over his mother. Avigdor tried to comfort him by saying he'd be back as soon as he made some plans and together they would go to America. That he would always protect him. It was then Shemuel gave him one of their mother's red curls. The other he always kept in his own pocket.

≈ ≈ ≈ ≈ ≈

Avigdor left. He waved goodbye, shouting his promise to quickly come back for him. Shemuel waited and waited, until the waiting became too much and he, too, left. How he ran and ran looking for him—a boy of eight, a wild child, running into the explosions of World War I. The surgeries to his face.

He remembers the mud-flooded trenches in France. A young soldier who *did* take him with—the poet Wilfred Owen. At Craiglockhart War Hospital both he and his "older brother," as he came to call him, mended. Owen even made him an editorial assistant at *Hydra*, a journal Owen founded, when they were both at the Edinburgh hospital.

Then Wilfred Owen went back to the war and was killed one week before the Armistice.

≈ ≈ ≈ ≈ ≈

Once, after Avigdor's death, Dr. Sam Guttmacher visited his brother's office, and on the enormous carved-oak desk he saw a small, oval-shaped onyx frame, its background black velvet, that held a single red curl inside it.

His own had dissolved from the heat and fire when he was hit. Wilfred Owen had told him this after he began to heal at the hospital and that he was sorry he couldn't save it. He understood its importance.

≈ ≈ ≈ ≈ ≈

Sometimes Dr. Sam Guttmacher goes to his office and thumbs through his just-published book, *The Oedipus Complex, Even More Complex*, but often he just sits in his chair and stares at, or reads—with large tears in his eyes—Owen's poem, signed to him, that he had framed and placed on his desk, entitled "Arms and the Boy."

> Let the boy try along this bayonet-blade
> How cold steel is, and keen with hunger of blood;
> Blue with all malice, like a madman's flash;
> And thinly drawn with famishing for flesh.
>
> Lend him to stroke these blind, blunt bullet-leads,
> Which long to nuzzle in the hearts of lads,
> Or give him cartridges of fine zinc teeth
> Sharp with the sharpness of grief and death.
>
> For his teeth seem for laughing round an apple.
> There lurk no claws behind his fingers supple;

And God will grow no talons at his heels,
Nor antlers through the thickness of his curls.

≈ ≈ ≈ ≈ ≈

Dr. Sam Guttmacher knows of loss, the rage of just being left, and the sometimes healing power of art . . .

XXXIII

He watches Christiane cross the street—the same street she has crossed for fifty-six years. She was his patient and he both listened and stayed quiet about who he was. Like his brother, he fell fiercely in love with her—how she looked, who she was—all the time living that love vicariously through her presence, her words. She let him read everything she wrote and he'd praise her talent and encourage her to nourish it.

At twenty-one she had arrived here from Nebraska, all golden curls, cherubic and innocent—straight from the heartland—her talent and heart in her hand. A play, a novel, and a book of poems are secured and ready to be mailed in the bag she holds with her right hand—with more soon to be sent. Under her left arm she carries *The Unauthorized, Unabridged Biography of Avigdor Element*. He knows it is incomplete as he believes all true, told stories are, but he's pleased it does exist. The editor-in-chief of the most coveted publishing house awaits her work. No one except he yet notices this old woman—her now-white curls, embellished by the glow from the street lights and the full moon, look like a halo or a laurel wreath.

DISCUSSION QUESTIONS

1. How are Jennie Silver, Cecilia Slaughter, Idy Cometh, and Christiane Juul similar to each other? How are they different?

2. Have you ever known anyone who has been in a troubled relationship such as Beck's and Jennie Silver's?

3. Did Avigdor Element love Christiane Juul or was he just obsessed with her? Would you consider her strong or weak?

4. What roles do fathers or father figures play in this book?

5. Are the questions asked in the play answered? Can the power of art save the artist? Can it save someone else who experiences the art?

6. Why is Avigdor Element's need to find his brother so large? Is it out of guilt or love? Or is it just the one thing he finds himself unable to control?

7. How is Jennie Silver's relationship with her brother John similar to Idy Cometh's relationship with her "stepbrother" David Adler? How is it different? What role do brothers play in this book?

8. After all this writing—the Diary, the Play, and the Novella—do you believe Jennie Silver gets over Beck?

9. Do you think many people would be vulnerable to men such as Avigdor Element or Benedict Eck (Beck)?

10. What actual historical events affected you the most and/or developed a character or characters' behavior further?

BIOGRAPHICAL NOTE

Susan Hahn is a best-selling, award-winning, Illinois poet, playwright, and novelist. She is also a Guggenheim fellow. She was born Susan Firestone in Chicago, Illinois and attended Highland Park High School. After receiving a B.A. and an M.A. in psychology from Northwestern University she began working at the Woodlawn Mental Health Center and became licensed as a group therapist. Incorporating writing and art into her therapy, she started writing her own work and submitted her first poems to *Poetry* magazine, where they were accepted. In 1997 she was appointed Editor of *TriQuarterly* literary magazine and remained there until 2010. She was also co-founder and co-editor of TriQuarterly Books. During the period 2013–2014 she was the inaugural Writer-in-Residence at the Ernest Hemingway Foundation.